The King could not contain himself for joy.

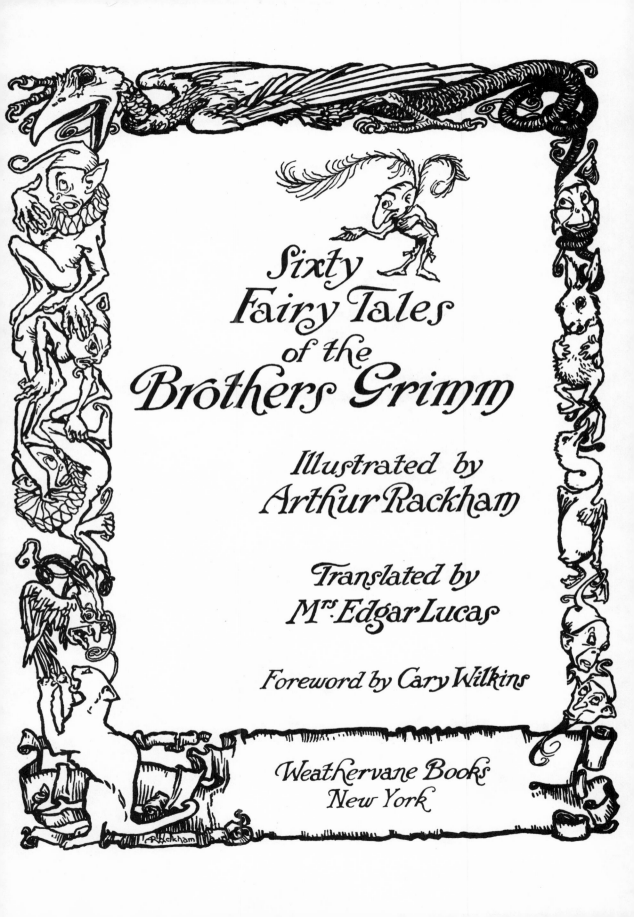

Sixty Fairy Tales of the Brothers Grimm

Illustrated by
Arthur Rackham

Translated by
Mrs. Edgar Lucas

Foreword by Cary Wilkins

Weathervane Books
New York

Special material copyright © MCMLXXIX by Crown Publishers, Inc.
All rights reserved.
This edition is published by Weathervane Books,
distributed by Crown Publishers, Inc.
a b c d e f g h
WEATHERVANE 1979 EDITION
Manufactured in the United States of America

Library of Congress Cataloging in Publication Data

Grimm, Jakob Ludwig Karl, 1785-1863.
  Sixty fairy tales of the Brothers Grimm.

    Translation of Kinder- und Hausmärchen.
    SUMMARY: Sixty tales from the collections of the
Grimm brothers.
    1. Fairy tales, German. [1. Fairy tales. 2. Folk-
lore—Germany] I. Grimm, Wilhelm Karl, 1786-1859,
joint author. II. Rackham, Arthur, 1867-1939.
III. Lucas, Alice. IV. Title.
PZ8.G882Fai 1979   398.2'1'0924   79-14513
ISBN 0-517-28525-8

Contents

List of Illustrations

iv

LIST OF ILLUSTRATIONS

v

GRIMM'S FAIRY TALES

vi

LIST OF ILLUSTRATIONS

List of Coloured Illustrations

GRIMM'S FAIRY TALES

LIST OF COLOURED ILLUSTRATIONS

Foreword

Mentioning the Brothers Grimm to an adult, one sometimes hears this reaction: "Those stories *were* pretty grim, weren't they?" No, they weren't! Only when people reacquaint themselves with these delightful stories of their childhood, do they remember how much pleasure the tales gave them. One wonders if Germans have a similar problem with the brothers' name, since the word *Grimm* in German means "fury, rage, wrath."

These words never come up, however, when describing these dedicated men who devoted their lives to preserving and expanding German language and literature. Scholars, philologists, historians, and philosophers, Jacob and Wilhelm Grimm set out to collect genuine folktales in order to study ancient German customs, laws, religion, and literature. A happy outcome of this venture was the popular and lasting pleasure that these tales have given children and adults all over the world.

The *Kinder- und Hausmärchen*, or *Nursery and Household Tales*, were published between 1812 and 1824. Out of the more than two hundred stories, sixty of the most popular ones are in this collection. A few of the old favorites might not be recognized, because in this translation they have different names: Sleeping Beauty is called Briar Rose, Snow White is found in the story "Snowdrop," and Cinderella is given the name Ashenputtel.

Because the Grimms faithfully recorded most of these folktales from oral sources, without changing or embellishing them, the tales reflect the attitudes and beliefs of the common people. Some of the stories seem excessively nationalistic and show contempt for the outsider. A few stories reveal anti-Semitic attitudes. One such story, which appeared in the original edition of this book, is "The Jew Among the Thorns"; it has been changed here to "The Man Among the Thorns."

For the most part, however, these tales continue to enchant and delight us. They have had many imaginative illustrators, one of the best being Arthur Rackham. He could make it seem perfectly natural for a dragon to rest its head in the lap of a princess; on the other hand, a scene of two women running through the woods is made eerily frightening and dramatic. Full of marvelous detail and extraordinary color, Rackham's fantastic and often grotesque creations excite our imagination and transport us to the mystical world of fairyland.

CARY WILKINS

The Golden Bird.

A LONG time ago there was a King who had a lovely pleasure-garden round his palace, and in it stood a tree which bore golden apples. When the apples were nearly ripe they were counted, but the very next morning one was missing.

This was reported to the King, and he ordered a watch to be set every night under the tree.

The King had three sons, and he sent the eldest into the garden at nightfall; but by midnight he was overcome with sleep, and in the morning another apple was missing.

On the following night the second son had to keep watch, but he fared no better. When the clock struck twelve, he too was fast asleep, and in the morning another apple was gone.

The turn to watch now came to the third son. He was quite ready, but the King had not much confidence in him, and thought that he would accomplish even less than his brothers. At last, however, he gave his permission; so the youth lay down under the tree to watch, determined not to let sleep get the mastery over him.

As the clock struck twelve there was a rustling in the air,

1

and by the light of the moon he saw a Bird, whose shining feathers were of pure gold. The Bird settled on the tree, and was just plucking an apple when the young Prince shot an arrow at it. The Bird flew away, but the arrow hit its plumage, and one of the golden feathers fell to the ground. The Prince picked it up, and in the morning took it to the King and told him all that he had seen in the night.

The King assembled his council, and everybody declared that a feather like that was worth more than the whole kingdom. 'If the feather is worth so much,' said the King, 'one will not satisfy me; I must and will have the whole Bird.'

The eldest, relying on his cleverness, set out in search of the Bird, and thought that he would be sure to find it soon.

When he had gone some distance he saw a Fox sitting by the edge of a wood; he raised his gun and aimed at it. The Fox cried out, 'Do not shoot me, and I will give you some good advice. You are going to look for the Golden Bird; you will come to a village at nightfall, where you will find two inns opposite each other. One of them will be brightly lighted, and there will be noise and revelry going on in it. Be sure you do not choose that one, but go into the other, even if you don't like the look of it so well.'

'How can a stupid animal like that give me good advice?' thought the King's son, and he pulled the trigger, but missed the Fox, who turned tail and made off into the wood.

Thereupon the Prince continued his journey, and at nightfall reached the village with the two inns. Singing and dancing were going on in the one, and the other had a poverty-stricken and decayed appearance.

'I should be a fool,' he said, 'if I were to go to that miserable place with this good one so near.'

So he went into the noisy one, and lived there in rioting and revelry, forgetting the Bird, his father, and all his good counsels.

When some time had passed and the eldest son did not come back, the second prepared to start in quest of the

2

Golden Bird. He met the Fox, as the eldest son had done, and it gave him the same good advice, of which he took just as little heed.

He came to the two inns, and saw his brother standing at the window of the one whence sounds of revelry proceeded. He could not withstand his brother's calling, so he went in and gave himself up to a life of pleasure.

Again some time passed, and the King's youngest son wanted to go out to try his luck; but his father would not let him go.

'It is useless,' he said. 'He will be even less able to find the Golden Bird than his brothers, and when any ill luck overtakes him, he will not be able to help himself; he has no backbone.'

But at last, because he gave him no peace, he let him go. The Fox again sat at the edge of the wood, begged for its life, and gave its good advice. The Prince was good-natured, and said : 'Be calm, little Fox, I will do thee no harm.'

'You won't repent it,' answered the Fox; 'and so that you may get along faster, come and mount on my tail.'

No sooner had he seated himself than the Fox began to run, and away they flew over stock and stone, at such a pace that his hair whistled in the wind.

When they reached the village, the Prince dismounted, and following the good advice of the Fox, he went straight to the mean inn without looking about him, and there he passed a peaceful night. In the morning when he went out into the fields, there sat the Fox, who said : 'I will now tell you what you must do next. Walk straight on till you come to a castle, in front of which a whole regiment of soldiers is encamped. Don't be afraid of them; they will all be asleep and snoring. Walk through the midst of them straight into the castle, and through all the rooms, and at last you will reach an apartment where the Golden Bird will be hanging in a common wooden cage. A golden cage stands near it for show, but beware ! whatever you do, you must not take

3

the bird out of the wooden cage to put it into the other, or it will be the worse for you.'

After these words the Fox again stretched out his tail, the Prince took his seat on it, and away they flew over stock and stone, till his hair whistled in the wind.

When he arrived at the castle, he found everything just as the Fox had said.

The Prince went to the room where the Golden Bird hung in the wooden cage, with a golden cage standing by, and the three golden apples were scattered about the room. He thought it would be absurd to leave the beautiful Bird in the common old cage, so he opened the door, caught it, and put it into the golden cage. But as he did it, the Bird uttered a piercing shriek. The soldiers woke up, rushed in, and carried him away to prison. Next morning he was taken before a judge, and, as he confessed all, he was sentenced to death. The King, however, said that he would spare his life on one condition, and this was that he should bring him the Golden Horse which runs faster than the wind. In addition, he should have the Golden Bird as a reward.

So the Prince set off with many sighs; he was very sad, for where was he to find the Golden Horse?

Then suddenly he saw his old friend the Fox sitting on the road. 'Now you see,' said the Fox, 'all this has happened because you did not listen to me. All the same, keep up your spirits; I will protect you and tell you how to find the Golden Horse. You must keep straight along the road, and you will come to a palace, in the stable of which stands the Golden Horse. The grooms will be lying round the stable, but they will be fast asleep and snoring, and you can safely lead the horse through them. Only, one thing you must beware of. Put the old saddle of wood and leather upon it, and not the golden one hanging near, or you will rue it.'

Then the Fox stretched out his tail, the Prince took his seat, and away they flew over stock and stone, till his hair whistled in the wind.

4

Everything happened just as the Fox had said. The Prince came to the stable where the Golden Horse stood, but when he was about to put the old saddle on its back, he thought, ' Such a beautiful animal will be disgraced if I don't put the good saddle upon him, as he deserves.' Hardly had the golden saddle touched the horse than he began neighing loudly. The grooms awoke, seized the Prince, and threw him into a dungeon.

The next morning he was taken before a judge, and condemned to death ; but the King promised to spare his life, and give him the Golden Horse as well, if he could bring him the beautiful Princess out of the golden palace. With a heavy heart the Prince set out, when to his delight he soon met the faithful Fox.

' I ought to leave you to your fate,' he said ; ' but I will have pity on you and once more help you out of your trouble. Your road leads straight to the golden palace,—you will reach it in the evening ; and at night, when everything is quiet, the beautiful Princess will go to the bathroom to take a bath. As she goes along, spring forward and give her a kiss, and she will follow you. Lead her away with you ; only on no account allow her to bid her parents good-bye, or it will go badly with you.'

Again the Fox stretched out his tail, the Prince seated himself upon it, and off they flew over stock and stone, till his hair whistled in the wind.

When he got to the palace, it was just as the Fox had said. He waited till midnight, and when the whole palace was wrapped in sleep, and the Maiden went to take a bath, he sprang forward and gave her a kiss. She said she was quite willing to go with him, but she implored him to let her say good-bye to her parents. At first he refused ; but as she cried, and fell at his feet, at last he gave her leave. Hardly had the Maiden stepped up to her father's bed, when he and every one else in the palace woke up. The Prince was seized, and thrown into prison.

Next morning the King said to him, ' Your life is forfeited, and it can only be spared if you clear away the mountain in front of my window, which shuts out the view. It must be done in eight days, and if you accomplish the task you shall have my daughter as a reward.'

So the Prince began his labours, and he dug and shovelled without ceasing. On the seventh day, when he saw how little he had done, he became very sad, and gave up all hope. However, in the evening the Fox appeared and said, ' You do not deserve any help from me, but lie down and go to sleep ; I will do the work.' In the morning when he woke and looked out of the window, the mountain had disappeared.

Overjoyed, the Prince hurried to the King and told him that his condition was fulfilled, and, whether he liked it or not, he must keep his word and give him his daughter.

So they both went away together, and before long the faithful Fox joined them.

' You certainly have got the best thing of all,' said he ; ' but to the Maiden of the golden palace the Golden Horse belongs.'

' How am I to get it ? ' asked the Prince.

' Oh ! I will tell you that,' answered the Fox. ' First take the beautiful Maiden to the King who sent you to the golden palace. There will be great joy when you appear, and they will bring out the Golden Horse to you. Mount it at once, and shake hands with everybody, last of all with the beautiful Maiden ; and when you have taken her hand firmly, pull her up beside you with a swing and gallop away. No one will be able to catch you, for the horse goes faster than the wind.'

All this was successfully done, and the Prince carried off the beautiful Maiden on the Golden Horse.

The Fox was not far off, and he said to the Prince, ' Now I will help you to get the Golden Bird, too. When you approach the castle where the Golden Bird lives, let the Maiden dismount, and I will take care of her. Then ride with the Golden Horse into the courtyard of the castle ; there will be great rejoicing when they see you, and they will bring out the

6

Away they flew over stock and stone, at such a pace that
his hair whistled in the wind.

By day she made herself into a cat.

. . . Or a screech owl.

Once there was a poor old woman who lived in a village.

Golden Bird to you. As soon as you have the cage in your hand, gallop back to us and take up the Maiden again.'

When these plans had succeeded, and the Prince was ready to ride on with all his treasures, the Fox said to him :

'Now you must reward me for my help.'

'What do you want?' asked the Prince.

'When you reach that wood, shoot me dead and cut off my head and my paws.'

'That would indeed be gratitude!' said the Prince. 'I can't possibly promise to do such a thing.'

The Fox said, 'If you won't do it, I must leave you; but before I go I will give you one more piece of advice. Beware of two things —buy no gallows-birds, and don't sit on the edge of a well.' Saying which, he ran off into the wood.

The Prince thought, 'That is a strange animal; what whims he has. Who on earth would want to buy gallows-birds! And the desire to sit on the edge of a well has never yet seized me!'

He rode on with the beautiful Maiden, and the road led him through the village where his two brothers had stayed behind. There was a great hubbub in the village, and when he asked what it was about, he was told that two persons were going to be hanged. When he got nearer he saw that they

The Prince carried off the beautiful Maiden on the Golden Horse.

were his brothers, who had wasted their possessions and done all sorts of evil deeds. He asked if they could not be set free.

7

'Yes, if you'll ransom them,' answered the people; 'but why will you throw your money away in buying off such wicked people?'

He did not stop to reflect, however, but paid the ransom for them, and when they were set free they all journeyed on together.

They came to the wood where they had first met the Fox. It was deliciously cool there, while the sun was broiling outside, so the two brothers said, 'Let us sit down here by the well to rest a little and eat and drink.' The Prince agreed, and during the conversation he forgot what he was about, and, never dreaming of any foul play, seated himself on the edge of the well. But his two brothers threw him backwards into it, and went home to their father, taking with them the Maiden, the Horse, and the Bird.

'Here we bring you not only the Golden Bird, but the Golden Horse, and the Maiden from the golden palace, as our booty.'

Thereupon there was great rejoicing; but the Horse would not eat, the Bird would not sing, and the Maiden sat and wept all day.

The youngest brother had not perished, however. Happily the well was dry, and he fell upon soft moss without taking any harm; only, he could not get out.

Even in this great strait the faithful Fox did not forsake him, but came leaping down and scolded him for not taking his advice. 'I can't leave you to your fate, though; I must help you to get back to the light of day.' He told him to take tight hold of his tail, and then he dragged him up. 'You are not out of every danger even now,' said the Fox. 'Your brothers were not sure of your death, so they have set watchers all over the wood to kill you if they see you.'

A poor old man was sitting by the roadside, and the Prince exchanged clothes with him, and by this means he succeeded in reaching the King's court.

Nobody recognised him, but the Bird began to sing, the

Horse began to eat, and the beautiful Maiden left off crying.

In astonishment the King asked, 'What does all this mean ?'

The Maiden answered : 'I do not know ; but I was very sad, and now I am gay. It seems to me that my true bridegroom must have come.'

She told the King all that had happened, although the two brothers had threatened her with death if she betrayed anything. The King ordered every person in the palace to be brought before him. Among them came the Prince disguised as an old man in all his rags ; but the Maiden knew him at once, and fell on his neck. The wicked brothers were seized and put to death ; but the Prince was married to the beautiful Maiden, and proclaimed heir to the King.

But what became of the poor Fox ? Long afterwards, when the Prince went out into the fields one day, he met the Fox, who said : 'You have everything that you can desire, but there is no end to my misery. It still lies in your power to release me.' And again he implored the Prince to shoot him dead, and to cut off his head and his paws.

At last the Prince consented to do as he was asked, and no sooner was it done than the Fox was changed into a man ; no other than the brother of the beautiful Princess, at last set free from the evil spell which so long had lain upon him.

There was nothing now wanting to their happiness for the rest of their lives.

Hans in Luck

HANS had served his master for seven years, when he one day said to him: 'Master, my time is up, I want to go home to my mother; please give me my wages.'

His master answered, 'You have served me well and faithfully, and as the service has been, so shall the wages be'; and he gave him a lump of gold as big as his head.

Hans took out his pocket-handkerchief and tied up the gold in it, and then slung the bundle over his shoulder, and started on his homeward journey.

As he walked along, just dragging one foot after the other, a man on horseback appeared, riding, fresh and gay, along on his spirited horse.

'Ah!' said Hans, quite loud as he passed, 'what a fine thing riding must be. You are as comfortable as if you were in an easy-chair; you don't stumble over any stones; you save your shoes, and you get over the road you needn't bother how.'

The horseman, who heard him, stopped and said, 'Hullo, Hans, why are you on foot?'

'I can't help myself,' said Hans, 'as I have this bundle to carry home. It is true that it is a lump of gold, but I can hardly hold my head up for it, and it weighs down my shoulder frightfully.'

'I'll tell you what,' said the horseman, 'we will change. I will give you my horse, and you shall give me your bundle.'

'With all my heart,' said Hans; 'but you will be rarely burdened with it.'

The horseman dismounted, took the gold, and helped Hans

10

up, put the bridle into his hands, and said : ' When you want to go very fast, you must click your tongue and cry " Gee-up, Gee-up." '

Hans was delighted when he found himself so easily riding along on horseback. After a time it occurred to him that he might be going faster, and he began to click with his tongue, and to cry ' Gee-up, Gee-up.' The horse broke into a gallop, and before Hans knew where he was, he was thrown off into a ditch which separated the fields from the high road. The horse would have run away if a peasant coming along the road leading a cow had not caught it. Hans felt himself all over, and picked himself up ; but he was very angry, and said to the peasant : ' Riding is poor fun at times, when you have a nag like mine, which stumbles and throws you, and puts you in danger of breaking your neck. I will never mount it again. I think much more of that cow of yours. You can walk comfortably behind her, and you have her milk into the bargain every day, as well as butter and cheese. What would I not give for a cow like that ! '

' Well,' said the peasant, ' if you have such a fancy for it as all that, I will exchange the cow for the horse.'

Hans accepted the offer with delight, and the peasant mounted the horse and rode rapidly off.

Hans drove his cow peacefully on, and thought what a lucky bargain he had made. ' If only I have a bit of bread, and I don't expect ever to be without that, I shall always have butter and cheese to eat with it. If I am thirsty, I only have to milk my cow and I have milk to drink. My heart ! what more can you desire ? '

When he came to an inn he made a halt, and in great joy he ate up all the food he had with him, all his dinner and his supper too, and he gave the last coins he had for half a glass of beer. Then he went on further in the direction of his mother's village, driving his cow before him. The heat was overpowering, and, as midday drew near, Hans found himself on a heath which it took him an hour to cross. He was so

11

hot and thirsty, that his tongue was parched and clung to the roof of his mouth.

'This can easily be set to rights,' thought Hans. 'I will milk my cow and sup up the milk.' He tied her to a tree, and as he had no pail, he used his leather cap instead; but, try as hard as he liked, not a single drop of milk appeared. As he was very clumsy in his attempts, the impatient animal gave him a severe kick on his forehead with one of her hind legs. He was stunned by the blow, and fell to the ground, where he lay for some time, not knowing where he was.

Happily just then a butcher came along the road, trundling a young pig in a wheel-barrow.

'What is going on here?' he cried, as he helped poor Hans up.

Hans told him all that had happened.

The butcher handed him his flask, and said: 'Here, take a drink, it will do you good. The cow can't give any milk I suppose; she must be too old, and good for nothing but to be a beast of burden, or to go to the butcher.'

'Oh dear!' said Hans, smoothing his hair. 'Now who would ever have thought it! Killing the animal is all very well, but what kind of meat will it be? For my part, I don't like cow's flesh; it's not juicy enough. Now, if one had a nice young pig like that, it would taste ever so much better; and then, all the sausages!'

'Listen, Hans!' then said the butcher, 'for your sake I will exchange, and let you have the pig instead of the cow.'

'God reward your friendship!' said Hans, handing over the cow, as the butcher untied the pig, and put the halter with which it was tied into his hand.

Hans went on his way, thinking how well everything was turning out for him. Even if a mishap befell him, something else immediately happened to make up for it. Soon after this, he met a lad carrying a beautiful white goose under his arm. They passed the time of day, and Hans began to tell him how lucky he was, and what successful bargains he had

12

made. The lad told him that he was taking the goose for a christening feast. 'Just feel it,' he went on, holding it up by the wings. 'Feel how heavy it is; it's true they have been stuffing it for eight weeks. Whoever eats that roast goose will have to wipe the fat off both sides of his mouth.'

Just then a butcher came along the road, trundling a young pig
in a wheel-barrow.

'Yes, indeed!' answered Hans, weighing it in his hand; 'but my pig is no light weight either.'

Then the lad looked cautiously about from side to side, and shook his head. 'Now, look here,' he began, 'I don't

13

think it's all quite straight about your pig. One has just been stolen out of Schultze's sty, in the village I have come from. I fear, I fear it is the one you are leading. They have sent people out to look for it, and it would be a bad business for you if you were found with it; the least they would do, would be to put you in the black hole.'

Poor Hans was very much frightened at this. ' Oh, dear! oh dear!' he said. 'Do help me out of this trouble. You are more at home here; take my pig, and let me have your goose.'

' Well, I shall run some risk if I do, but I won't be the means of getting you into a scrape.'

So he took the rope in his hand, and quickly drove the pig up a side road; and honest Hans, relieved of his trouble, plodded on with the goose under his arm.

' When I really come to think it over,' he said to himself, ' I have still had the best of the bargain. First, there is the delicious roast goose, and then all the fat that will drip out of it in roasting, will keep us in goose-fat to eat on our bread for three months at least; and, last of all, there are the beautiful white feathers which I will stuff my pillow with, and then I shall need no rocking to send me to sleep. How delighted my mother will be.'

As he passed through the last village he came to a knife-grinder with his cart, singing to his wheel as it buzzed merrily round—

> ' Scissors and knives I grind so fast,
> And hang up my cloak against the blast.'

Hans stopped to look at him, and at last he spoke to him and said, ' You must be doing a good trade to be so merry over your grinding.'

' Yes,' answered the grinder. ' The work of one's hands is the foundation of a golden fortune. A good grinder finds money whenever he puts his hand into his pocket. But where did you buy that beautiful goose ? '

' I did not buy it; I exchanged my pig for it.'

14

' And the pig ? '

' Oh, I got that instead of my cow.'

' And the cow ? '

' I got that for a horse.'

' And the horse ? '

' I gave a lump of gold as big as my head for it.'

' And the gold ? '

' Oh, that was my wages for seven years' service.'

' You certainly have known how to manage your affairs,' said the grinder. ' Now, if you could manage to hear the money jingling in your pockets when you got up in the morning, you would indeed have made your fortune.'

' How shall I set about that ? ' asked Hans.

' You must be a grinder like me—nothing is needed for it but a whetstone ; everything else will come of itself. I have one here which certainly is a little damaged, but you need not give me anything for it but your goose. Are you willing ? '

' How can you ask me such a question ? ' said Hans. ' Why, I shall be the happiest person in the world. If I can have some money every time I put my hand in my pocket, what more should I have to trouble about ? '

So he handed him the goose, and took the whetstone in exchange.

' Now,' said the grinder, lifting up an ordinary large stone which lay near on the road, ' here is another good stone into the bargain. You can hammer out all your old nails on it to straighten them. Take it, and carry it off.'

Hans shouldered the stone, and went on his way with a light heart, and his eyes shining with joy. ' I must have been born in a lucky hour,' he cried ; ' everything happens just as I want it, and as it would happen to a Sunday's child.'

In the meantime, as he had been on foot since daybreak, he began to feel very tired, and he was also very hungry, as he had eaten all his provisions at once in his joy at his bargain over the cow. At last he could hardly walk any further, and he was obliged to stop every minute to rest. Then the

15

stones were frightfully heavy, and he could not get rid of the
thought that it would be very nice if he were not obliged to
carry them any further. He dragged himself like a snail
to a well in the fields, meaning to rest and refresh himself
with a draught of the cool water. So as not to injure the
stones by sitting on them, he laid them carefully on the edge
of the well. Then he sat down, and was about to stoop down
to drink when he inadvertently gave them a little push, and
both the stones fell straight into the water.

When Hans saw them disappear before his very eyes he
jumped for joy, and then knelt down and thanked God, with
tears in his eyes, for having shown him this further grace,
and relieved him of the heavy stones (which were all that
remained to trouble him) without giving him anything to
reproach himself with. 'There is certainly no one under the
sun so happy as I.'

And so, with a light heart, free from every care, he now
bounded on home to his mother.

Jorinda and Joringel

THERE was once an old castle in the middle of a vast thick wood; in it there lived an old woman quite alone, and she was a witch. By day she made herself into a cat or a screech-owl, but regularly at night she became a human being again. In this way she was able to decoy wild beasts and birds, which she would kill, and boil or roast. If any man came within a hundred paces of the castle, he was forced to stand still and could not move from the place till she gave the word of release; but if an innocent maiden came within the circle she changed her into a bird, and shut her up in a cage which she carried into a room in the castle. She must have had seven thousand cages of this kind, containing pretty birds.

Now, there was once a maiden called Jorinda who was more beautiful than all other maidens. She had promised to marry a very handsome youth named Joringel, and it was in the days of their courtship, when they took the greatest joy in being alone together, that one day they wandered out into the forest. 'Take care,' said Joringel; 'do not let us go too near the castle.'

It was a lovely evening. The sunshine glanced between the tree-trunks of the dark green-wood, while the turtle-doves sang plaintively in the old beech-trees. Yet Jorinda sat down in the sunshine, and could not help weeping and bewailing, while Joringel, too, soon became just as mournful. They both felt as miserable as if they had been going to die. Gazing round them, they found they had lost their way, and did not know how they should find the path home. Half the sun still appeared above the mountain; half had sunk below. Joringel peered into the bushes and saw the old walls of the castle quite close to them ; he was terror-struck, and became pale as death. Jorinda was singing :

> 'My birdie with its ring so red
> Sings sorrow, sorrow, sorrow ;
> My love will mourn when I am dead,
> To-morrow, morrow, mor—— jug, jug.'

Joringel looked at her, but she was changed into a nightingale who sang ' Jug, jug.'

A screech-owl with glowing eyes flew three times round her, and cried three times ' Shu hu-hu.' Joringel could not stir ; he stood like a stone without being able to speak, or cry, or move hand or foot. The sun had now set ; the owl flew into a bush, out of which appeared almost at the same moment a crooked old woman, skinny and yellow ; she had big, red eyes and a crooked nose whose tip reached her chin. She mumbled something, caught the nightingale, and carried it away in her hand. Joringel could not say a word nor move from the spot, and the nightingale was gone. At last the old woman came back, and said in a droning voice : ' Greeting to thee, Zachiel ! When the moon shines upon the cage, unloose the captive, Zachiel ! '

Then Joringel was free. He fell on his knees before the witch, and implored her to give back his Jorinda ; but she said he should never have her again, and went away. He pleaded, he wept, he lamented, but all in vain. ' Alas ! what is to become of me ? ' said Joringel. At last he went away, and arrived at a strange village, where he spent a long time as a shepherd. He often wandered round about the castle, but did not go too near it. At last he dreamt one night that he found a blood-red flower, in the midst of which was a beautiful large pearl. He plucked the flower, and took it to the castle. Whatever he touched with it was made free of enchantment. He dreamt, too, that by this means he had found his Jorinda again. In the morning when he awoke he

18

At last the old woman came back, and said in a droning voice: 'Greeting to thee, Zachiel!'

began to search over hill and dale, in the hope of finding a flower like this ; he searched till the ninth day, when he found the flower early in the morning. In the middle was a big dewdrop, as big as the finest pearl. This flower he carried day and night, till he reached the castle. He was not held fast as before when he came within the hundred paces of the castle, but walked straight up to the door.

Joringel was filled with joy ; he touched the door with the flower, and it flew open. He went in through the court, and listened for the sound of birds. He went on, and found the hall, where the witch was feeding the birds in the seven thousand cages. When she saw Joringel she was angry, very angry—scolded, and spat poison and gall at him. He paid no attention to her, but turned away and searched among the bird-cages. Yes, but there were many hundred nightingales ; how was he to find his Jorinda ?

While he was looking about in this way he noticed that the old woman was secretly removing a cage with a bird inside, and was making for the door. He sprang swiftly towards her, touched the cage and the witch with the flower, and then she no longer had power to exercise her spells. Jorinda stood there, as beautiful as before, and threw her arms round Joringel's neck. After that he changed all the other birds back into maidens again, and went home with Jorinda, and they lived long and happily together.

The Bremen Town Musicians

ONCE upon a time a man had an Ass which for many
years carried sacks to the mill without tiring. At
last, however, its strength was worn out ; it was
no longer of any use for work. Accordingly its master began
to ponder as to how best to cut down its keep ; but the Ass,
seeing there was mischief in the air, ran away and started
on the road to Bremen ; there he thought he could become
a town-musician.

When he had been travelling a short time, he fell in with a
hound, who was lying panting on the road as though he had
run himself off his legs.

' Well, what are you panting so for, Growler ? ' said the Ass.

' Ah,' said the Hound, ' just because I am old, and every
day I get weaker, and also because I can no longer keep
up with the pack, my master wanted to kill me, so I took my
departure. But now, how am I to earn my bread ? '

' Do you know what,' said the Ass. ' I am going to Bremen,
and shall there become a town-musician ; come with me and
take your part in the music. I shall play the lute, and you
shall beat the kettle-drum.'

The Hound agreed, and they went on.

A short time after they came upon a Cat, sitting in the road,
with a face as long as a wet week.

' Well, what has been crossing you, Whiskers ? ' asked the
Ass.

' Who can be cheerful when he is out at elbows ? ' said
the Cat. ' I am getting on in years, and my teeth are blunted
and I prefer to sit by the stove and purr instead of hunting
round after mice. Just because of this my mistress wanted

21

to drown me. I made myself scarce, but now I don't know where to turn.'

'Come with us to Bremen,' said the Ass. 'You are a great hand at serenading, so you can become a town-musician.'

A short time after they came upon a Cat, sitting in the road, with a face as long as a wet week.

The Cat consented, and joined them.

Next the fugitives passed by a yard where a barn-door fowl was sitting on the door, crowing with all its might.

'You crow so loud you pierce one through and through,' said the Ass. 'What is the matter?'

'Why! didn't I prophesy fine weather for Lady Day, when Our Lady washes the Christ Child's little garment and wants to dry it? But, notwithstanding this, because Sunday visitors are coming to-morrow, the mistress has no pity, and she has ordered the cook to make me into soup, so I shall have my neck wrung to-night. Now I am crowing with all my might while I have the chance.'

'Come along, Red-comb,' said the Ass; 'you had much better come with us. We are going to Bremen, and you will find a much better fate there. You have a good voice,

22

and when we make music together, there will be quality in it.'

The Cock allowed himself to be persuaded, and they all four went off together. They could not, however, reach the town in one day, and by evening they arrived at a wood, where they determined to spend the night. The Ass and the Hound lay down under a big tree; the Cat and the Cock settled themselves in the branches, the Cock flying right up to the top, which was the safest place for him. Before going to sleep he looked round once more in every direction; suddenly it seemed to him that he saw a light burning in the distance. He called out to his comrades that there must be a house not far off, for he saw a light.

' Very well,' said the Ass, ' let us set out and make our way to it, for the entertainment here is very bad.'

The Hound thought some bones or meat would suit him too, so they set out in the direction of the light, and soon saw it shining more clearly, and getting bigger and bigger, till they reached a brightly-lighted robbers' den. The Ass, being the tallest, approached the window and looked in.

' What do you see, old Jackass ? ' asked the Cock.

' What do I see ? ' answered the Ass ; ' why, a table spread with delicious food and drink, and robbers seated at it enjoying themselves.'

' That would just suit us,' said the Cock.

' Yes ; if we were only there,' answered the Ass.

Then the animals took counsel as to how to set about driving the robbers out. At last they hit upon a plan.

The Ass was to take up his position with his fore-feet on the window-sill, the Hound was to jump on his back, the Cat to climb up on to the Hound, and last of all the Cock flew up and perched on the Cat's head. When they were thus arranged, at a given signal they all began to perform their music ; the Ass brayed, the Hound barked, the Cat mewed, and the Cock crowed ; then they dashed through the window, shivering the panes. The robbers jumped up at the terrible

23

noise; they thought nothing less than that a demon was coming in upon them, and fled into the wood in the greatest alarm. Then the four animals sat down to table, and helped themselves according to taste, and ate as though they had been starving for weeks. When they had finished they extinguished the light, and looked for sleeping places, each one to suit his nature and taste.

The Ass lay down on the manure heap, the Hound behind the door, the Cat on the hearth near the warm ashes, and the Cock flew up to the rafters. As they were tired from the long journey, they soon went to sleep.

When midnight was past, and the robbers saw from a distance that the light was no longer burning, and that all seemed quiet, the chief said:

'We ought not to have been scared by a false alarm,' and ordered one of the robbers to go and examine the house.

The Ass brayed, the Hound barked, the Cat mewed, and the Cock crowed.

Finding all quiet, the messenger went into the kitchen to kindle a light, and taking the Cat's glowing, fiery eyes for live coals, he held a match close to them so as to light it. But the Cat would stand no nonsense; it flew at his face, spat and scratched. He was terribly frightened and ran away.

24

THE BREMEN TOWN MUSICIANS

He tried to get out by the back door, but the Hound, who was lying there, jumped up and bit his leg. As he ran across the manure heap in front of the house, the Ass gave him a good sound kick with his hind legs, while the Cock, who had awoken at the uproar quite fresh and gay, cried out from his perch : ' Cock-a-doodle-doo.' Thereupon the robber ran back as fast as he could to his chief, and said : ' There is a gruesome witch in the house, who breathed on me and scratched me with her long fingers. Behind the door there stands a man with a knife, who stabbed me ; while in the yard lies a black monster, who hit me with a club ; and upon the roof the judge is seated, and he called out, " Bring the rogue here," so I hurried away as fast as I could.'

Thenceforward the robbers did not venture again to the house, which, however, pleased the four Bremen musicians so much that they never wished to leave it again.

And he who last told the story has hardly finished speaking yet.

Old Sultan

A PEASANT once had a faithful dog called Sultan, who had grown old and lost all his teeth, and could no longer keep fast hold of his quarry. One day when the peasant was standing in front of his house with his wife, he said : 'To-morrow I intend to shoot old Sultan ; he is no longer any use.'

His wife, who pitied the faithful animal, answered : 'Since he has served us so long and honestly, we might at least keep him and feed him to the end of his days.'

'What nonsense,' said her husband ; 'you are a fool. He has not a tooth left in his head ; thieves are not a bit afraid of him now that they can get away from him. Even if he has served us well, he has been well fed in return.'

The poor dog, who lay near, stretched out in the sun, heard all they said, and was sad at the thought that the next day was to be his last. Now, he had a good friend who was a wolf, and in the evening he slunk off into the wood, and complained to him of the fate which awaited him.

'Listen, comrade,' said the Wolf, 'be of good cheer ; I will help you in your need, for I have thought of a plan. To-morrow your master and mistress are going hay-making, and

26

they will take their little child with them because there will be nobody left at home. During their work they usually lay it under the hedge in the shade; you lie down as though to guard it. I will then come out of the wood and steal the child. You must rush quickly after me, as though you wanted to rescue the child. I will let it fall, and you will take it back to its parents again; they will think that you have saved it, and will be far too thankful to do you any harm. On the contrary, you will come into high favour, and they will never let you want again.'

The plot pleased the dog, and it was carried out just as it was planned. The father cried out when he saw the Wolf run across the field with his child in its mouth; but when old Sultan brought it back he was overjoyed, stroked him, and said: 'Not a hair of your coat shall be hurt; you shall have plenty to eat as long as you live.' Then he said to his wife: 'Go home immediately and prepare some broth for old Sultan which he won't need to bite, and bring the pillow out of my bed. I will give it to him to lie upon.'

Henceforward old Sultan was as well off as he could wish. Soon afterwards the Wolf paid him a visit, and rejoiced that all had turned out so well. 'But, comrade,' he said, 'you must shut your eyes. Suppose some fine day I carry off one of your master's fat sheep? Nowadays it is hard to get one's living.'

'Don't count on that,' answered the dog. 'I must remain true to my master—I shall never permit it?'

The Wolf, thinking that he had not spoken in earnest, came and crept in at night, and tried to carry off a sheep. But the peasant, to whom the faithful Sultan had betrayed the Wolf's intention, spied him and belaboured him soundly with a threshing-flail. The Wolf was forced to retreat, but he called out to the dog, 'Wait a bit, you wicked creature—you shall suffer for this.'

The next morning he sent the Boar to invite the Dog into the wood, there to settle matters by a duel. Old Sultan could find no second except the Cat, who had only three legs. When they came out the poor Cat hobbled along, lifting up its tail with pain.

The Wolf and his second were already in position; but when they saw their opponent coming they thought that he was bringing a sword, for they took the outstretched tail of the Cat for one. And because the poor animal hobbled on three legs, they thought nothing less than that it was picking up stones to throw at them every time it stooped. Then both became frightened; the Boar crept away into a thicket, and the Wolf jumped up into a tree. The Dog and the Cat were astonished, when they arrived, at seeing no one about. The Boar, however, had not been able to conceal himself completely; his ears still stuck out. While the Cat was looking round cautiously, the Boar twitched its ears; the Cat, who thought that it was a mouse moving, sprang upon it, and began biting with a will. The Boar jumped up and ran away, calling out: 'The guilty party is up in that tree.' The Cat and the Dog looked up and perceived the Wolf, who, ashamed of having shown himself such a coward, made peace with the Dog.

The Straw, the Coal, and the Bean

ONCE there was a poor old woman who lived in a village; she had collected a bundle of beans, and was going to cook them. So she prepared a fire on her hearth, and to make it burn up quickly she lighted it with a handful of straw. When she threw the beans into the pot, one escaped her unnoticed and slipped on to the floor, where it lay by a straw. Soon after a glowing coal jumped out of the fire and joined the others. Then the Straw began, and said : 'Little friends, how came ye hither ? '

The Coal answered : ' I have happily escaped the fire ; and if I had not done so by force of will, my death would certainly have been a most cruel one ; I should have been burnt to a cinder.'

The Bean said : ' I also have escaped so far with a whole skin ; but if the old woman had put me into the pot, I should have been pitilessly boiled down to broth like my comrades.'

' Would a better fate have befallen me, then ? ' asked the Straw ; ' the old woman packed all my brothers into the fire and smoke, sixty of them all done for at once. Fortunately, I slipped through her fingers.'

' What are we to do now, though ? ' asked the Coal.

' My opinion is,' said the Bean, ' that, as we have escaped death, we must all keep together like good comrades ; and so that we may run no further risks, we had better quit the country.'

This proposal pleased both the others, and they set out together. Before long they came to a little stream, and, as there was neither path nor bridge, they did not know how to get over. The Straw at last had an idea, and said, ' I will throw myself over and then you can walk across upon me like a bridge.' So the Straw stretched himself across from one side to the other, and the Coal, which was of a fiery nature, tripped gaily over the newly-built bridge. But when it got to the middle and heard the water rushing below, it was frightened, and remained speechless, not daring to go any further. The Straw beginning to burn, broke in two and fell into the stream; the Coal, falling with it, fizzled out in the water. The Bean, who had cautiously remained on the bank, could not help laughing over the whole business, and, having begun, could not stop, but laughed till she split her sides. Now, all would have been up with her had not, fortunately, a wandering tailor been taking a rest by the stream. As he had a sympathetic heart, he brought out a needle and thread and stitched her up again; but, as he used black thread, all beans have a black seam to this day.

Briar Rose

ALONG time ago there lived a King and Queen, who said every day, 'If only we had a child'; but for a long time they had none.

It fell out once, as the Queen was bathing, that a frog crept out of the water on to the land, and said to her : 'Your wish shall be fulfilled ; before a year has passed you shall bring a daughter into the world.'

The frog's words came true. The Queen had a little girl who was so beautiful that the King could not contain himself for joy, and prepared a great feast. He invited not only his relations, friends, and acquaintances, but the fairies, in order that they might be favourably and kindly disposed towards the child. There were thirteen of them in the kingdom, but as the King had only twelve golden plates for them to eat from, one of the fairies had to stay at home.

The feast was held with all splendour, and when it came to an end the fairies all presented the child with a magic gift. One gave her virtue, another beauty, a third riches, and so on, with everything in the world that she could wish for.

When eleven of the fairies had said their say, the thirteenth suddenly appeared. She wanted to revenge herself for not having been invited. Without greeting any one, or even glancing at the company, she called out in a loud voice : 'The Princess shall prick herself with a distaff in her fifteenth year and shall fall down dead'; and without another word she turned and left the hall.

Every one was terror-struck, but the twelfth fairy, whose wish was still unspoken, stepped forward. She could not cancel the curse, but could only soften it, so she said : 'It shall not be death, but a deep sleep lasting a hundred years, into which your daughter shall fall.'

The King was so anxious to guard his dear child from the

'The Thirteenth Fairy.'

misfortune, that he sent out a command that all the distaffs in the whole kingdom should be burned.

As time went on all the promises of the fairies came true. The Princess grew up so beautiful, modest, kind, and clever

32

that every one who saw her could not but love her. Now it happened that on the very day when she was fifteen years old the King and Queen were away from home, and the Princess was left quite alone in the castle. She wandered about over the whole place, looking at rooms and halls as she pleased, and at last she came to an old tower. She ascended a narrow, winding staircase and reached a little door. A rusty key was sticking in the lock, and when she turned it the door flew open. In a little room sat an old woman with a spindle, spinning her flax busily.

'Good day, Granny,' said the Princess; 'what are you doing?'

'I am spinning,' said the old woman, and nodded her head.

'What is the thing that whirls round so merrily?' asked the Princess; and she took the spindle and tried to spin too.

But she had scarcely touched it before the curse was fulfilled, and she pricked her finger with the spindle. The instant she felt the prick she fell upon the bed which was standing near, and lay still in a deep sleep which spread over the whole castle.

The King and Queen, who had just come home and had stepped into the hall, went to sleep, and all their courtiers with them. The horses went to sleep in the stable, the dogs in the yard, the doves on the roof, the flies on the wall; yes, even the fire flickering on the hearth grew still and went to sleep, and the roast meat stopped crackling; the cook, who was pulling the scullion's hair because he had made some mistake, let him go and went to sleep. The wind dropped, and on the trees in front of the castle not a leaf stirred.

But round the castle a hedge of briar roses began to grow up; every year it grew higher, till at last it surrounded the whole castle so that nothing could be seen of it, not even the flags on the roof.

But there was a legend in the land about the lovely sleeping Briar Rose, as the King's daughter was called, and from time to time princes came and tried to force a way through the hedge into the castle. They found it impossible, for the thorns, as though they had hands, held them fast, and the princes remained caught in them without being able to free themselves, and so died a miserable death.

After many, many years a Prince came again to the country and heard an old man tell of the castle which stood behind the briar hedge, in which a most beautiful maiden called Briar

But round the castle a hedge of briar roses began to grow up.

Rose had been asleep for the last hundred years, and with her slept the King, Queen, and all her courtiers. He knew also, from his grandfather, that many princes had already come and sought to pierce through the briar hedge, and had remained caught in it and died a sad death.

Then the young Prince said, 'I am not afraid; I am determined to go and look upon the lovely Briar Rose.'

34

BRIAR ROSE

The good old man did all in his power to dissuade him, but the Prince would not listen to his words.

Now, however, the hundred years were just ended, and the day had come when Briar Rose was to wake up again. When the Prince approached the briar hedge it was in blossom, and was covered with beautiful large flowers which made way for him of their own accord and let him pass unharmed, and then closed up again into a hedge behind him.

In the courtyard he saw the horses and brindled hounds lying asleep, on the roof sat the doves with their heads under their wings : and when he went into the house the flies were asleep on the walls, and near the throne lay the King and Queen ; in the kitchen was the cook, with his hand raised as though about to strike the scullion, and the maid sat with the black fowl in her lap which she was about to pluck.

He went on further, and all was so still that he could hear his own breathing. At last he reached the tower, and opened the door into the little room where Briar Rose was asleep. There she lay, looking so beautiful that he could not take his eyes off her ; he bent down and gave her a kiss. As he touched her, Briar Rose opened her eyes and looked lovingly at him. Then they went down together ; and the King woke up, and the Queen, and all the courtiers, and looked at each other with astonished eyes. The horses in the stable stood up and shook themselves, the hounds leaped about and wagged their tails, the doves on the roof lifted their heads from under their wings, looked round, and flew into the fields ; the flies on the walls began to crawl again, the fire in the kitchen roused itself and blazed up and cooked the food, the meat began to crackle, and the cook boxed the scullion's ears so soundly that he screamed aloud, while the maid finished plucking the fowl. Then the wedding of the Prince and Briar Rose was celebrated with all splendour, and they lived happily till they died.

The Dog and the Sparrow

THERE was once a sheep-dog who had not got a kind master, but one who left him to suffer from hunger. When he could bear it no longer, he went sadly away. On the road he met a Sparrow, who said, 'Brother Dog, why are you so sad?'

On the road he met a Sparrow.

The Dog answered, 'Because I am hungry and I have nothing to eat.'

'Then,' said the Sparrow, 'Brother Dog, come with me to the town, and I will satisfy your hunger.'

So they went to the town together, and when they came to

36

a butcher's shop, the Sparrow said to the Dog, 'Stay where you are out there and I will peck down a piece of meat.' He perched upon the stall, and looked about to see that he was not noticed ; then he pecked, pulled, and pushed a piece of meat lying near the edge, till at last it fell to the ground. The Dog seized it and ran off with it to a corner, where he devoured it. Then the Sparrow said to him, ' Now come with me to another shop, and I will pull down another piece so that you may have enough.'

When the Dog had gobbled up the second piece of meat, the Sparrow said, ' Brother Dog, have you had enough ? '

' Yes, I have had enough meat,' replied the Dog ; ' but I haven't had any bread.'

' Oh, you shall have some bread too,' said the Sparrow. ' Come with me.' And then he led him to a baker's shop, where he pecked at a couple of rolls till they fell down. Then, as the Dog still wanted more, he took him to another shop where he pulled down some more bread.

When that was consumed, the Sparrow said, ' Brother Dog, is your hunger satisfied ? '

' Yes,' he answered ; ' now let us go and walk about outside the town for a bit.'

So they both went out on to the high-road. Now it was very warm weather, and when they had walked a little way the Dog said, ' I am tired, and I want to go to sleep.'

' Oh, by all means,' answered the Sparrow ; ' I will sit upon this branch in the meantime.'

So the Dog lay down upon the road and fell fast asleep. While he lay there sleeping, a Carter came along driving a wagon with three horses. The wagon was laden with two casks of wine. The Sparrow saw that he was not going to turn aside, but was going on in the track in which the Dog lay, and he called out, ' Carter, don't do it, or I will ruin you ! '

But the Carter grumbled to himself, ' You won't ruin me,' cracked his whip, and drove the wheels of his wagon right over the Dog and killed him.

The Sparrow cried out after him, ' Carter, you have killed my brother Dog ; it will cost you your wagon and your team.'

' My wagon and my team indeed, what harm can you do me ? ' asked the Carter, as he drove on. The Sparrow crept under the tarpaulin and pecked at the bunghole of one of the casks till the bung came out, and all the wine trickled away without the Carter's being aware of it. When he looked round and saw the wine dripping from the wagon, he examined the casks and found that one was empty.

' Alas, poor man that I am ! ' he cried.

' Not poor enough yet,' said the Sparrow, as he flew on to the head of one of the horses and pecked out its eyes. When the Carter saw what he was doing, he seized his chopper to throw it at the Sparrow ; but the bird flew away, and the chopper hit the horse on the head, and he dropped down dead.

' Alas, poor man that I am ! ' he cried.

' Not poor enough yet,' said the Sparrow. As the Carter drove on with his two horses, the Sparrow again crept under the tarpaulin and pecked the bung out of the second cask, so that all the wine ran out.

When the Carter perceived it, he cried again, ' Alas, poor man that I am ! '

But the Sparrow answered, ' Not poor enough yet ' ; and he seated himself on the head of the second horse and pecked its eyes out. The Carter ran up with his big chopper and struck at him ; but the Sparrow flew away, and the blow hit the horse and killed it.

' Alas, poor man that I am ! ' cried the Carter.

' Not poor enough yet,' said the Sparrow, as he perched on the head of the third horse and pecked out its eyes. In his rage, the Carter struck out at the Sparrow with his chopper without taking aim, missed the Sparrow, but hit his last horse on the head, and it fell down dead.

' Alas, poor man that I am ! '

' Not poor enough yet,' said the Sparrow. ' Now, I will bring poverty to your home ' ; and he flew away.

The King could not contain himself for joy.

The young Prince said, ' I am not afraid; I am determined
to go and look upon the lovely Briar Rose.'

At the third sting the **Fox** screamed, and down went his tail
between his legs.

So she seized him with two fingers, and carried him upstairs.

THE DOG AND THE SPARROW

The Carter had to leave his wagon standing, and he went home full of rage and fury.

'Ah!' he said to his wife, 'what misfortunes I have had to-day; the wine has all run out of the casks, and my three horses are dead.'

'Alas! husband,' she answered, 'whatever kind of evil bird is this which has come into our house. He has assembled all the birds in the world, and they have settled on our maize and they are eating it clean up.'

He went up into the loft, where thousands and thousands of birds were sitting on the floor. They had eaten up all the maize, and the Sparrow sat in the middle of them.

Then the Carter cried out, 'Alas, poor man that I am!'

'Not poor enough,' answered the Sparrow, 'Carter, it will cost you your life yet'; and he flew away.

Now the Carter, having lost all that he possessed, went downstairs and sat down beside the stove, very angry and ill-tempered. But the Sparrow sat outside the window and cried, 'Carter, it will cost you your life.'

The Carter seized his chopper and threw it at the Sparrow, but it only smashed the window and did not hit the bird.

Then the Sparrow hopped in and perched on the stove, and cried, 'Carter, it will cost you your life.'

The Carter, mad, and blind with rage, smashed the stove to atoms, but the Sparrow fluttered hither and thither till all the furniture,—the little looking-glass, the bench, the table,—and at last the very walls of his house were destroyed, but without ever hitting the Sparrow. At last he caught it in his hand.

'Then,' said his wife, 'shall I kill it?'

'No,' he cried; 'that would be too good for it; it shall die a much worse death. I will swallow it.' And he took it and gulped it down whole.

But the bird began to flutter about in his inside, and at last fluttered up into the man's mouth. He stretched out his head and cried, 'Carter, it will cost you your life yet.'

39

The Carter handed his chopper to his wife and said, ' Wife, kill the bird in my mouth.' The woman hit out, but she aimed badly and hit the Carter on the head, and down he fell, dead.

The Sparrow, however, flew out and right away.

The Twelve
Dancing Princesses

THERE was once a King who had twelve daughters, each more beautiful than the other. They slept together in a hall where their beds stood close to one another; and at night, when they had gone to bed, the King locked the door and bolted it. But when he unlocked it in the morning, he noticed that their shoes had been danced to pieces, and nobody could explain how it happened. So the King sent out a proclamation saying that any one who could discover where the Princesses did their night's dancing should choose one of them to be his wife and should reign after his death; but whoever presented himself, and failed to make the discovery after three days and nights, was to forfeit his life.

A Prince soon presented himself and offered to take the risk. He was well received, and at night was taken into a room adjoining the hall where the Princesses slept. His bed was made up there, and he was to watch and see where they went to dance; so that they could not do anything, or go anywhere else, the door of his room was left open too. But the eyes of the King's son grew heavy, and he fell asleep. When he woke up in the morning all the twelve had been dancing, for the soles of their shoes were full of holes. The second and third evenings passed with the same results, and then the Prince found no mercy, and his head was cut off.

41

Many others came after him and offered to take the risk, but they all had to lose their lives.

Now it happened that a poor Soldier, who had been wounded and could no longer serve, found himself on the road to the town where the King lived. There he fell in with an old woman who asked him where he intended to go.

'I really don't know, myself,' he said; and added, in fun, 'I should like to discover where the King's daughters dance their shoes into holes, and after that to become King.'

'That is not so difficult,' said the old woman. 'You must not drink the wine which will be brought to you in the evening, but must pretend to be fast asleep.' Whereupon she gave him a short cloak, saying: 'When you wear this you will be invisible, and then you can slip out after the Twelve Princesses.'

As soon as the Soldier heard this good advice he took it up seriously, plucked up courage, appeared before the King, and offered himself as suitor. He was as well received as the others, and was dressed in royal garments.

In the evening, when bed-time came, he was conducted to the ante-room. As he was about to go to bed the eldest Princess appeared, bringing him a cup of wine; but he had fastened a sponge under his chin and let the wine run down into it, so that he did not drink one drop. Then he lay down, and when he had been quiet a little while he began to snore as though in the deepest sleep.

The Twelve Princesses heard him, and laughed. The eldest said: 'He, too, must forfeit his life.'

Then they got up, opened cupboards, chests, and cases, and brought out their beautiful dresses. They decked themselves before the glass, skipping about and revelling in the prospect of the dance. Only the youngest sister said: 'I don't know what it is. You may rejoice, but I feel so strange; a misfortune is certainly hanging over us.'

'You are a little goose,' answered the eldest; 'you are always frightened. Have you forgotten how many Princes

42

have come here in vain ? Why, I need not have given the Soldier a sleeping draught at all ; the blockhead would never have awakened.'

When they were all ready they looked at the Soldier ; but his eyes were shut and he did not stir. So they thought they would soon be quite safe. Then the eldest went up to one of the beds and knocked on it ; it sank into the earth, and they descended through the opening, one after another, the eldest first.

The Soldier, who had noticed everything, did not hesitate long, but threw on his cloak and went down behind the youngest. Half-way down he trod on her dress. She was frightened, and said : ' What was that ? who is holding on to my dress ? '

' Don't be so foolish. You must have caught on a nail,' said the eldest. Then they went right down, and when they got quite underground, they stood in a marvellously beautiful avenue of trees ; all the leaves were silver, and glittered and shone.

The Soldier thought, ' I must take away some token with me.' And as he broke off a twig, a sharp crack came from the tree.

The youngest cried out, ' All is not well ; did you hear that sound ? '

' Those are triumphal salutes, because we shall soon have released our Princes,' said the eldest.

Next they came to an avenue where all the leaves were of gold, and, at last, into a third, where they were of shining diamonds. From both these he broke off a twig, and there was a crack each time which made the youngest Princess start with terror ; but the eldest maintained that the sounds were only triumphal salutes. They went on faster, and came to a great lake. Close to the bank lay twelve little boats, and in every boat sat a handsome Prince. They had expected the Twelve Princesses, and each took one with him ; but the Soldier seated himself by the youngest.

Then said the Prince, ' I don't know why, but the boat is much heavier to-day, and I am obliged to row with all my strength to get it along.'

' I wonder why it is,' said the youngest, ' unless, perhaps, it is the hot weather ; it is strangely hot.'

On the opposite side of the lake stood a splendid brightly-lighted castle, from which came the sound of the joyous music of trumpets and drums. They rowed across, and every Prince danced with his love ; and the Soldier danced too, unseen. If one of the Princesses held a cup of wine he drank out of it, so that it was empty when she lifted it to her lips. This frightened the youngest one, but the eldest always silenced her. They danced till three next morning, when their shoes were danced into holes, and they were obliged to stop. The Princes took them back across the lake, and this time the Soldier took his seat beside the eldest. On the bank they said farewell to their Princes, and promised to come again the next night. When they got to the steps, the Soldier ran on ahead, lay down in bed, and when the twelve came lagging by, slowly and wearily, he began to snore again, very loud, so that they said, ' We are quite safe as far as he is concerned.' Then they took off their beautiful dresses, put them away, placed the worn-out shoes under their beds, and lay down.

The next morning the Soldier determined to say nothing, but to see the wonderful doings again. So he went with them the second and third nights. Everything was just the same as the first time, and they danced each time till their shoes were in holes ; but the third time the Soldier took away a wine-cup as a token.

When the appointed hour came for his answer, he took the three twigs and the cup with him and went before the King. The Twelve Princesses stood behind the door listening to hear what he would say. When the King put the question, ' Where did my daughters dance their shoes to pieces in the night ? ' he answered : ' With twelve Princes in an underground castle.' Then he produced the tokens.

44

On the opposite side of the lake stood a splendid brightly-lighted Castle.

The King sent for his daughters and asked them whether the Soldier had spoken the truth. As they saw that they were betrayed, and would gain nothing by lies, they were obliged to admit all. Thereupon the King asked the Soldier which one he would choose as his wife. He answered : ' I am no longer young, give me the eldest.'

So the wedding was celebrated that very day, and the kingdom was promised to him on the King's death. But for every night which the Princes had spent in dancing with the Princesses a day was added to their time of enchantment.

The Fisherman and his Wife

THERE was once a Fisherman, who lived with his Wife in a miserable little hovel close to the sea. He went to fish every day, and he fished and fished, and at last one day, as he was sitting looking deep down into the shining water, he felt something on his line. When he hauled it up there was a great Flounder on the end of the line. The Flounder said to him, 'Listen, Fisherman, I beg you not to kill me: I am no common Flounder, I am an enchanted prince! What good will it do you to kill me?

47

I shan't be good to eat; put me back into the water, and leave me to swim about.'

'Ho! ho!' said the Fisherman, 'you need not make so many words about it. I am quite ready to put back a Flounder that can talk.' And so saying, he put back the Flounder into the shining water, and it sank down to the bottom, leaving a streak of blood behind it.

Then the Fisherman got up and went back to his Wife in the hovel. 'Husband,' she said, 'hast thou caught nothing to-day?'

'No,' said the Man; 'all I caught was one Flounder, and he said he was an enchanted prince, so I let him go swim again.'

'Didst thou not wish for anything then?' asked the Good-wife.

'No,' said the Man; 'what was there to wish for?'

'Alas!' said his Wife, 'isn't it bad enough always to live in this wretched hovel! Thou mightst at least have wished for a nice clean cottage. Go back and call him, tell him I want a pretty cottage: he will surely give us that.'

'Alas!' said the Man, 'what am I to go back there for?'

'Well,' said the Woman, 'it was thou who didst catch him and let him go again; for certain he will do that for thee. Be off now!'

The Man was still not very willing to go, but he did not want to vex his Wife, and at last he went back to the sea.

He found the sea no longer bright and shining, but dull and green. He stood by it and said—

> 'Flounder, Flounder in the sea,
> Prythee, hearken unto me:
> My Wife, Ilsebil, must have her own will,
> And sends me to beg a boon of thee.'

The Flounder came swimming up, and said, 'Well, what do you want?'

'Alas,' said the Man, 'I had to call you, for my Wife said I ought to have wished for something as I caught you. She doesn't want to live in our miserable hovel any longer, she wants a pretty cottage.'

'Go home again then,' said the Flounder, 'she has her wish fully.'

The Man went home and found his Wife no longer in the old hut, but a pretty little cottage stood in its place, and his Wife was sitting on a bench by the door.

She took him by the hand, and said, 'Come and look in here—isn't this much better ? '

They went inside and found a pretty sitting-room, and a bedroom with a bed in it, a kitchen and a larder furnished with everything of the best in tin and brass and every possible requisite. Outside there was a little yard with chickens and ducks, and a little garden full of vegetables and fruit.

'Look ! ' said the Woman, 'is not this nice ? '

'Yes,' said the Man, 'and so let it remain. We can live here very happily.'

'We will see about that,' said the Woman. With that they ate something and went to bed.

Everything went well for a week or more, and then said the Wife, 'Listen, husband, this cottage is too cramped, and the garden is too small. The Flounder could have given us a bigger house. I want to live in a big stone castle. Go to the Flounder, and tell him to give us a castle.'

'Alas, Wife,' said the Man, 'the cottage is good enough for us : what should we do with a castle ? '

'Never mind,' said his Wife, 'do thou but go to the Flounder, and he will manage it.'

'Nay, Wife,' said the Man, 'the Flounder gave us the cottage. I don't want to go back ; as likely as not he 'll be angry.'

'Go, all the same,' said the Woman. 'He can do it easily enough, and willingly into the bargain. Just go ! '

The Man's heart was heavy, and he was very unwilling to go. He said to himself, 'It 's not right.' But at last he went.

He found the sea was no longer green; it was still calm, but dark violet and grey. He stood by it and said—

> 'Flounder, Flounder in the sea,
> Prythee, hearken unto me:
> My Wife, Ilsebil, must have her own will,
> And sends me to beg a boon of thee.'

'Now, what do you want?' said the Flounder.

'Alas,' said the Man, half scared, 'my wife wants a big stone castle.'

'Go home again,' said the Flounder, 'she is standing at the door of it.'

Then the man went away thinking he would find no house, but when he got back he found a great stone palace, and his Wife standing at the top of the steps, waiting to go in.

She took him by the hand and said, 'Come in with me.'

With that they went in and found a great hall paved with marble slabs, and numbers of servants in attendance, who opened the great doors for them. The walls were hung with beautiful tapestries, and the rooms were furnished with golden chairs and tables, while rich carpets covered the floors, and crystal chandeliers hung from the ceilings. The tables groaned under every kind of delicate food and the most costly wines. Outside the house there was a great courtyard, with stabling for horses, and cows, and many fine carriages. Beyond this there was a great garden filled with the loveliest flowers, and fine fruit-trees. There was also a park, half a mile long, and in it were stags and hinds, and hares, and everything of the kind one could wish for.

'Now,' said the Woman, 'is not this worth having?'

'Oh yes,' said the Man; 'and so let it remain. We will live in this beautiful palace and be content.'

'We will think about that,' said his Wife, 'and sleep upon it.'

With that they went to bed.

Next morning the Wife woke up first; day was just dawn-

50

ing, and from her bed she could see the beautiful country around her. Her husband was still asleep, but she pushed him with her elbow, and said, ' Husband, get up and peep out of the window. See here, now, could we not be King over all this land ? Go to the Flounder. We will be King.'

' Alas, Wife,' said the Man, ' what should we be King for ? I don't want to be King.'

' Ah,' said his Wife, ' if thou wilt not be King, I will. Go to the Flounder. I will be King.'

' Alas, Wife,' said the Man, ' whatever dost thou want to be King for ? I don't like to tell him.'

' Why not ? ' said the Woman. ' Go thou must. I will be King.'

So the Man went ; but he was quite sad because his Wife would be King.

' It is not right,' he said ; ' it is not right.'

When he reached the sea, he found it dark, grey, and rough, and evil smelling. He stood there and said—

> ' Flounder, Flounder in the sea,
>   Prythee, hearken unto me :
>   My Wife, Ilsebil, must have her own will,
>   And sends me to beg a boon of thee.'

' Now, what does she want ? ' said the Flounder.

' Alas,' said the Man, ' she wants to be King now.'

' Go back. She is King already,' said the Flounder.

So the Man went back, and when he reached the palace he found that it had grown much larger, and a great tower had been added with handsome decorations. There was a sentry at the door, and numbers of soldiers were playing drums and trumpets. As soon as he got inside the house, he found everything was marble and gold ; and the hangings were of velvet, with great golden tassels. The doors of the saloon were thrown wide open, and he saw the whole court assembled. His Wife was sitting on a lofty throne of gold and diamonds ; she wore a golden crown, and carried in one hand a sceptre of pure gold. On each side of her stood her ladies in a long row, every one a head shorter than the next.

He stood before her, and said : ' Alas, Wife, art thou now King ? '

' Yes,' she said ; ' now I am King.'

He stood looking at her for some time, and then he said : ' Ah, Wife, it is a fine thing for thee to be King ; now we will not wish to be anything more.'

' Nay, husband,' she answered, quite uneasily ; ' I find the time hang very heavy on my hands. I can't bear it any longer. Go back to the Flounder. King I am, but I must also be Emperor.'

' Alas, Wife,' said the Man, ' why dost thou now want to be Emperor ? '

' Husband,' she answered, ' go to the Flounder. Emperor I will be.'

' Alas, Wife,' said the Man, ' Emperor he can't make thee, and I won't ask him. There is only one Emperor in the country ; and Emperor the Flounder cannot make thee, that he can't.'

' What ? ' said the Woman. ' I am King, and thou art but my husband. To him thou must go, and that right quickly. If he can make a King, he can also make an Emperor. Emperor I will be, so go quickly.'

He had to go, but he was quite frightened. And as he went, he thought, ' This won't end well ; Emperor is too shameless. The Flounder will make an end of the whole thing.'

With that he came to the sea, but now he found it quite black, and heaving up from below in great waves. It tossed to and fro, and a sharp wind blew over it, and the man trembled. So he stood there, and said—

> ' Flounder, Flounder in the sea,
> Prythee, hearken unto me :
> My Wife, Ilsebil, must have her own will,
> And sends me to beg a boon of thee.'

'What does she want now?' said the Flounder.

'Alas, Flounder,' he said, 'my Wife wants to be Emperor.'

'Go back,' said the Flounder. 'She is Emperor.'

So the man went back, and when he got to the door, he found that the whole palace was made of polished marble, with alabaster figures and golden decorations. Soldiers marched up and down before the doors, blowing their trumpets and beating their drums. Inside the palace, counts, barons, and dukes walked about as attendants, and they opened to him the doors, which were of pure gold.

He went in, and saw his Wife sitting on a huge throne made of solid gold. It was at least two miles high. She had on her head a great golden crown set with diamonds three yards high. In one hand she held the sceptre, and in the other the orb of empire. On each side of her stood the gentlemen-at-arms in two rows, each one a little smaller than the other, from giants two miles high down to the tiniest dwarf no bigger than my little finger. She was surrounded by princes and dukes.

Her husband stood still, and said: 'Wife, art thou now Emperor?'

'Yes,' said she; 'now I am Emperor.'

Then he looked at her for some time, and said: 'Alas, Wife, how much better off art thou for being Emperor?'

'Husband,' she said, 'what art thou standing there for? Now I am Emperor, I mean to be Pope! Go back to the Flounder.'

'Alas, Wife,' said the Man, 'what wilt thou not want? Pope thou canst not be. There is only one Pope in Christendom. That's more than the Flounder can do.'

'Husband,' she said, 'Pope I will be; so go at once. I must be Pope this very day.'

'No, Wife,' he said, 'I dare not tell him. It's no good; it's too monstrous altogether. The Flounder cannot make thee Pope.'

'Husband,' said the Woman, 'don't talk nonsense. If

he can make an Emperor, he can make a Pope. Go immediately. I am Emperor, and thou art but my husband, and thou must obey.'

So he was frightened, and went; but he was quite dazed. He shivered and shook, and his knees trembled.

A great wind arose over the land, the clouds flew across the sky, and it grew as dark as night; the leaves fell from the trees, and the water foamed and dashed upon the shore. In the distance the ships were being tossed to and fro on the waves, and he heard them firing signals of distress. There was still a little patch of blue in the sky among the dark clouds, but towards the south they were red and heavy, as in a bad storm. In despair, he stood and said—

> 'Flounder, Flounder in the sea,
> Prythee, hearken unto me:
> My Wife, Ilsebil, must have her own will,
> And sends me to beg a boon of thee.'

'Now, what does she want?' said the Flounder.

'Alas,' said the Man, 'she wants to be Pope!'

'Go back. Pope she is,' said the Flounder.

So back he went, and he found a great church surrounded with palaces. He pressed through the crowd, and inside he found thousands and thousands of lights, and his Wife, entirely clad in gold, was sitting on a still higher throne, with three golden crowns upon her head, and she was surrounded with priestly state. On each side of her were two rows of candles, the biggest as thick as a tower, down to the tiniest little taper. Kings and Emperors were on their knees before her, kissing her shoe.

'Wife,' said the Man, looking at her, 'art thou now Pope?'

'Yes,' said she; 'now I am Pope.'

So there he stood gazing at her, and it was like looking at a shining sun.

'Alas, Wife,' he said, 'art thou better off for being Pope?' At first she sat as stiff as a post, without stirring. Then he said : 'Now, Wife, be content with being Pope ; higher thou canst not go.'

'I will think about that,' said the Woman, and with that they both went to bed. Still she was not content, and could not sleep for her inordinate desires. The Man slept well and soundly, for he had walked about a great deal in the day ; but his Wife could think of nothing but what further grandeur

'Flounder, Flounder in the sea,
Prythee, hearken unto me.'

she could demand. When the dawn reddened the sky she raised herself up in bed and looked out of the window, and when she saw the sun rise, she said :

'Ha ! can I not cause the sun and the moon to rise ? Husband ! ' she cried, digging her elbow into his side, ' wake up and go to the Flounder. I will be Lord of the Universe.'

Her husband, who was still more than half asleep, was so

shocked that he fell out of bed. He thought he must have heard wrong. He rubbed his eyes, and said :

'Alas, Wife, what didst thou say ? '

'Husband,' she said, ' if I cannot be Lord of the Universe, and cause the sun and moon to set and rise, I shall not be able to bear it. I shall never have another happy moment.'

She looked at him so wildly that it caused a shudder to run through him.

'Alas, Wife,' he said, falling on his knees before her, ' the Flounder can't do that. Emperor and Pope he can make, but that is indeed beyond him. I pray thee, control thyself and remain Pope.'

Then she flew into a terrible rage. Her hair stood on end ; she kicked him and screamed—

'I won't bear it any longer ; wilt thou go ! '

Then he pulled on his trousers and tore away like a madman. Such a storm was raging that he could hardly keep his feet : houses and trees quivered and swayed, and mountains trembled, and the rocks rolled into the sea. The sky was pitchy black ; it thundered and lightened, and the sea ran in black waves mountains high, crested with white foam. He shrieked out, but could hardly make himself heard—

> 'Flounder, Flounder in the sea,
> Prythee, hearken unto me :
> My Wife, Ilsebil, must have her own will,
> And sends me to beg a boon of thee.'

'Now, what does she want ? ' asked the Flounder.

'Alas,' he said, ' she wants to be Lord of the Universe.'

'Now she must go back to her old hovel ; and there she is.'

So there they are to this very day.

The Wren and the Bear

ONCE upon a time, in the summer, a Bear and a Wolf were taking a walk in a wood when the Bear heard a bird singing most beautifully, and he said, ' Brother Wolf, what kind of bird is that singing so beautifully ? '

' That is the King of the birds, and we must bow down to it.'

But really it was a Wren.

' If that is so,' said the Bear, ' I should like to see his royal palace.   Come, you must take me to it.'

' That 's not so easy,' said the Wolf.   ' You must wait till the Queen comes.'

Soon after, the Queen made her appearance, bringing food in her beak, and the King came with her to feed their little ones.   The Bear would have liked to go in at once, but the Wolf held him by the sleeve, and said, ' No ; now you must wait till the King and Queen fly away again.'

So they marked the opening of the nest, and trudged on. But the Bear had no rest till he could see the royal palace, and before long he went back.

The King and the Queen had gone out again.   He peeped in, and saw five or six young ones lying in the nest.

' Is that the royal palace ? ' cried the Bear.   ' What a miserable place !   And do you mean to say that you are royal children ?   You must be changelings ! '

When the young Wrens heard this, they were furious, and shrieked, ' No, indeed we 're not.   Our parents are honest people ; we must have this out with you.'

The Bear and the Wolf were very much frightened.   They turned round and ran home to their dens.

But the young Wrens continued to shriek and scream aloud; and when their parents came back with more food, they said, ' We won't touch so much as the leg of a fly, even if we starve, till you tell us whether we are really your lawful children or not. The Bear has been here calling us names.'

Then said the old King, ' Only be quiet, and this shall be seen to.'

Thereupon he and his wife the Queen flew off to the Bear in his den, and called in to him, ' Old Bruin, why have you been calling our children names? It will turn out badly for you, and it will lead to a bloody war between us.'

So war was declared, and all the four-footed animals were called together—the ox, the ass, the cow, the stag, the roedeer, and every other creature on the earth.

But the Wren called together every creature which flew in the air, not only birds both large and small, but also the gnats, the hornets, the bees, and the flies.

When the time came for the war to begin, the Wren sent out scouts to discover where the commanding generals of the enemy were to be found. The gnats were the most cunning of all. They swarmed in the wood where the enemy were assembled, and at last they hid themselves under a leaf of the tree where the orders were being given.

The Bear called the Fox up to him and said, ' You are the slyest of all the animals, Reynard. You shall be our general, and lead us.'

' Very good,' said the Fox; ' but what shall we have for a signal?' But nobody could think of anything. Then said the Fox, ' I have a fine, long, bushy tail, which almost looks like a red feather brush. When I hold my tail erect, things are going well, and you must march forward at once; but if it droops, you must all run away as hard as ever you can.'

When the gnats heard this they flew straight home and told the Wrens every detail.

When the day broke, all the four-footed animals came

58

rushing to the spot where the battle was to take place. They came with such a tramping that the earth shook.

The Wren and his army also came swarming through the air; they fluttered and buzzed enough to terrify one. And then they made for one another.

The Wren sent the Hornet down with orders to seat herself under the tail of the Fox and to sting him with all her might.

When the Fox felt the first sting he quivered, and raised one leg in the air; but he bore it bravely, and kept his tail erect. At the second sting he was forced to let it droop for a moment, but the third time he could bear it no longer; he screamed, and down went his tail between his legs. When the animals saw this they thought all was lost, and off they ran helter-skelter, as fast as they could go, each to his own den.

So the birds won the battle.

When it was over the King and the Queen flew home to their children, and cried, 'Children, be happy! Eat and drink to your hearts' content; we have won the battle.'

But the young Wrens said, 'We won't eat till the Bear comes here to make an apology, and says that we are really and truly your lawful children.'

The Wren flew to the Bear's den, and cried, 'Old Bruin, you will have to come and apologise to my children for calling them names, or else you will have all your ribs broken.'

So in great terror the Bear crept to the nest and apologised, and at last the young Wrens were satisfied, and they ate and drank and made merry till far into the night.

The Frog Prince

IN the olden time, when wishing was some good, there lived a King whose daughters were all beautiful, but the youngest was so lovely that even the sun, that looked on many things, could not but marvel when he shone upon her face.

Near the King's palace there was a large dark forest, and in the forest, under an old lime-tree, was a well. When the day was very hot the Princess used to go into the forest and sit upon the edge of this cool well; and when she was tired of doing nothing she would play with a golden ball, throwing it up in the air and catching it again, and this was her favourite game. Now on one occasion it so happened that the ball did not fall back into her hand stretched up to catch it, but dropped to the ground and rolled straight into the well. The Princess followed it with her eyes, but it disappeared, for the well was so very deep that it was quite impossible to see the bottom. Then she began to cry bitterly, and nothing would comfort her.

As she was lamenting in this manner, some one called out to her, 'What is the matter, Princess? Your lamentations would move the heart of a stone.'

She looked round towards the spot whence the voice came, and saw a Frog stretching its broad, ugly face out of the water.

'Oh, it's you, is it, old splasher? I am crying for my golden ball which has fallen into the water.'

'Be quiet then, and stop crying,' answered the Frog. 'I know what to do; but what will you give me if I get you back your plaything?'

'Whatever you like, you dear old Frog,' she said. 'My
60

clothes, my pearls and diamonds, or even the golden crown upon my head.'

The Frog answered, ' I care neither for your clothes, your pearls and diamonds, nor even your golden crown ; but if you will be fond of me, and let me be your playmate, sit by you at table, eat out of your plate, drink out of your cup, and sleep in your little bed—if you will promise to do all this, I will go down and fetch your ball.'

' I will promise anything you like to ask, if only you will get me back my ball.'

She thought, ' What is the silly old Frog chattering about ? He lives in the well, croaking with his mates, and he can't be the companion of a human being.'

As soon as the Frog received her promise, he ducked his head under the water and disappeared. After a little while, back he came with the ball in his mouth, and threw it on to the grass beside her.

The Princess was full of joy when she saw her pretty toy again, picked it up, and ran off with it.

' Wait, wait,' cried the Frog. ' Take me with you ; I can't run as fast as you can.'

But what was the good of his crying ' Croak, croak,' as loud as he could ? She did not listen to him, but hurried home, and forgot all about the poor Frog ; and he had to go back to his well.

The next day, as she was sitting at dinner with the King and all the courtiers, eating out of her golden plate, something came flopping up the stairs, flip, flap, flip, flap. When it reached the top it knocked at the door, and cried : ' Youngest daughter of the King, you must let me in.' She ran to see who it was. When she opened the door and saw the Frog she shut it again very quickly, and went back to the table, for she was very much frightened.

The King saw that her heart was beating very fast, and he said : ' My child, what is the matter ? Is there a giant at the door wanting to take you away ? '

'Oh no!' she said: 'it's not a giant, but a hideous Frog.'

'What does the Frog want with you?'

'Oh, father dear, last night, when I was playing by the well in the forest, my golden ball fell into the water. And I cried, and the Frog got it out for me; and then, because he insisted on it, I promised that he should be my playmate. But I never thought that he would come out of the water, but there he is, and he wants to come in to me.'

He knocked at the door for the second time, and sang—

> 'Youngest daughter of the King,
> Take me up, I sing;
> Know'st thou not what yesterday
> Thou to me didst say
> By the well in forest dell.
> Youngest daughter of the King,
> Take me up, I sing.'

Then said the King, 'What you have promised you must perform. Go and open the door for him.'

So she opened the door, and the Frog shuffled in, keeping close to her feet, till he reached her chair. Then he cried, 'Lift me up beside you.' She hesitated, till the King ordered her to do it. When the Frog was put on the chair, he demanded to be placed upon the table, and then he said, 'Push your golden plate nearer that we may eat together.' She did as he asked her, but very unwillingly, as could easily be seen. The Frog made a good dinner, but the Princess could not swallow a morsel. At last he said, 'I have eaten enough, and I am tired, carry me into your bedroom and arrange your silken bed, that we may go to sleep.'

The Princess began to cry, for she was afraid of the clammy Frog, which she did not dare to touch, and which was now to sleep in her pretty little silken bed. But the King grew very angry, and said, 'You must not despise any one who has helped you in your need.'

So she seized him with two fingers, and carried him upstairs, where she put him in a corner of her room. When she got into bed, he crept up to her, and said, 'I am tired, and I want to go to sleep as well as you. Lift me up, or I will tell your father.'

She was very angry, picked him up, and threw him with all her might against the wall, saying, 'You may rest there as well as you can, you hideous Frog.' But when he fell to the ground, he was no longer a hideous Frog, but a handsome Prince with beautiful friendly eyes.

And at her father's wish he became her beloved companion and husband. He told her that he had been bewitched by a wicked fairy, and nobody could have released him from the spells but she herself.

Next morning, when the sun rose, a coach drove up drawn by eight milk-white horses, with white ostrich plumes on their heads, and golden harness. Behind stood faithful Henry, the Prince's body-servant. The faithful fellow had been so distressed when his master was changed into a Frog, that he had caused three iron bands to be placed round his heart, lest it should break from grief and pain.

The coach had come to carry the young pair back into the Prince's own kingdom. The faithful Henry helped both of them into the coach and mounted again behind, delighted at his master's deliverance.

They had only gone a little way when the Prince heard a cracking behind him, as if something were breaking. He turned round, and cried—

'"Henry, the coach is giving way!"
"No, Sir, the coach is safe, I say,
A band from my heart has fall'n in twain,
For long I suffered woe and pain,
While you a frog within a well
Enchanted were by witch's spell!"'

Once more he heard the same snapping and cracking, and then again. The Prince thought it must be some part of the carriage giving way, but it was only the bands round faithful Henry's heart which were snapping, because of his great joy at his master's deliverance and happiness.

63

The Cat and Mouse in Partnership

A CAT once made the acquaintance of a Mouse, and she said so much to it about her love and friendship that at last the Mouse agreed to go into partnership and live with her.

'We must take precautions for the winter,' said the Cat, 'or we shall suffer from hunger. You, little Mouse, dare not venture everywhere, and in the end you will get me into a fix.'

So the good advice was followed, and a pot of fat was purchased. They did not know where to keep it, but, after much deliberation, the Cat said, ' I know no place where it would be safer than in the church; nobody dare venture to take anything there. We will put it under the altar, and will not touch it till we are obliged to.'

So the pot was deposited in safety; but, before long, the Cat began to hanker after it, and said to the Mouse:

' Oh, little Mouse, my cousin has asked me to be godmother. She has brought a son into the world. He is white, with brown spots; and I am to hold him at the font. Let me go out to-day, and you stay alone to look after the house.'

' Oh yes,' said the Mouse, ' by all means go; and if you have anything nice to eat, think of me. I would gladly have a drop of sweet raspberry wine myself.'

64

THE CAT AND MOUSE IN PARTNERSHIP

Now there wasn't a word of truth in all this. The Cat had no cousin, and she had not been invited to be godmother at all. She went straight to the church, crept to the pot of fat, and began to lick it, and she licked and licked the whole of the top off it. Then she took a stroll on the house-tops and reflected on her proceedings, after which she stretched herself in the sun, and wiped her whiskers every time she thought of the pot of fat. She did not go home till evening.

' Oh, there you are again,' said the Mouse ; ' you must have had a merry time.'

' Oh, well enough,' answered the Cat.

' What kind of name was given to the child ? ' asked the Mouse.

' Top-off,' answered the Cat, drily.

' Top-off ! ' cried the Mouse. ' What an extraordinary name ; is it a common one in your family ? '

' What does it matter ! ' said the Cat. ' It 's not worse than crumbstealers, as your godchildren are called.'

Not long after the Cat was again overcome by her desires. She said to the Mouse, ' You must oblige me again by looking after the house alone. For the second time I have been asked to be sponsor, and, as the child has a white ring round its neck, I can't refuse.'

The good little Mouse was quite ready to oblige, and the Cat stole away behind the city walls to the church, and ate half of the pot of fat. ' Nothing tastes better,' she said, ' than what one eats by oneself ' ; and she was quite satisfied with her day's work. When she got home, the Mouse asked what this child had been named.

' Half-gone.'

' What do you say ? I have never heard such a name in my life. I don't believe you would find it in the calendar.'

Soon the Cat's mouth watered again for the dainty morsel.

' Good things always come in threes,' she said to the Mouse ; ' again I am to stand sponsor. This child is quite black, with big white paws, but not another white hair on its body. Such

65

a thing only occurs once in a few years. You will let me go out again, won't you ? '

' Top-off ! Half-gone ! They are such curious names ; they set me thinking.'

' You sit at home in your dark grey velvet coat,' said the Cat, ' getting your head full of fancies. It all comes of not going out in the daytime.'

During the Cat's absence, the Mouse cleared up and made the house tidy ; but the greedy Cat ate up all the fat. ' When it 's all gone, one can be at peace,' said she to herself, as she went home, late at night, fat and satiated.

The Mouse immediately asked what name had been given to the third child.

' I don't suppose it will please you any better,' said the Cat. ' He is called All-gone ! '

' All-gone ! ' exclaimed the Mouse. ' I have never seen it in print. All-gone ! What is the meaning of it ? '

She shook her head, rolled herself up, and went to sleep.

From this time nobody asked the Cat to be sponsor. But when the winter came, and it grew very difficult to get food, the Mouse remembered their store, and said,'Come, Cat, we will go to our pot of fat which we have saved up ; won't it be good now ? '

' Yes, indeed ! ' answered the Cat ; ' it will do you just as much good as putting your tongue out of the window.'

They started off to the church, and when they got there they found the fat-pot still in its place, but it was quite empty.

' Alas,' said the Mouse, ' now I see it all. Everything has come to the light of day. You have indeed been a true friend ! You ate it all up when you went to be godmother. First Top-off, then Half-gone, then——'

' Hold your tongue,' cried the Cat. ' Another word, and I 'll eat you too.'

But the unfortunate Mouse had ' All-gone ' on its lips, and hardly had it come out than the Cat made a spring, seized the Mouse, and gobbled it up.

Now, that 's the way of the world, you see.

The Goosegirl

THERE was once an old Queen whose husband had been dead for many years, and she had a very beautiful daughter. When she grew up she was betrothed to a Prince in a distant country. When the time came for the maiden to be sent into this distant country to be married, the old Queen packed up quantities of clothes and jewels, gold and silver, cups and ornaments, and, in fact, everything suitable to a royal outfit, for she loved her daughter very dearly.

She also sent a Waiting-woman to travel with her, and to put her hand into that of the bridegroom. They each had a horse. The Princess's horse was called Falada, and it could speak.

When the hour of departure came, the old Queen went to her bedroom, and with a sharp little knife cut her finger and made it bleed. Then she held a piece of white cambric under it, and let three drops of blood fall on to it. This cambric she gave to her daughter, and said, ' Dear child, take good care of this ; it will stand you in good stead on the journey.' They then bade each other a sorrowful farewell. The Princess hid the piece of cambric in her bosom, mounted her horse, and set out to her bridegroom's country.

When they had ridden for a time the Princess became very thirsty, and said to the Waiting-woman, ' Get down and fetch me some water in my cup from the stream. I must have something to drink.'

' If you are thirsty,' said the Waiting-woman, ' dismount yourself, lie down by the water and drink. I don't choose to be your servant.'

So, in her great thirst, the Princess dismounted and stooped down to the stream and drank, as she might not have her golden cup. The poor Princess said, 'Alas!' and the drops of blood answered, 'If your mother knew this, it would break her heart.'

The royal bride was humble, so she said nothing, but mounted her horse again. Then they rode several miles further; but the day was warm, the sun was scorching, and the Princess was soon thirsty again.

When they reached a river she called out again to her Waiting-woman, 'Get down, and give me some water in my golden cup!'

She had forgotten all about the rude words which had been said to her. But the Waiting-woman answered more haughtily than ever, 'If you want to drink, get the water for yourself. I won't be your servant.'

Being very thirsty, the Princess dismounted, and knelt by the flowing water. She cried, and said, 'Ah me!' and the drops of blood answered, 'If your mother knew this it would break her heart.'

While she stooped over the water to drink, the piece of cambric with the drops of blood on it fell out of her bosom, and floated away on the stream; but she never noticed this in her great fear. The Waiting-woman, however, had seen it, and rejoiced at getting more power over the bride, who, by losing the drops of blood, had become weak and powerless.

Now, when she was about to mount her horse Falada again, the Waiting-woman said, 'By rights, Falada belongs to me; this jade will do for you!'

The poor little Princess was obliged to give way. Then the Waiting-woman, in a harsh voice, ordered her to take off her royal robes, and to put on her own mean garments. Finally, she forced her to swear before heaven that she would not tell a creature at the Court what had taken place. Had she not taken the oath she would have been killed on the spot. But Falada saw all this and marked it.

THE GOOSEGIRL

The Waiting - woman then mounted Falada and put the real bride on her poor jade, and they continued their journey.

There was great rejoicing when they arrived at the castle. The Prince hurried towards them, and lifted the Waiting-woman from her horse, thinking she was his bride. She was led upstairs, but the real Princess had to stay below.

The old King looked out of the window and saw the delicate, pretty little creature standing in the courtyard; so he went to the bridal apartments and asked the bride about her companion, who was left standing in the courtyard, and wished to know who she was.

'I picked her up on the way, and brought her with me for company. Give the girl something to do to keep her from idling.'

But the old King had no work for her, and could not think of anything. At last he said, 'I have a little lad who looks after the geese; she may help him.'

The boy was called little Conrad, and the real bride was sent with him to look after the geese.

Soon after, the false bride said to the Prince, 'Dear husband, I pray you do me a favour.'

He answered, 'That will I gladly.'

'Well, then, let the knacker be called to cut off the head of the horse I rode; it angered me on the way.'

Really, she was afraid that the horse would speak, and tell of her treatment of the Princess. So it was settled, and the faithful Falada had to die.

When this came to the ear of the real Princess, she promised the knacker a piece of gold if he would do her a slight service. There was a great dark gateway to the town, through which she had to pass every morning and evening. 'Would he nail up Falada's head in this gateway, so that she might see him as she passed?'

The knacker promised to do as she wished, and when the horse's head was cut off, he hung it up in the dark gateway.

69

In the early morning, when she and Conrad went through the gateway, she said in passing—

> 'Alas! dear Falada, there thou hangest.'

And the Head answered—

> 'Alas! Queen's daughter, there thou gangest.
> If thy mother knew thy fate,
> Her heart would break with grief so great.'

Then they passed on out of the town, right into the fields, with the geese. When they reached the meadow, the Princess sat down on the grass and let down her hair. It shone like pure gold, and when little Conrad saw it, he was so delighted that he wanted to pluck some out; but she said—

> 'Blow, blow, little breeze,
> And Conrad's hat seize.
> Let him join in the chase
> While away it is whirled,
> Till my tresses are curled
> And I rest in my place.'

Then a strong wind sprang up, which blew away Conrad's hat right over the fields, and he had to run after it. When he came back, she had finished combing her hair, and it was all put up again; so he could not get a single hair. This made him very sulky, and he would not say another word to her. And they tended the geese till evening, when they went home.

Next morning, when they passed under the gateway, the Princess said—

> 'Alas! dear Falada, there thou hangest.'

Falada answered :—

> 'Alas! Queen's daughter, there thou gangest.
> If thy mother knew thy fate,
> Her heart would break with grief so great.'

The Cat stole away behind the city walls to the church.

Alas! dear Falada, there thou hangest.

Blow, blow, little breeze, And Conrad's hat seize.

Now we will go up the hill and have a good feast before the squirrel
carries off all the nuts.

Again, when they reached the meadows, the Princess undid her hair and began combing it. Conrad ran to pluck some out ; but she said quickly—

'Blow, blow, little breeze,
And Conrad's hat seize.
Let him join in the chase
While away it is whirled,
Till my tresses are curled
And I rest in my place.'

The wind sprang up and blew Conrad's hat far away over the fields, and he had to run after it. When he came back the hair was all put up again, and he could not pull a single hair out. And they tended the geese till the evening. When they got home Conrad went to the old King, and said, ' I won't tend the geese with that maiden again.'

' Why not ? ' asked the King.

' Oh, she vexes me every day.'

The old King then ordered him to say what she did to vex him.

Conrad said, ' In the morning, when we pass under the dark gateway with the geese, she talks to a horse's head which is hung up on the wall. She says—

' Alas ! Falada, there thou hangest,'

and the Head answers—

' Alas ! Queen's daughter, there thou gangest.
If thy mother knew thy fate,
Her heart would break with grief so great.'

Then Conrad went on to tell the King all that happened in the meadow, and how he had to run after his hat in the wind.

The old King ordered Conrad to go out next day as usual. Then he placed himself behind the dark gateway, and heard the Princess speaking to Falada's head. He also followed her into the field, and hid himself behind a bush, and with his own eyes he saw the Goosegirl and the lad come driving

71

the geese into the field. Then, after a time, he saw the girl
let down her hair, which glittered in the sun. Directly after
this, she said—

> ' Blow, blow, little breeze,
> And Conrad's hat seize.
> Let him join in the chase
> While away it is whirled,
> Till my tresses are curled
> And I rest in my place.'

Then came a puff of wind, which carried off Conrad's hat
and he had to run after it. While he was away, the maiden
combed and did up her hair ; and all this the old King
observed. Thereupon he went away unnoticed ; and in the
evening, when the Goosegirl came home, he called her aside
and asked why she did all these things.

'That I may not tell you, nor may I tell any human
creature ; for I have sworn it under the open sky, because if
I had not done so I should have lost my life.'

He pressed her sorely, and gave her no peace, but he could
get nothing out of her. Then he said, ' If you won't tell me,
then tell your sorrows to the iron stove there ' ; and he went
away.

She crept up to the stove, and, beginning to weep and
lament, unburdened her heart to it, and said : ' Here I am,
forsaken by all the world, and yet I am a Princess. A false
Waiting-woman brought me to such a pass that I had to take
off my royal robes. Then she took my place with my bridegroom, while I have to do mean service as a Goosegirl. If
my mother knew it she would break her heart.'

The old King stood outside by the pipes of the stove, and
heard all that she said. Then he came back, and told her to
go away from the stove. He caused royal robes to be put
upon her, and her beauty was a marvel. The old King called
his son, and told him that he had a false bride—she was only a
Waiting-woman ; but the true bride was here, the so-called
Goosegirl.

72

THE GOOSEGIRL

The young Prince was charmed with her youth and beauty. A great banquet was prepared, to which all the courtiers and good friends were bidden. The bridegroom sat at the head of the table, with the Princess on one side and the Waiting-Woman at the other; but she was dazzled, and did not recognise the Princess in her brilliant apparel.

When they had eaten and drunk and were all very merry, the old King put a riddle to the Waiting-woman. 'What does a person deserve who deceives his master?' telling the whole story, and ending by asking, 'What doom does he deserve?'

The false bride answered, 'No better than this. He must be put stark naked into a barrel stuck with nails, and be dragged along by two white horses from street to street till he is dead.'

'That is your own doom,' said the King, 'and the judgment shall be carried out.'

When the sentence was fulfilled, the young Prince married his true bride, and they ruled their kingdom together in peace and happiness.

The Adventures of Chanticleer
and Partlet

I. HOW THEY WENT TO THE HILLS TO EAT NUTS

CHANTICLEER said to Partlet one day, 'The nuts must be ripe; now we will go up the hill together and have a good feast before the squirrel carries them all off.'

'All right,' said Partlet, 'come along; we'll have a fine time.' So they went away up the hill, and, as it was a bright day, they stayed till evening.

Now whether they really had grown fat, or whether it was merely pride, I do not know, but, whatever the reason, they would not walk home, and Chanticleer had to make a little carriage of nut-shells. When it was ready, Partlet took her seat in it, and said to Chanticleer, 'Now you get between the shafts.'

'That's all very fine,' said Chanticleer, 'but I would sooner go home on foot than put myself in harness. I will sit on the box and drive, but draw it myself I never will.'

As they were squabbling over this, a Duck quacked out, 'You thievish folk! Who told you to come to my nut-hill? Just you wait, you will suffer for it.'

Then she rushed at Chanticleer with open bill, but he was not to be taken by surprise, and fell upon her with his spurs till she cried out for mercy. At last she allowed herself to be harnessed to the carriage. Chanticleer seated himself on the box as coachman, and cried out unceasingly, 'Now, Duck, run as fast as you can.'

When they had driven a little way they met two foot
74

passengers, a Pin and a Needle. They called out, 'Stop! stop!' They said it would soon be pitch dark, and they couldn't walk a step further, the road was so dirty; might they not have a lift? They had been to the *Tailor's Inn* by the gate, and had lingered over their beer.

As they were both very thin, and did not take up much room, Chanticleer allowed them to get in, but he made them promise not to tread either on his toes, or on Partlet's. Late in the evening they came to an inn, and as they did not want to drive any further in the dark, and the Duck was getting rather uncertain on her feet, tumbling from side to side, they drove in.

The Landlord at first made many objections to having them, and said the house was already full; perhaps he thought they were not very grand folk. But at last, by dint of persuasive words, and promising him the egg which Mrs. Partlet had laid on the way, and also that he should keep the Duck, who laid an egg every day, he consented to let them stay the night.

Then they had a meal served to them, and feasted, and passed the time in rioting.

In the early dawn, before it grew light, and every one was asleep, Partlet woke up Chanticleer, fetched the egg, pecked a hole in it, and between them they ate it all up, and threw the shells on to the hearth. Then they went to the Needle, which was still asleep, seized it by the head and stuck it in the cushion of the Landlord's arm-chair; the Pin they stuck in his towel, and then, without more ado, away they flew over the heath. The Duck, which preferred to sleep in the open air, and had stayed in the yard, heard them whizzing by, and bestirred herself. She found a stream, and swam away down it; it was a much quicker way to get on than being harnessed to a carriage.

A couple of hours later, the Landlord, who was the first to leave his pillow, got up and washed. When he took up the towel to dry himself, he scratched his face and made a long red line from ear to ear. Then he went to the kitchen to light

75

his pipe, but when he stooped over the hearth the egg-shells
flew into his eye.

'Everything goes to my head this morning,' he said
angrily, as he dropped on to the cushion of his Grandfather's
arm-chair. But he quickly bounded up again, and shouted,
'Gracious me!' for the Needle had run into him, and this
time not in the head. He grew furious, and his suspicions
immediately fell on the guests who had come in so late the
night before. When he went to look for them, they were
nowhere to be seen. Then he swore never to take such
ragamuffins into his house again; for they ate a great deal,
paid nothing, and played tricks, by way of thanks, into the
bargain.

II. THE VISIT TO MR. KORBES

ANOTHER day, when Partlet and Chanticleer were about to take
a journey, Chanticleer built a fine carriage with four red
wheels, and harnessed four little mice to it. Mrs. Partlet
seated herself in it with Chanticleer, and they drove off together.

Before long they met a Cat. 'Whither away?' said she.
Chanticleer answered—

> 'All on our way
> A visit to pay
> To Mr. Korbes at his house to-day.'

'Take me with you,' said the Cat.

Chanticleer answered, 'With pleasure; sit down behind,
so that you don't fall out forwards.'

> 'My wheels so red, pray have a care
> From any splash of mud to spare.
> Little wheels hurry!
> Little mice scurry!
> All on our way
> A visit to pay
> To Mr. Korbes at his house to-day.'

Then came a Millstone, an Egg, a Duck, a Pin, and, last of all, a Needle. They all took their places in the carriage and went with the rest.

But when they arrived at Mr. Korbes' house, he wasn't in. The mice drew the carriage into the coach-house, Partlet and Chanticleer flew on to a perch, the Cat sat down by the fire, the Duck lay down by the well-pole. The Egg rolled itself up in the towel, the Pin stuck itself into the cushion, the Needle sprang into the pillow on the bed, and the Millstone laid itself over the door.

When Mr. Korbes came home, and went to the hearth to make a fire, the Cat threw ashes into his face. He ran into the kitchen to wash, and the Duck squirted water into his face; seizing the towel to dry himself, the Egg rolled out, broke, and stuck up one of his eyes. He wanted to rest, and sat down in his arm-chair, when the Pin pricked him. He grew very angry, threw himself on the bed and laid his head on the pillow, when the Needle ran into him and made him cry out. In a fury he wanted to rush into the open air, but when he got to the door, the Millstone fell on his head and killed him. What a bad man Mr. Korbes must have been!

III. THE DEATH OF PARTLET

PARTLET and Chanticleer went to the nut-hill on another occasion, and they arranged that whichever of them found a nut should share it with the other.

Partlet found a huge nut, but said nothing about it, and meant to eat it all herself; but the kernel was so big that she could not swallow it. It stuck in her throat, and she was afraid she would be choked. She shrieked, ' Chanticleer, Chanticleer, run and fetch some water as fast as you can, or I shall choke! '

So Chanticleer ran as fast as he could to the Well, and said, ' Well, Well, you must give me some water! Partlet is out on the nut-hill; she has swallowed a big nut, and is choking.'

The Well answered, 'First you must run to my Bride, and tell her to give you some red silk.'

Chanticleer ran to the Bride, and said, 'Bride, Bride, give me some red silk: I will give the silk to the Well, and the Well will give me some water to take to Partlet, for she has swallowed a big nut, and is choking.'

The Bride answered, 'Run first and fetch me a wreath which I left hanging on a willow.'

So Chanticleer ran to the willow, pulled the wreath off the branch, and brought it to the Bride. The Bride gave him the red silk, which he took to the Well, and the Well gave him the water for it. Then Chanticleer took the water to Partlet; but as it happened she had choked in the meantime, and lay there dead and stiff. Chanticleer's grief was so great that he cried aloud, and all the animals came and condoled with him.

Six mice built a little car to draw Partlet to the grave; and when the car was ready they harnessed themselves to it, and drew Partlet away.

On the way, Reynard the fox joined them. 'Where are you going, Chanticleer?'

'I 'm going to bury my wife, Partlet.'

'May I go with you?'

'Jump up behind, we 're not yet full,
A weight in front, my nags can't pull.'

So the Fox took a seat at the back, and he was followed by the wolf, the bear, the stag, the lion, and all the other animals of the forest. The procession went on, till they came to a stream.

'How shall we ever get over?' said Chanticleer.

A Straw was lying by the stream, and it said, 'I will stretch myself across, and then you can pass over upon me.'

But when the six mice got on to the Straw it collapsed, and the mice fell into the water with it, and they were all drowned.

So their difficulty was as great as ever. Then a Coal came along, and said, ' I am big enough, I will lie down, and you can pass over me.'

So the Coal laid itself across the stream, but unfortunately it just touched the water, hissed, went out, and was dead. A stone, seeing this, had pity on them, and, wanting to help Chanticleer, laid itself over the water. Now Chanticleer drew the car, and he just managed to get across himself with the hen. Then he wanted to pull the others over who were hanging on behind, but it was too much for him, and the car fell back and they all fell into the water and were drowned.

So Chanticleer was left alone with the dead hen, and he dug a grave and laid her in it. Then he made a mound over it, and seated himself upon it and grieved till he died; and then they were all dead.

Rapunzel

THERE was once a man and his wife who had long wished in vain for a child, when at last they had reason to hope that Heaven would grant their wish. There was a little window at the back of their house, which overlooked a beautiful garden, full of lovely flowers and shrubs. It was, however, surrounded by a high wall, and nobody dared to enter it, because it belonged to a powerful Witch, who was feared by everybody.

One day the woman, standing at this window and looking into the garden, saw a bed planted with beautiful rampion. It looked so fresh and green that it made her long to eat some of it. This longing increased every day, and as she knew it could never be satisfied, she began to look pale and miserable, and to pine away. Then her husband was alarmed, and said : ' What ails you, my dear wife ? '

' Alas ! ' she answered, ' if I cannot get any of the rampion from the garden behind our house to eat, I shall die.'

Her husband, who loved her, thought, ' Before you let your wife die, you must fetch her some of that rampion, cost what it may.' So in the twilight he climbed over the wall into the Witch's garden, hastily picked a handful of rampion, and took it back to his wife. She immediately dressed it, and ate it up very eagerly. It was so very, very nice, that the next day her longing for it increased threefold. She could have no peace unless her husband fetched her some more. So in the twilight he set out again ; but when he got over the wall he was terrified to see the Witch before him.

' How dare you come into my garden like a thief, and steal my rampion ? ' she said, with angry looks. ' It shall be the worse for you ! '

80

RAPUNZEL

' Alas ! ' he answered, ' be merciful to me ; I am only here from necessity. My wife sees your rampion from the window, and she has such a longing for it, that she would die if she could not get some of it.'

The anger of the Witch abated, and she said to him, ' If it is as you say, I will allow you to take away with you as much rampion as you like, but on one condition. You must give me the child which your wife is about to bring into the world. I will care for it like a mother, and all will be well with it.' In his fear the man consented to everything, and when the baby was born, the Witch appeared, gave it the name of Rapunzel (rampion), and took it away with her.

Rapunzel was the most beautiful child under the sun. When she was twelve years old, the Witch shut her up in a tower which stood in a wood. It had neither staircase nor doors, and only a little window quite high up in the wall. When the Witch wanted to enter the tower, she stood at the foot of it, and cried—

' Rapunzel, Rapunzel, let down your hair.'

Rapunzel had splendid long hair, as fine as spun gold. As soon as she heard the voice of the Witch, she unfastened her plaits and twisted them round a hook by the window. They fell twenty ells downwards, and the Witch climbed up by them.

It happened a couple of years later that the King's son rode through the forest, and came close to the tower. From thence he heard a song so lovely, that he stopped to listen. It was Rapunzel, who in her loneliness made her sweet voice resound to pass away the time. The King's son wanted to join her, and he sought for the door of the tower, but there was none to find.

He rode home, but the song had touched his heart so deeply that he went into the forest every day to listen to it. Once, when he was hidden behind a tree, he saw a Witch come to the tower and call out—

' Rapunzel, Rapunzel, let down your hair.'

Then Rapunzel lowered her plaits of hair and the Witch climbed up to her.

'If that is the ladder by which one ascends,' he thought, 'I will try my luck myself.' And the next day, when it began to grow dark, he went to the tower and cried—

'Rapunzel, Rapunzel, let down your hair.'

The hair fell down at once, and the King's son climbed up by it.

At first Rapunzel was terrified, for she had never set eyes on a man before, but the King's son talked to her kindly, and told her that his heart had been so deeply touched by her song that he had no peace, and he was obliged to see her. Then Rapunzel lost her fear, and when he asked if she would have him for her husband, and she saw that he was young and handsome, she thought, 'He will love me better than old Mother Gothel.' So she said, 'Yes,' and laid her hand in his. She said, 'I will gladly go with you, but I do not know how I am to get down from this tower. When you come, will you bring a skein of silk with you every time. I will twist it into a ladder, and when it is long enough I will descend by it, and you can take me away with you on your horse.'

She arranged with him that he should come and see her every evening, for the old Witch came in the daytime.

The Witch discovered nothing, till suddenly Rapunzel said to her, 'Tell me, Mother Gothel, how can it be that you are so much heavier to draw up than the young Prince who will be here before long?'

'Oh, you wicked child, what do you say? I thought I had separated you from all the world, and yet you have deceived me.' In her rage she seized Rapunzel's beautiful hair, twisted it twice round her left hand, snatched up a pair of shears and cut off the plaits, which fell to the ground. She was so merciless that she took poor Rapunzel away into a wilderness, where she forced her to live in the greatest grief and misery.

In the evening of the day on which she had banished

RAPUNZEL

Rapunzel, the Witch fastened the plaits which she had cut off to the hook by the window, and when the Prince came and called—

'Rapunzel, Rapunzel, let down your hair,'
she lowered the hair. The Prince climbed up, but there he found, not his beloved Rapunzel, but the Witch, who looked at him with angry and wicked eyes.

'Ah!' she cried mockingly, "you have come to fetch your ladylove, but the pretty bird is no longer in her nest; and she can sing no more, for the cat has seized her, and it will scratch your own eyes out too. Rapunzel is lost to you; you will never see her again.'

The Prince was beside himself with grief, and in his despair he sprang out of the window. He was not killed, but his eyes were scratched out by the thorns among which he fell. He wandered about blind in the wood, and had nothing but roots and berries to eat. He did nothing but weep and lament over the loss of his beloved wife Rapunzel. In this way he wandered about for some years, till at last he reached the wilderness where Rapunzel had been living in great poverty with the twins who had been born to her, a boy and a girl.

He heard a voice which seemed very familiar to him, and he went towards it. Rapunzel knew him at once, and fell weeping upon his neck. Two of her tears fell upon his eyes, and they immediately grew quite clear, and he could see as well as ever.

He took her to his kingdom, where he was received with joy, and they lived long and happily together.

Fundevogel

THERE was once a Forester who went into the woods to hunt, and he heard a cry like that of a little child. He followed the sound, and at last came to a big tree where a tiny child was sitting high up on one of the top branches. The mother had gone to sleep under the tree, and a bird of prey, seeing the child on her lap, had flown down and carried it off in its beak to the top of the tree.

The Forester climbed the tree and brought down the child, thinking to himself, ' I will take it home, and bring it up with my own little Lina.'

So he took it home, and the two children were brought up together. The foundling was called Fundevogel, because it had been found by a bird. Fundevogel and Lina were so fond of each other, that they could not bear to be out of each other's sight.

Now the Forester had an old Cook, who one evening took two pails, and began carrying water. She did not go once but many times, backwards and forwards to the well.

Lina saw this, and said : ' Dear me, Sanna, why are you carrying so much water ? '

' If thou wilt not tell any one, I will tell thee why.'

Lina said no, she would not tell any one.

So then the Cook said : ' To-morrow morning early, when the Forester goes out hunting, I am going to boil the water, and when it bubbles in the kettle, I am going to throw Fundevogel into it to boil him.'

Next morning the Forester got up very early, and went out hunting, leaving the children still in bed.

84

She did not go once but many times, backwards and forwards to the well.

Then said Lina to Fundevogel : 'Never forsake me, and I will never forsake thee.'

And Fundevogel answered : 'I will never forsake thee.'

Then Lina said : 'I must tell thee now. Old Sanna brought in so many pails of water last night, that I asked her what she was doing. She said if I would not tell anybody, she would tell me what it was for. So I promised not to tell anybody, and she said that in the morning, when the father had gone out hunting, she would fill the kettle, and when it was boiling, she would throw thee into it and boil thee. Now we must get up quickly, dress ourselves, and run away.'

So the children got up, dressed quickly, and left the house.

When the water boiled, the Cook went to their bedroom to fetch Fundevogel to throw him into it. But when she entered the room, and went up to the bed, both the children were gone. She was terribly frightened, and said to herself : 'Whatever am I to say to the Forester when he comes home and finds the children gone ? We must hurry after them and get them back.' So the Cook despatched three men-servants to catch up the children and bring them back.

The children were sitting near a wood, and when they saw the three men a great way off, Lina said to Fundevogel, 'Do not forsake me, and I will never forsake thee.'

And Fundevogel answered, 'I will never forsake thee as long as I live.'

Then Lina said, 'Thou must turn into a rosebush, and I will be a rosebud upon it.'

When the three men reached the wood, they found nothing but a rosebush with one rosebud on it ; no children were to be seen. They said to each other, 'There is nothing to be done here.' And they went home and told the Cook that they had seen nothing whatever but a rosebush, with one rosebud on it.

The old Cook scolded them, and said : 'You boobies, you ought to have hacked the rosebush to pieces, broken off the bud, and brought it home to me. Off with you at once and do it.' So they had to start off again on the search.

86

FUNDEVOGEL

But the children saw them a long way off, and Lina said to Fundevogel, ' Do not forsake me, and I will never forsake thee.'

Fundevogel said : ' I will never forsake thee as long as I live.'

Then said Lina : ' Thou must become a church, and I will be the chandelier in it.'

Now when the three men came up they found nothing but a church with a chandelier in it ; and they said to each other : ' What are we to do here ?   We had better go home again.'

When they reached the house, the Cook asked if they had not found anything.   They said : ' Nothing but a church with a chandelier in it.'

' You fools,' screamed the Cook, ' why did you not destroy the church and bring me the chandelier ? '   Then the old Cook put her best foot foremost, and started herself with the three men in pursuit of the children.

But the children saw the three men in the distance, and the old Cook waddling behind them.   Then said Lina : ' Fundevogel, do not forsake me, and I will never forsake thee.'

And he said : ' I will never forsake thee as long as I live.'

Lina said : ' Thou must become a pond, and I will be the duck swimming upon it.'

When the Cook reached the pond, she lay down beside it to drink it up, but the duck swam quickly forward, seized her head with his bill and dragged her under water ; so the old witch was drowned.

Then the children went home together as happy as possible, and if they are not dead yet, then they are still alive.

The Valiant Tailor

A TAILOR was sitting on his table at the window one summer morning. He was a good fellow, and stitched with all his might. A peasant woman came down the street, crying, 'Good jam for sale! good jam for sale!'

This had a pleasant sound in the Tailor's ears; he put his pale face out of the window, and cried, 'You'll find a sale for your wares up here, good Woman.'

The Woman went up the three steps to the Tailor, with the heavy basket on her head, and he made her unpack all her pots. He examined them all, lifted them up, smelt them, and at last said, 'The jam seems good; weigh me out four ounces, good Woman, and should it come over the quarter pound, it will be all the same to me.'

The Woman, who had hoped for a better sale, gave him what he asked for, but went away cross, and grumbling to herself.

'That jam will be a blessing to me,' cried the Tailor; 'it will give me strength and power.' He brought his bread out of the cupboard, cut a whole slice, and spread the jam on it. 'It won't be a bitter morsel,' said he, 'but I will finish this waistcoat before I stick my teeth into it.'

He put the bread down by his side, and went on with his sewing, but in his joy the stitches got bigger and bigger. The smell of the jam rose to the wall, where the flies were clustered in swarms, and tempted them to come down, and they settled on the jam in masses.

'Ah! who invited you?' cried the Tailor, chasing away his unbidden guests. But the flies, who did not understand

88

his language, were not to be got rid of so easily, and came back in greater numbers than ever. At last the Tailor came to the end of his patience, and seizing a bit of cloth, he cried, 'Wait a bit, and I'll give it you!' So saying, he struck out at them mercilessly. When he looked, he found no fewer than seven dead and motionless. 'So that's the kind of fellow you are,' he said, admiring his own valour. 'The whole town shall know of this.'

In great haste he cut out a belt for himself, and stitched on it, in big letters, 'Seven at one blow!' 'The town!' he then said, 'the whole world shall know of it!' And his heart wagged for very joy like the tail of a lamb. The Tailor fastened the belt round his waist, and wanted to start out into the world at once; he found his workshop too small for his valour. Before starting, he searched the house to see if there was anything to take with him. He only found an old cheese, but this he put into his pocket. By the gate he saw a bird entangled in a thicket, and he put that into his pocket with the cheese. Then he boldly took to the road, and as he was

'Wait a bit, and I'll give it you!' So saying, he struck out at them mercilessly.

light and active, he felt no fatigue. The road led up a mountain, and when he reached the highest point, he found a huge Giant sitting there comfortably looking round him.

The Tailor went pluckily up to him, and addressed him.

'Good-day, Comrade, you are sitting there surveying the

wide world, I suppose. I am just on my way to try my luck. Do you feel inclined to go with me ? '

The Giant looked scornfully at the Tailor, and said, ' You jackanapes ! you miserable ragamuffin ! '

' That may be,' said the Tailor, unbuttoning his coat and showing the Giant his belt. ' You may just read what kind of fellow I am.'

The Giant read, ' Seven at one blow,' and thought that it was people the Tailor had slain ; so it gave him a certain amount of respect for the little fellow. Still, he thought he would try him ; so he picked up a stone and squeezed it till the water dropped out of it.

' Do that,' he said, ' if you have the strength.'

' No more than that ! ' said the Tailor ; ' why, it 's a mere joke to me.'

He put his hand into his pocket, and pulling out the bit of soft cheese, he squeezed it till the moisture ran out.

' I guess that will equal you,' said he.

The Giant did not know what to say, and could not have believed it of the little man.

Then the Giant picked up a stone, and threw it up so high that one could scarcely follow it with the eye.

' Now, then, you sample of a mannikin, do that after me.'

' Well thrown ! ' said the Tailor, ' but the stone fell to the ground again. Now I will throw one for you which will never come back again.'

So saying, he put his hand into his pocket, took out the bird, and threw it into the air. The bird, rejoiced at its freedom, soared into the air, and was never seen again.

' What do you think of that, Comrade ? ' asked the Tailor.

' You can certainly throw ; but now we will see if you are in a condition to carry anything,' said the Giant.

He led the Tailor to a mighty oak which had been felled, and which lay upon the ground.

' If you are strong enough, help me out of the wood with this tree,' he said.

90

' Willingly,' answered the little man. ' You take the trunk on your shoulder, and I will take the branches ; they must certainly be the heaviest.'

The Giant accordingly took the trunk on his shoulder; but the Tailor seated himself on one of the branches, and the Giant, who could not look round, had to carry the whole tree, and the Tailor into the bargain. The Tailor was very merry on the end of the tree, and whistled ' Three Tailors rode merrily out of the town,' as if tree-carrying were a joke to him.

When the Giant had carried the tree some distance, he could go no further, and exclaimed, ' Look out, I am going to drop the tree.'

The Tailor sprang to the ground with great agility, and seized the tree with both arms, as if he had been carrying it all the time. He said to the Giant : ' Big fellow as you are, you can't carry a tree.'

After a time they went on together, and when they came to a cherry-tree, the Giant seized the top branches, where the cherries ripened first, bent them down, put them in the Tailor's hand, and told him to eat. The Tailor, however, was much too weak to hold the tree, and when the Giant let go, the tree sprang back, carrying the Tailor with it into the air. When he reached the ground again, without any injury, the Giant said, ' What 's this ? Haven't you the strength to hold a feeble sapling ? '

' It 's not strength that 's wanting,' answered the Tailor. ' Do you think that would be anything to one who killed seven at a blow ? I sprang over the tree because some sportsmen were shooting among the bushes. Spring after me if you like.'

The Giant made the attempt, but he could not clear the tree, and stuck among the branches. So here, too, the Tailor had the advantage of him.

The Giant said, ' If you are such a gallant fellow, come with me to our cave, and stay the night with us.'

The Tailor was quite willing, and went with him. When

91

they reached the cave, they found several other **Giants** sitting round a fire, and each one held a roasted sheep in his hand, which he was eating. The Tailor looked about him, and thought, ' It is much more roomy here than in my workshop.'

The Giant showed him a bed, and told him to lie down and have a good sleep. The bed was much too big for the Tailor, so he did not lie down in it, but crept into a corner. At midnight, when the Giant thought the Tailor would be in a heavy sleep, he got up, took a big oak club, and with one blow crashed right through the bed, and thought he had put an end to the grasshopper. Early in the morning the Giants went out into the woods, forgetting all about the Tailor, when all at once he appeared before them, as lively as possible. They were terrified, and thinking he would strike them all dead, they ran off as fast as ever they could.

The Tailor went on his way, always following his own pointed nose. When he had walked for a long time, he came to the courtyard of a royal palace. He was so tired that he lay down on the grass and went to sleep. While he lay and slept, the people came and inspected him on all sides, and they read on his belt, ' Seven at one blow.' ' Alas ! ' they said, ' why does this great warrior come here in time of peace ; he must be a mighty man.'

They went to the King and told him about it ; and they were of opinion that, should war break out, he would be a useful and powerful man, who should on no account be allowed to depart. This advice pleased the King, and he sent one of his courtiers to the Tailor to offer him a military appointment when he woke up. The messenger remained standing by the Tailor, till he opened his eyes and stretched himself, and then he made the offer.

' For that very purpose have I come,' said the Tailor. ' I am quite ready to enter the King's service.'

So he was received with honour, and a special dwelling was assigned to him.

The Soldiers, however, bore him a grudge, and wished him

a thousand miles away. ' What will be the end of it ? ' they said to each other. ' When we quarrel with him, and he strikes out, seven of us will fall at once. One of us can't cope with him.' So they took a resolve, and went all together to the King, and asked for their discharge. ' We are not made,' said they, ' to hold our own with a man who strikes seven at one blow.'

It grieved the King to lose all his faithful servants for the sake of one man ; he wished he had never set eyes on the Tailor, and was quite ready to let him go. He did not dare, however, to give him his dismissal, for he was afraid that he would kill him and all his people, and place himself on the throne. He pondered over it for a long time, and at last he thought of a plan. He sent for the Tailor, and said that as he was so great a warrior, he would make him an offer. In a forest in his kingdom lived two giants, who, by robbery, murder, burning, and laying waste, did much harm. No one dared approach them without being in danger of his life. If he could subdue and kill these two Giants, he would give him his only daughter to be his wife, and half his kingdom as a dowry ; also he would give him a hundred Horsemen to accompany and help him.

' That would be something for a man like me,' thought the Tailor. ' A beautiful Princess and half a kingdom are not offered to one every day.' ' Oh yes,' was his answer, ' I will soon subdue the Giants, and that without the hundred Horsemen. He who slays seven at a blow need not fear two.' The Tailor set out at once, accompanied by the hundred Horsemen ; but when he came to the edge of the forest, he said to his followers, ' Wait here, I will soon make an end of the Giants by myself.'

Then he disappeared into the wood ; he looked about to the right and to the left. Before long he espied both the Giants lying under a tree fast asleep, and snoring. Their snores were so tremendous that they made the branches of the tree dance up and down. The Tailor, who was no fool, filled his pockets with stones, and climbed up the tree. When he got half-way up, he slipped on to a branch just above the sleepers, and then hurled the stones, one after another, on to one of them.

It was some time before the Giant noticed anything; then he woke up, pushed his companion, and said, 'What are you hitting me for?'

'You're dreaming,' said the other. 'I didn't hit you.' They went to sleep again, and the Tailor threw a stone at the other one. 'What's that?' he cried. 'What are you throwing at me?'

'I'm not throwing anything,' answered the first one, with a growl.

They quarrelled over it for a time, but as they were sleepy, they made it up, and their eyes closed again.

The Tailor began his game again, picked out his biggest stone, and threw it at the first Giant as hard as he could.

'This is too bad,' said the Giant, flying up like a madman. He pushed his companion against the tree with such violence that it shook. The other paid him back in the same coin, and they worked themselves up into such a rage that they tore up trees by the roots, and hacked at each other till they both fell dead upon the ground.

Then the Tailor jumped down from his perch. 'It was very lucky,' he said, 'that they did not tear up the tree I was sitting on, or I should have had to spring on to another like a squirrel, but we are nimble fellows.' He drew his sword, and gave each of the Giants two or three cuts in the chest. Then he went out to the Horsemen, and said, 'The work is done. I have given both of them the finishing stroke, but it was a difficult job. In their distress they tore trees up by the root to defend themselves; but all that's no good when a man like me comes, who slays seven at a blow.'

'Are you not wounded?' then asked the Horsemen.

'There was no danger,' answered the Tailor. 'Not a hair of my head was touched.'

94

The Horsemen would not believe him, and rode into the forest to see. There, right enough, lay the Giants in pools of blood, and, round about them, the uprooted trees.

The Tailor now demanded his promised reward from the King; but he, in the meantime, had repented of this promise, and was again trying to think of a plan to shake him off.

' Before I give you my daughter and the half of my kingdom, you must perform one more doughty deed. There is a Unicorn which runs about in the forests doing vast damage; you must capture it.'

' I have even less fear of one Unicorn than of two Giants. Seven at one stroke is my style.' He took a rope and an axe, and went into the wood, and told his followers to stay outside. He did not have long to wait. The Unicorn soon appeared, and dashed towards the Tailor, as if it meant to run him through with its horn on the spot. ' Softly, softly,' cried the Tailor. ' Not so fast.' He stood still, and waited till the animal got quite near, and then he very nimbly dodged behind a tree. The Unicorn rushed at the tree, and ran its horn so hard into the trunk that it had not strength to pull it out again, and so it was caught. ' Now I have the prey,' said the Tailor, coming from behind the tree. He fastened the rope round the creature's neck, and, with his axe, released the horn from the tree. When this was done he led the animal away, and took it to the King.

Still the King would not give him the promised reward, but made a third demand of him. Before the marriage, the Tailor must catch a Boar which did much damage in the woods : the Huntsmen were to help him.

' Willingly,' said the Tailor. ' That will be mere child's play.'

He did not take the Huntsmen into the wood with him, at which they were well pleased, for they had already more than once had such a reception from the Boar that they had no wish to encounter him again. When the Boar saw the Tailor, it flew at him with foaming mouth, and, gnashing its teeth,

95

tried to throw him to the ground; but the nimble hero darted into a little chapel which stood near. He jumped out again immediately by the window. The Boar rushed in after the Tailor; but he by this time was hopping about outside, and quickly shut the door upon the Boar. So the raging animal was caught, for it was far too heavy and clumsy to jump out of the window. The Tailor called the Huntsmen up to see the captive with their own eyes.

The hero then went to the King, who was now obliged to keep his word, whether he liked it or not; so he handed over his daughter and half his kingdom to him. Had he known that it was no warrior but only a Tailor who stood before him, he would have taken it even more to heart. The marriage was held with much pomp, but little joy, and a King was made out of a Tailor.

After a time the young Queen heard her husband talking in his sleep, and saying, 'Apprentice, bring me the waistcoat, and patch the trousers, or I will break the yard measure over your head.' So in this manner she discovered the young gentleman's origin. In the morning she complained to the King, and begged him to rid her of a husband who was nothing more than a Tailor.

The King comforted her, and said, 'To-night, leave your bedroom door open. My servants shall stand outside, and when he is asleep they shall go in and bind him. They shall then carry him away, and put him on board a ship which will take him far away.'

The lady was satisfied with this; but the Tailor's armour-bearer, who was attached to his young lord, told him the whole plot.

' I will put a stop to their plan,' said the Tailor.

At night he went to bed as usual with his wife. When she thought he was asleep, she got up, opened the door, and went to bed again. The Tailor, who had only pretended to be asleep, began to cry out in a clear voice, ' Apprentice, bring me the waistcoat, and you patch the trousers, or I will break

96

the yard measure over your head. I have slain seven at a blow, killed two Giants, led captive a Unicorn, and caught a Boar ; should I be afraid of those who are standing outside my chamber door ? '

When they heard the Tailor speaking like this, the servants were overcome by fear, and ran away as if wild animals were after them, and none of them would venture near him again.

So the Tailor remained a King till the day of his death.

Hansel and Grethel

CLOSE to a large forest there lived a Woodcutter with his Wife and his two children. The boy was called Hansel, and the girl Grethel. They were always very poor, and had very little to live on; and at one time, when there was famine in the land, he could no longer procure daily bread.

One night he lay in bed worrying over his troubles, and he sighed and said to his Wife: 'What is to become of us? How are we to feed our poor children when we have nothing for ourselves?'

'I'll tell you what, Husband,' answered the Woman, 'to-morrow morning we will take the children out quite early into the thickest part of the forest. We will light a fire, and give each of them a piece of bread; then we will go to our work and leave them alone. They won't be able to find their way back, and so we shall be rid of them.'

'Nay, Wife,' said the Man; 'we won't do that. I could never find it in my heart to leave my children alone in the forest; the wild animals would soon tear them to pieces.'

'What a fool you are!' she said. 'Then we must all four die of hunger. You may as well plane the boards for our coffins at once.'

She gave him no peace till he consented. 'But I grieve over the poor children all the same,' said the Man.

The two children could not go to sleep for hunger either, and they heard what their Stepmother said to their Father.

Grethel wept bitterly, and said: 'All is over with us now!'

'Be quiet, Grethel!' said Hansel. 'Don't cry; I will find some way out of it.'

98

HANSEL AND GRETHEL

When the old people had gone to sleep, he got up, put on his little coat, opened the door, and slipped out. The moon was shining brightly, and the white pebbles round the house shone like newly-minted coins. Hansel stooped down and put as many into his pockets as they would hold.

Then he went back to Grethel, and said : ' Take comfort, little sister, and go to sleep. God won't forsake us.' And then he went to bed again.

When the day broke, before the sun had risen, the Woman came and said : ' Get up, you lazybones ; we are going into the forest to fetch wood.'

Then she gave them each a piece of bread, and said : ' Here is something for your dinner, but mind you don't eat it before, for you 'll get no more.'

Grethel put the bread under her apron, for Hansel had the stones in his pockets. Then they all started for the forest.

When they had gone a little way, Hansel stopped and looked back at the cottage, and he did the same thing again and again.

His Father said : ' Hansel, what are you stopping to look back at ? Take care, and put your best foot foremost.'

' O Father ! ' said Hansel, ' I am looking at my white cat, it is sitting on the roof, wanting to say good-bye to me.'

' Little fool ! that 's no cat, it 's the morning sun shining on the chimney.'

But Hansel had not been looking at the cat, he had been dropping a pebble on to the ground each time he stopped. When they reached the middle of the forest, their Father said:

' Now, children, pick up some wood, I want to make a fire to warm you.'

Hansel and Grethel gathered the twigs together and soon made a huge pile. Then the pile was lighted, and when it blazed up, the Woman said : ' Now lie down by the fire and rest yourselves while we go and cut wood ; when we have finished we will come back to fetch you.'

Hansel and Grethel sat by the fire, and when dinner-time came they each ate their little bit of bread, and they thought

'Hansel picked up the glittering white pebbles and filled his pockets with **them**.'

their Father was quite near because they could hear the sound of an axe. It was no axe, however, but a branch which the Man had tied to a dead tree, and which blew backwards and forwards against it. They sat there such a long time that they got tired, their eyes began to close, and they were soon fast asleep.

When they woke it was dark night. Grethel began to cry : 'How shall we ever get out of the wood ! '

But Hansel comforted her, and said : 'Wait a little till the moon rises, then we will soon find our way.'

When the full moon rose, Hansel took his little sister's hand, and they walked on, guided by the pebbles, which glittered like newly-coined money. They walked the whole night, and at daybreak they found themselves back at their Father's cottage.

They knocked at the door, and when the Woman opened it and saw Hansel and Grethel, she said : ' You bad children, why did you sleep so long in the wood ? We thought you did not mean to come back any more.'

But their Father was delighted, for it had gone to his heart to leave them behind alone.

Not long after they were again in great destitution, and the children heard the Woman at night in bed say to their Father : ' We have eaten up everything again but half a loaf, and then we are at the end of everything. The children must go away ; we will take them further into the forest so that they won't be able to find their way back. There is nothing else to be done.'

The Man took it much to heart, and said : ' We had better share our last crust with the children.'

But the Woman would not listen to a word he said, she only scolded and reproached him. Any one who once says A must also say B, and as he had given in the first time, he had to do so the second also. The children were again wide awake and heard what was said.

When the old people went to sleep Hansel again got up,

meaning to go out and get some more pebbles, but the Woman had locked the door and he couldn't get out. But he consoled his little sister, and said :

'Don't cry, Grethel ; go to sleep. God will help us.'

In the early morning the Woman made the children get up, and gave them each a piece of bread, but it was smaller than the last. On the way to the forest Hansel crumbled it up in his pocket, and stopped every now and then to throw a crumb on to the ground.

'Hansel, what are you stopping to look about you for ? ' asked his Father.

'I am looking at my dove which is sitting on the roof and wants to say good-bye to me,' answered Hansel.

'Little fool ! ' said the Woman, 'that is no dove, it is the morning sun shining on the chimney.'

Nevertheless, Hansel strewed the crumbs from time to time on the ground. The Woman led the children far into the forest where they had never been in their lives before. Again they made a big fire, and the Woman said :

'Stay where you are, children, and when you are tired you may go to sleep for a while. We are going further on to cut wood, and in the evening when we have finished we will come back and fetch you.'

At dinner-time Grethel shared her bread with Hansel, for he had crumbled his up on the road. Then they went to sleep, and the evening passed, but no one came to fetch the poor children.

It was quite dark when they woke up, and Hansel cheered his little sister, and said : 'Wait a bit, Grethel, till the moon rises, then we can see the bread-crumbs which I scattered to show us the way home.'

When the moon rose they started, but they found no bread-crumbs, for all the thousands of birds in the forest had pecked them up and eaten them.

Hansel said to Grethel : 'We shall soon find the way.'

But they could not find it. They walked the whole night,

102

When he went over the wall he was terrified to see the Witch
before him.

The Witch climbed up.

Pulling the piece of soft cheese out of his pocket, he squeezed
it till the moisture ran out.

They worked themselves up into such a rage that they tore up trees
by the roots, and hacked at each other till they both fell dead.

and all the next day from morning till night, but they could not get out of the wood.

They were very hungry, for they had nothing to eat but a few berries which they found. They were so tired that their legs would not carry them any further, and they lay down under a tree and went to sleep.

When they woke in the morning, it was the third day since they had left their Father's cottage. They started to walk again, but they only got deeper and deeper into the wood, and if no help came they must perish.

At midday they saw a beautiful snow-white bird sitting on a tree. It sang so beautifully that they stood still to listen to it. When it stopped, it fluttered its wings and flew round them. They followed it till they came to a little cottage, on the roof of which it settled itself.

When they got quite near, they saw that the little house was made of bread, and it was roofed with cake ; the windows were transparent sugar.

'This will be something for us,' said Hansel. 'We will have a good meal. I will have a piece of the roof, Grethel, and you can have a bit of the window, it will be nice and sweet.'

Hansel stretched up and broke off a piece of the roof to try what it was like. Grethel went to the window and nibbled at that. A gentle voice called out from within :

> 'Nibbling, nibbling like a mouse,
> Who's nibbling at my little house?'

The children answered :

> 'The wind, the wind doth blow
> From heaven to earth below,'

and went on eating without disturbing themselves. Hansel, who found the roof very good, broke off a large piece for himself ; and Grethel pushed a whole round pane out of the window, and sat down on the ground to enjoy it.

All at once the door opened and an old, old **Woman,** supporting herself on a crutch, came hobbling out. Hansel and Grethel were so frightened, that they dropped what they held in their hands.

But the old Woman only shook her head, and said : ' Ah, dear children, who brought you here ? Come in and stay with me ; you will come to no harm.'

She took them by the hand and led them into the little house. A nice dinner was set before them, pancakes and sugar, milk, apples, and nuts. After this she showed them two little white beds into which they crept, and felt as if they were in Heaven.

Although the old Woman appeared to be so friendly, she was really a wicked old Witch who was on the watch for children, and she had built the bread house on purpose to lure them to her. Whenever she could get a child into her clutches she cooked it and ate it, and considered it a grand feast. Witches have red eyes, and can't see very far, but they have keen scent like animals, and can perceive the approach of human beings.

When Hansel and Grethel came near her, she laughed wickedly to herself, and said scornfully · ' Now I have them, they shan't escape me.'

She got up early in the morning, before the children were awake, and when she saw them sleeping, with their beautiful rosy cheeks, she murmured to herself : ' They will be dainty morsels.'

She seized Hansel with her bony hand and carried him off to a little stable, where she shut him up with a barred door ; he might shriek as loud as he liked, she took no notice of him. Then she went to Grethel and shook her till she woke, and cried :

' Get up, little lazy-bones, fetch some water and cook something nice for your brother ; he is in the stable, and has to be fattened. When he is nice and fat, I will eat him.'

Grethel began to cry bitterly, but it was no use, she had

HANSEL AND GRETHEL

to obey the Witch's orders. The best food was now cooked for poor Hansel, but Grethel only had the shells of cray-fish.

The old Woman hobbled to the stable every morning, and cried: 'Hansel, put your finger out for me to feel how fat you are.'

Hansel put out a knuckle-bone, and the old Woman, whose eyes were dim, could not see, and thought it was his finger, and she was much astonished that he did not get fat.

When four weeks had passed, and Hansel still kept thin, she became very impatient and would wait no longer.

'Now then, Grethel,' she cried, 'bustle along and fetch the water. Fat or thin, to-morrow I will kill Hansel and eat him.'

Oh, how his poor little sister grieved. As she carried the water, the tears streamed down her cheeks.

'Dear God, help us!' she cried. 'If only the wild animals in the forest had devoured us, we should, at least, have died together.'

'You may spare your lamentations; they will do you no good,' said the old Woman.

Early in the morning Grethel had to go out to fill the kettle with water, and then she had to kindle a fire and hang the kettle over it.

'We will bake first,' said the old Witch. 'I have heated the oven and kneaded the dough.'

She pushed poor Grethel towards the oven, and said: 'Creep in and see if it is properly heated, and then we will put the bread in.'

She meant, when Grethel had got in, to shut the door and roast her.

But Grethel saw her intention, and said: 'I don't know how to get in. How am I to manage it?'

'Stupid goose!' cried the Witch. 'The opening is big enough; you can see that I could get into it myself.'

She hobbled up, and stuck her head into the oven. But

Grethel gave her a push which sent the Witch right in, and then she banged the door and bolted it.

'Oh! oh!' she began to howl horribly. But Grethel ran away and left the wicked Witch to perish miserably.

Grethel ran as fast as she could to the stable. She opened the door, and cried : 'Hansel, we are saved. The old Witch is dead.'

'Stupid goose !' cried the Witch. 'The opening is big enough ; you can see that I could get into it myself.'

Hansel sprang out, like a bird out of a cage when the door is set open. How delighted they were. They fell upon each other's necks, and kissed each other, and danced about for joy.

As they had nothing more to fear, they went into the Witch's house, and they found chests in every corner full of pearls and precious stones.

106

'These are better than pebbles,' said Hansel, as he filled his pockets.

Grethel said : 'I must take something home with me too.' And she filled her apron.

'But now we must go,' said Hansel, 'so that we may get out of this enchanted wood.'

Before they had gone very far, they came to a great piece of water.

'We can't get across it,' said Hansel ; 'I see no stepping-stones and no bridge.'

'And there are no boats either,' answered Grethel. 'But there is a duck swimming, it will help us over if we ask it.'

So she cried—

> 'Little duck, that cries quack, quack,
> Here Grethel and here Hansel stand.
> Quickly, take us on your back,
> No path nor bridge is there at hand !'

The duck came swimming towards them, and Hansel got on its back, and told his sister to sit on his knee.

'No,' answered Grethel, 'it will be too heavy for the duck ; it must take us over one after the other.'

The good creature did this, and when they had got safely over and walked for a while, the wood seemed to grow more and more familiar to them, and at last they saw their Father's cottage in the distance. They began to run, and rushed inside, where they threw their arms round their Father's neck. The Man had not had a single happy moment since he had deserted his children in the wood, and in the meantime his Wife was dead.

Grethel shook her apron and scattered the pearls and precious stones all over the floor, and Hansel added handful after handful out of his pockets.

So all their troubles came to an end, and they lived together as happily as possible.

The Mouse, the Bird, and the Sausage

ONCE upon a time, a Mouse, a Bird, and a Sausage went into partnership; they kept house together long and amicably, and thus had increased their possessions. It was the Bird's work to fly to the forest every day and bring back wood. The Mouse had to carry water, make up the fire, and set the table, while the Sausage did the cooking.

Whoever is too well off is always eager for something new.

One day the Bird met a friend, to whom it sang the praises of its comfortable circumstances. But the other bird scolded it, and called it a poor creature who did all the hard work, while the other two had an easy time at home. For when the Mouse had made up the fire, and carried the water, she betook herself to her little room to rest till she was called to lay the table. The Sausage only had to stay by the hearth and take care that the food was nicely cooked; when it was nearly dinner-time, she passed herself once or twice through the broth and the vegetables, and they were then buttered, salted, and flavoured, ready to eat. Then the Bird came home, laid his burden aside, and they all sat down to table; and after their meal they slept their fill till morning. It was indeed a delightful life.

Another day the Bird, owing to the instigations of his friend, declined to go and fetch any more wood, saying that he had been drudge long enough, and had only been their dupe; they must now make a change and try some other arrangement.

In spite of the fervent entreaties of the Mouse and the Sausage, the Bird got his way. They decided to draw lots,

108

THE MOUSE, THE BIRD, AND THE SAUSAGE

and the lot fell on the Sausage, who was to carry the wood; the Mouse became cook, and the Bird was to fetch water.

What was the result?

The Sausage went out into the forest, the Bird made up the fire, while the Mouse put on the pot and waited alone for the Sausage to come home, bringing wood for the next day. But the Sausage stayed away so long that the other two suspected something wrong, and the Bird flew out to take the air in the hope of meeting her. Not far off he fell in with

The Mouse had to carry water, while the Sausage did the cooking.

a Dog which had met the poor Sausage and fallen upon her as lawful prey, seized her, and quickly swallowed her.

The Bird complained bitterly to the Dog of his barefaced robbery, but it was no good; for the Dog said he had found forged letters on the Sausage, whereby her life was forfeit to him.

The Bird took the wood and flew sadly home with it, and related what he had seen and heard. They were much upset, but they determined to do the best they could and stay together. So the Bird laid the table, and the Mouse prepared their meal. She tried to cook it, and, like the Sausage, to dip herself in the vegetables so as to flavour them. But before

109

she got well into the midst of them she came to a stand-still, and in the attempt lost her hair, skin, and life itself.

When the Bird came back and wanted to serve up the meal, there was no cook to be seen. The Bird in his agitation threw the wood about, called and searched everywhere, but could not find his cook. Then, owing to his carelessness, the wood caught fire and there was a blaze. The Bird hastened to fetch water, but the bucket fell into the well and the Bird with it; he could not recover himself, and so he was drowned.

The Bird took the wood and flew sadly home with it.

Mother Hulda

THERE was once a widow who had two daughters; one of them was beautiful and industrious, the other was ugly and lazy. She liked the ugly, lazy one best, because she was her own daughter. The other one had all the rough work, and was made the Cinderella at home. The poor girl had to sit in the street by a well, spinning till her fingers bled.

Now one day her bobbin got some blood upon it, and she stooped down to the well to rinse it, but it fell out of her hand into the water. She cried, and ran to tell her stepmother of her misfortune.

Her stepmother scolded her violently and without mercy, and at last said, ' If you have let the bobbin fall into the water, you must go in after it and fetch it out.'

The maiden went back to the well and did not know what to do, and in her terror she sprang into the water to try and find the bobbin.

She lost consciousness, and when she came to herself she was in a beautiful meadow dotted with flowers, and the sun was shining brightly. She walked on till she came to a baker's oven full of bread; the Loaves called out to her, ' Oh, draw us out, draw us out, or we shall burn ! We are over-baked already ! '

So she went up and drew them out one by one with a baker's shovel.

Then she went a little further, and came to an Apple-tree covered with apples, which called out to her. ' Oh, shake us down, shake us down, we are over-ripe ! '

So she shook the tree, and the apples fell like rain. She

111

shook till there were no more left, and when she had gathered them all into a heap, went on her way.

At last she came to a little house, out of which an old woman was looking. She had very large teeth, and the maiden was so frightened that she wanted to run away.

But the old woman called her, and said, 'What are you afraid of, dear child? Stay with me, and if you can do all kinds of housework well, I shall be very pleased. But you must be very particular how you make my bed; it must be

At last she came to a little house, out of which an old woman was looking.

thoroughly shaken, so that the feathers fly, then it snows in the world. I am Mother Hulda.'[1]

As the old woman spoke so kindly to her, she took heart and agreed to stay, and she began her duties at once.

She did everything to the old woman's satisfaction, and shook up the bed with such a will, that the feathers flew about like snow. So she led a very happy life; she had no hard words, but good food, both roast and boiled, every day.

Now after she had been some time with Mother Hulda, she grew sad. At first she did not know what was the matter,

[1] According to a Hessian legend, when it snows, Mother Hulda is making her bed.

but at last she discovered that she was homesick. Although everything here was a thousand times nicer than at home, still she had a yearning to go back.

At last she said to the old woman, ' Although I had nothing but misery at home, and happy as I have been here, still I must go back to my own people.'

Mother Hulda said, ' I am pleased that you ask to go home, and as you have been so faithful to me, I will take you back myself.'

She took her by the hand and led her to a great gate. The gate was opened, and as the maiden was passing through, a heavy shower of gold fell upon her, and remained sticking, so that she was covered from head to foot with it.

' This is your reward, because you have been so industrious,' said Mother Hulda. She also gave her back her bobbin which had fallen into the well.

Then the gate was shut, and the maiden found herself in the upper world not far from her mother's house.

When she reached the courtyard the Cock was sitting on the well, and he cried—

> ' Cock-a-doodle-doo,
> Our golden maid, I see,
> Has now come home to me.'

Then she went into her mother, and, as she was bedecked with gold, she was well received both by her mother and sister. The maiden told them all that had happened to her, and when her mother heard how she had got all her wealth, she wanted her ugly, lazy daughter to have the same. So she made her sit by the well and spin ; and so that there should be blood upon her bobbin, she scratched her finger, and thrust her hand into a blackthorn bush. Then she threw the bobbin into the water and jumped in after it. She found herself in the same beautiful meadow, and walked along the same path.

When she reached the baker's oven, the Loaves called out again, ' Draw us out, draw us out, or we shall be burnt ! '

113

Then the lazy girl answered, 'I should soil my fingers,' and went on.

Soon she came to the Apple-tree, and the apples cried, 'Shake us down, shake us down! We are all ripe!'

'A fine business indeed,' she answered. 'One of you might fall upon my head.' And she passed on.

When she came to Mother Hulda's house, she was not afraid of her big teeth, as she had heard all about them, and she immediately hired herself to the old woman. The first day she made a great effort; she was industrious, and obeyed the orders Mother Hulda gave her, for she thought of all the gold. But on the second day even, she began to be lazy, and on the third she was still more so. She would not get up in

So the lazy girl went home, but she was quite covered with pitch.

the morning, nor did she make Mother Hulda's bed as she
ought; nor shake it till the feathers
came out.

Mother Hulda soon grew tired
of this, and discharged her.

The lazy girl was well
enough pleased to go,
and thought now the

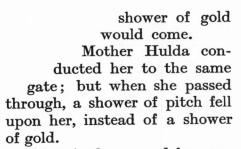

shower of gold
would come.

Mother Hulda con-
ducted her to the same
gate; but when she passed
through, a shower of pitch fell
upon her, instead of a shower
of gold.

' That is the reward for your
service,' said Mother Hulda, as she shut the gate behind her.

So the lazy girl went home, but she was quite covered
with pitch; and when the Cock on the well saw her, he cried—

' Cock-a-doodle-doo,
Our dirty maid, I see,
Has now come back to me.'

The pitch stuck to her as long as she lived; she could
never get rid of it.

Red Riding Hood

THERE was once a sweet little maiden, who was loved by all who knew her; but she was especially dear to her Grandmother, who did not know how to make enough of the child. Once she gave her a little red velvet cloak. It was so becoming, and she liked it so much, that she would never wear anything else; and so she got the name of Red Riding Hood.

One day her Mother said to her : ' Come here, Red Riding Hood, take this cake and a bottle of wine to Grandmother, she is weak and ill, and they will do her good. Go quickly, before it gets hot, and don't loiter by the way, or run, or you will fall down and break the bottle, and there would be no wine for Grandmother. When you get there, don't forget to say " Good morning " prettily, without staring about you.'

' I will do just as you tell me,' Red Riding Hood promised her Mother.

Her Grandmother lived away in the woods, a good half-hour from the village. When she got to the wood, she met a Wolf; but Red Riding Hood did not know what a wicked animal he was, so she was not a bit afraid of him.

' Good-morning, Red Riding Hood,' he said.

' Good-morning, Wolf,' she answered.

' Whither away so early, Red Riding Hood ? '

' To Grandmother's.'

' What have you got in your basket ? '

' Cake and wine; we baked yesterday, so I 'm taking a cake to Grannie; she wants something to make her well.'

' Where does your Grandmother live, Red Riding Hood ? '

116

RED RIDING HOOD

'A good quarter of an hour further into the wood. Her house stands under three big oak trees, near a hedge of nut trees which you must know,' said Red Riding Hood.

The Wolf thought : ' This tender little creature will be a plump morsel; she will be nicer than the old woman. I must be cunning, and snap them both up.'

He walked along with Red Riding Hood for a while, then he said : ' Look at the pretty flowers, Red Riding Hood. Why don't you look about you ? I don't believe you even hear the birds sing, you are just as solemn as if you were going to school : everything else is so gay out here in the woods.'

Red Riding Hood raised her eyes, and when she saw the sunlight dancing through the trees, and all the bright flowers, she thought : ' I 'm sure Grannie would be pleased if I took her a bunch of fresh flowers. It is still quite early, I shall have plenty of time to pick them.'

So she left the path, and wandered off among the trees to pick the flowers. Each time she picked one, she always saw another prettier one further on. So she went deeper and deeper into the forest.

In the meantime the Wolf went straight off to the Grandmother's cottage, and knocked at the door.

' Who is there ? '

' Red Riding Hood, bringing you a cake and some wine. Open the door ! '

' Press the latch ! ' cried the old woman. ' I am too weak to get up.'

The Wolf pressed the latch, and the door sprang open. He went straight in and up to the bed without saying a word, and ate up the poor old woman. Then he put on her nightdress and nightcap, got into bed and drew the curtains.

Red Riding Hood ran about picking flowers till she could carry no more, and then she remembered her Grandmother again. She was astonished when she got to the house to find the door open, and when she entered the room everything seemed so strange.

117

She felt quite frightened, but she did not know why. 'Generally I like coming to see Grandmother so much,' she thought. She cried : 'Good-morning, Grandmother,' but she received no answer.

Then she went up to the bed and drew the curtain back. There lay her Grandmother, but she had drawn her cap down over her face, and she looked very odd.

'O Grandmother, what big ears you have got,' she said.

'The better to hear with, my dear.'

'Grandmother, what big eyes you have got.'

'The better to see with, my dear.'

'What big hands you have got, Grandmother.'

'The better to catch hold of you with, my dear.'

'But, Grandmother, what big teeth you have got.'

'The better to eat you up with, my dear.'

Hardly had the Wolf said this, than he made a spring out of bed, and devoured poor little Red Riding Hood. When the Wolf had satisfied himself, he went back to bed and he was soon snoring loudly.

A Huntsman went past the house, and thought, 'How loudly the old lady is snoring ; I must see if there is anything the matter with her.'

So he went into the house, and up to the bed, where he found the Wolf fast asleep. 'Do I find you here, you old sinner ? ' he said. 'Long enough have I sought you.'

He raised his gun to shoot, when it just occurred to him that perhaps the Wolf had eaten up the old lady, and that she might still be saved. So he took a knife and began cutting open the sleeping Wolf. At the first cut he saw the little red cloak, and after a few more slashes, the little girl sprang out, and cried : 'Oh, how frightened I was, it was so dark inside the Wolf ! ' Next the old Grandmother came out, alive, but hardly able to breathe.

Red Riding Hood brought some big stones with which they filled the Wolf, so that when he woke and tried to spring away, they dragged him back, and he fell down dead.

118

All at once the door opened and an old, old Woman, supporting
herself on a crutch, came hobbling out.

Hansel put out a knuckle-bone, and the old Woman, whose eyes were dim, could not see, and thought it was his finger, and she was much astonished that he did not get fat.

When she got to the wood, she met a Wolf.

'O Grandmother, what big ears you have got,' she said.

RED RIDING HOOD

They were all quite happy now. The Huntsman skinned the Wolf, and took the skin home. The Grandmother ate the cake and drank the wine which Red Riding Hood had brought, and she soon felt quite strong. Red Riding Hood thought : ' I will never again wander off into the forest as long as I live, if my Mother forbids it.'

The Robber Bridegroom

THERE was once a Miller, who had a beautiful daughter. When she grew up, he wanted to have her married and settled. He thought, 'If a suitable bridegroom come and ask for my daughter, I will give her to him.'

Soon after a suitor came who appeared to be rich, and as the Miller knew nothing against him he promised his daughter to him. The Maiden, however, did not like him as a bride ought to like her bridegroom; nor had she any faith in him. Whenever she looked at him, or thought about him, a shudder came over her. One day he said to her, 'You are my betrothed, and yet you have never been to see me.'

The Maiden answered: 'I don't even know where your house is.'

Then the Bridegroom said, 'My house is in the depths of the forest.'

She made excuses, and said she could not find the way.

The Bridegroom answered: 'Next Sunday you must come and see me without fail. I have invited some other guests, and, so that you may be able to find the way, I will strew some ashes to guide you.'

When Sunday came, and the Maiden was about to start, she was frightened, though she did not know why. So that she should be sure of finding her way back she filled her pockets with peas and lentils. At the entrance to the forest she found the track of ashes, and followed it; but every step or two she scattered a few peas right and left.

She walked nearly the whole day, right into the midst of the forest, where it was almost dark. Here she saw a solitary house, which she did not like; it was so dark and dismal.

120

THE ROBBER BRIDEGROOM

She went in, but found nobody, and there was dead silence. Suddenly a voice cried—

> ' Turn back, turn back, thou bonnie Bride,
> Nor in this house of death abide.'

The Maiden looked up, and saw that the voice came from a bird in a cage hanging on the wall. Once more it made the same cry—

> ' Turn back, turn back, thou bonnie Bride,
> Nor in this house of death abide.'

The beautiful Bride went from room to room, all over the house, but they were all empty; not a soul was to be seen. At last she reached the cellar, and there she found an old, old woman with a shaking head.

' Can you tell me if my Bridegroom lives here ? '

' Alas ! poor child,' answered the old woman, ' little dost thou know where thou art; thou art in a murderer's den. Thou thoughtest thou wast about to be married, but death will be thy marriage. See here, I have had to fill this kettle with water, and when they have thee in their power they will kill thee without mercy, cook, and eat thee, for they are eaters of human flesh. Unless I take pity on thee and save thee, thou art lost.' Then the old woman led her behind a great cask, where she could not be seen. ' Be as quiet as a mouse,' she said. ' Don't stir, or all will be lost. To-night, when the murderers are asleep, we will fly. I have long waited for an opportunity.'

Hardly had she said this when the riotous crew came home. They dragged another maiden with them, but as they were quite drunk they paid no attention to her shrieks and lamentations. They gave her wine to drink, three glasses full—red, white, and yellow. After she had drunk them she fell down dead. The poor Bride hidden behind the cask was terrified; she trembled and shivered, for she saw plainly to what fate she was destined.

121

One of the men noticed a gold ring on the little finger of the murdered girl, and as he could not pull it off he took an axe and chopped the finger off; but it sprang up into the air, and fell right into the lap of the Bride behind the cask. The man took a light to look for it, but he could not find it. One of the others said, ' Have you looked behind the big cask ? '

They hurried away as quickly as they could.

But the old woman called out : ' Come and eat, and leave the search till to-morrow; the finger won't run away.'

The murderer said : ' The old woman is right,' and they gave up the search and sat down to supper. But the old woman dropped a sleeping draught into their wine, so they soon lay down, went to sleep, and snored lustily.

When the Bride heard them snoring she came out from behind the cask; but she was obliged to step over the sleepers, as they lay in rows upon the floor. She was dreadfully afraid of touching them, but God helped her, and she got through without mishap. The old woman went with her and opened

122

the door, and they hurried away as quickly as they could from this vile den.

All the ashes had been blown away by the wind, but the peas and lentils had taken root and shot up, and showed them the way in the moonlight.

They walked the whole night, and reached the mill in the morning. The Maiden told her father all that she had been through.

When the day which had been fixed for the wedding came, the Bridegroom appeared, and the Miller invited all his friends and relations. As they sat at table, each one was asked to tell some story. The Bride was very silent, but when it came to her turn, and the Bridegroom said, ' Come, my love, have you nothing to say ? Pray tell us something,' she answered :

' I will tell you a dream I have had. I was walking alone in a wood, and I came to a solitary house where not a soul was to be seen. A cage was hanging on the wall of one of the rooms, and in it there was a bird which cried—

> " Turn back, turn back, thou bonnie Bride,
> Nor in this house of death abide."

It repeated the same words twice. This was only a dream, my love ! I walked through all the rooms, but they were all empty and dismal. At last I went down to the cellar, and there sat a very old woman, with a shaking head. I asked her. " Does my Bridegroom live here ? " She answered, " Alas, you poor child, you are in a murderer's den ! Your Bridegroom indeed lives here, but he will cut you to pieces, cook you, and eat you." This was only a dream, my love ! Then the old woman hid me behind a cask, and hardly had she done so when the murderers came home, dragging a maiden with them. They gave her three kinds of wine to drink— red, white, and yellow ; and after drinking them she fell down dead. My love, I was only dreaming this ! Then they took her things off and cut her to pieces. My love, I was only dreaming ! One of the murderers saw a gold ring on the

123

girl's little finger, and, as he could not pull it off, he chopped off the finger; but the finger bounded into the air, and fell behind the cask on to my lap. Here is the finger with the ring.'

At these words she produced the finger and showed it to the company.

When the Bridegroom heard these words, he turned as pale as ashes, and tried to escape; but the guests seized him and handed him over to justice. And he and all his band were executed for their crimes.

Tom Thumb

A POOR Peasant sat one evening by his hearth and poked the fire, while his Wife sat opposite spinning. He said : 'What a sad thing it is that we have no children ; our home is so quiet, while other folk's houses are noisy and cheerful.'

'Yes,' answered his Wife, and she sighed ; 'even if it were an only one, and if it were no bigger than my thumb, I should be quite content ; we would love it with all our hearts.'

Now, some time after this, she had a little boy who was strong and healthy, but was no bigger than a thumb. Then they said : 'Well, our wish is fulfilled, and, small as he is, we will love him dearly'; and because of his tiny stature they called him Tom Thumb. They let him want for nothing, yet still the child grew no bigger, but remained the same size as when he was born. Still, he looked out on the world with intelligent eyes, and soon showed himself a clever and agile creature, who was lucky in all he attempted.

One day, when the Peasant was preparing to go into the forest to cut wood, he said to himself : 'I wish I had some one to bring the cart after me.'

'O Father !' said Tom Thumb, 'I will soon bring it. You leave it to me ; it shall be there at the appointed time.'

Then the Peasant laughed, and said : 'How can that be ? You are much too small even to hold the reins.'

'That doesn't matter, if only Mother will harness the horse,' answered Tom. 'I will sit in his ear and tell him where to go.'

'Very well,' said the Father ; 'we will try it for once.'

When the time came, the Mother harnessed the horse, set Tom in his ear, and then the little creature called out 'Gee-up'

125

Tom Thumb.

and ' Whoa ' in turn, and directed it where to go. It went quite well, just as though it were being driven by its master ; and they went the right way to the wood. Now it happened that while the cart was turning a corner, and Tom was calling to the horse, two strange men appeared on the scene.

' My goodness,' said one, ' what is this ? There goes a cart, and a driver is calling to the horse, but there is nothing to be seen.'

' There is something queer about this,' said the other ; ' we will follow the cart and see where it stops.'

The cart went on deep into the forest, and arrived quite safely at the place where the wood was cut.

When Tom spied his Father, he said : ' You see, Father, here I am with the cart ; now lift me down.' The Father held the horse with his left hand, and took his little son out of its ear with the right. Then Tom sat down quite happily on a straw.

When the two strangers noticed him, they did not know what to say for astonishment.

Then one drew the other aside, and said : ' Listen, that little creature might make our fortune if we were to show him in the town for money. We will buy him.'

So they went up to the Peasant, and said : ' Sell us the little man ; he shall be well looked after with us.'

' No,' said the Peasant ; ' he is the delight of my eyes, and I will not sell him for all the gold in the world.'

But Tom Thumb, when he heard the bargain, crept up by the folds of his Father's coat, placed himself on his shoulder, and whispered in his ear : ' Father, let me go ; I will soon come back again.'

Then his Father gave him to the two men for a fine piece of gold.

' Where will you sit ? ' they asked him.

' Oh, put me on the brim of your hat, then I can walk up and down and observe the neighbourhood without falling down.'

They did as he wished, and when Tom had said good-bye to his Father, they went away with him.

They walked on till it was twilight, when the little man said : ' You must lift me down.'

' Stay where you are,' answered the Man on whose head he sat.

' No,' said Tom ; ' I will come down. Lift me down immediately.'

The Man took off his hat and set the little creature in a field by the wayside. He jumped and crept about for a time, here and there among the sods, then slipped suddenly into a mouse-hole which he had discovered.

' Good evening, gentlemen, just you go home without me,' he called out to them in mockery.

They ran about and poked with sticks into the mouse-hole, but all in vain. Tom crept further and further back, and, as it soon got quite dark, they were forced to go home, full of anger, and with empty purses.

When Tom noticed that they were gone, he crept out of his underground hiding-place again. ' It is dangerous walking in this field in the dark,' he said ; ' one might easily break one's leg or one's neck.' Luckily, he came to an empty snail shell. ' Thank goodness,' he said ; ' I can pass the night in safety here,' and he sat down.

Not long after, just when he was about to go to sleep, he heard two men pass by. One said : ' How shall we set about stealing the rich parson's gold and silver ? '

' I can tell you,' interrupted Tom.

' What was that ? ' said one robber in a fright. ' I heard some one speak.'

They remained standing and listened.

Then Tom spoke again : ' Take me with you and I will help you.'

' Where are you ? ' they asked.

' Just look on the ground and see where the voice comes from,' he answered.

128

TOM THUMB

At last the thieves found him, and lifted him up. ' You little urchin, are *you* going to help us ? '

' Yes,' he said ; ' I will creep between the iron bars in the pastor's room, and will hand out to you what you want.'

' All right,' they said, ' we will see what you can do.'

When they came to the Parsonage, Tom crept into the room, but called out immediately with all his strength to the others : ' Do you want everything that is here ? '

The thieves were frightened, and said : ' Do speak softly, and don't wake any one.'

But Tom pretended not to understand, and called out again : ' What do you want ?   Everything ? '

The Cook, who slept above, heard him and sat up in bed and listened.   But the thieves were so frightened that they retreated a little way.   At last they summoned up courage again, and thought to themselves, ' The little rogue wants to tease us.'   So they came back and whispered to him : ' Now, do be serious, and hand us out something.'

Then Tom called out again, as loud as he could, ' I will give you everything if only you will hold out your hands.'

The Maid, who was listening intently, heard him quite distinctly, jumped out of bed, and stumbled to the door. The thieves turned and fled, running as though wild huntsmen were after them.   But the Maid, seeing nothing, went to get a light.   When she came back with it, Tom, without being seen, slipped out into the barn, and the Maid, after she had searched every corner and found nothing, went to bed again, thinking she had been dreaming with her eyes and ears open.

Tom Thumb climbed about in the hay, and found a splendid place to sleep.   There he determined to rest till day came, and then to go home to his parents.   But he had other experiences to go through first.   This world is full of trouble and sorrow !

The Maid got up in the grey dawn to feed the cows.   First she went into the barn, where she piled up an armful of hay, the very bundle in which poor Tom was asleep.   But he slept

129

so soundly that he knew nothing till he was almost in the mouth of the cow, who was eating him up with the hay.

'Heavens!' he said, 'however did I get into this mill?' but he soon saw where he was, and the great thing was to avoid being crushed between the cow's teeth. At last, whether he liked it or not, he had to go down the cow's throat.

'The windows have been forgotten in this house,' he said. 'The sun does not shine into it, and no light has been provided.'

Altogether he was very ill-pleased with his quarters, and, worst of all, more and more hay came in at the door, and the space grew narrower and narrower. At last he called out, in his fear, as loud as he could, 'Don't give me any more food. Don't give me any more food.'

The Maid was just milking the cow, and when she heard the same voice as in the night, without seeing any one, she was frightened, and slipped from her stool and spilt the milk. Then, in the greatest haste, she ran to her master, and said : 'Oh, your Reverence, the cow has spoken!'

'You are mad,' he answered ; but he went into the stable himself to see what was happening.

Scarcely had he set foot in the cow-shed before Tom began again, 'Don't bring me any more food.'

Then the Pastor was terrified too, and thought that the cow must be bewitched ; so he ordered it to be killed. It was accordingly slaughtered, but the stomach, in which Tom was hidden, was thrown into the manure heap. Tom had the greatest trouble in working his way out. Just as he stuck out his head, a hungry Wolf ran by and snapped up the whole stomach with one bite. But still Tom did not lose courage. 'Perhaps the Wolf will listen to reason,' he said. So he called out, 'Dear Wolf, I know where you would find a magnificent meal.'

'Where is it to be had?' asked the Wolf.

'Why, in such and such a house,' answered Tom. 'You must squeeze through the grating of the store-room window, and there you will find cakes, bacon, and sausages, as many as you can possibly eat '; and he went on to describe his father's house.

The Wolf did not wait to hear this twice, and at night forced himself in through the grating, and ate to his heart's content. When he was satisfied, he wanted to go away again; but he had grown so fat that he could not get out the same way. Tom had reckoned on this, and began to make a great commotion inside the Wolf's body, struggling and screaming with all his might.

'Be quiet,' said the Wolf; 'you will wake up the people of the house.'

'All very fine,' answered Tom. 'You have eaten your fill, and now I am going to make merry '; and he began to scream again with all his might.

At last his father and mother woke up, ran to the room, and looked through the crack of the door. When they saw a Wolf, they went away, and the husband fetched his axe, and the wife a scythe.

'You stay behind,' said the man, as they came into the room. 'If my blow does not kill him, you must attack him and rip up his body.'

When Tom Thumb heard his Father's voice, he called out: 'Dear Father, I am here, inside the Wolf's body.'

Full of joy, his Father cried, 'Heaven be praised! our dear child is found again,' and he bade his wife throw aside the scythe that it might not injure Tom.

Then he gathered himself together, and struck the Wolf a blow on the head, so that it fell down lifeless. Then with knives and shears they ripped up the body, and took their little boy out.

'Ah,' said his Father, 'what trouble we have been in about you.'

'Yes, Father, I have travelled about the world, and I am thankful to breathe fresh air again.'

'Wherever have you been?' they asked.

'Down a mouse-hole, in a Cow's stomach, and in a Wolf's maw,' he answered ; ' and now I shall stay with you.'

' And we will never sell you again, for all the riches in the world,' they said, kissing and fondling their dear child.

Then they gave him food and drink, and had new clothes made for him, as his own had been spoilt in his travels.

Rumpelstiltskin

THERE was once a Miller who was very poor, but he had a beautiful daughter. Now, it fell out that he had occasion to speak with the King, and, in order to give himself an air of importance, he said : ' I have a daughter who can spin gold out of straw.'

The King said to the Miller : ' That is an art in which I am much interested. If your daughter is as skilful as you say she is, bring her to my castle to-morrow, and I will put her to the test.'

Accordingly, when the girl was brought to the castle, the King conducted her to a chamber which was quite full of straw, gave her a spinning-wheel and winder, and said, ' Now, set to work, and if between to-night and to-morrow at dawn you have not spun this straw into gold you must die.' Thereupon he carefully locked the door of the chamber, and she remained alone.

There sat the unfortunate Miller's daughter, and for the life of her did not know what to do. She had not the least idea how to spin straw into gold, and she became more and more distressed, until at last she began to weep. Then all at once the door sprang open, and in stepped a little Mannikin, who said : ' Good evening, Mistress Miller, what are you weeping so for ? '

' Alas ! ' answered the Maiden, ' I 've got to spin gold out of straw, and don't know how to do it.'

Then the Mannikin said, ' What will you give me if I spin it for you ? '

' My necklace,' said the Maid.

The little Man took the necklace, sat down before the

spinning-wheel, and whir—whir—whir, in a trice the reel was full.

Then he fixed another reel, and whir—whir—whir, thrice round, and that too was full ; and so it went on until morning, when all the straw was spun and all the reels were full of gold.

Then all at once the door sprang open, and in stepped a little Mannikin.

Immediately at sunrise the King came, and when he saw the gold he was astonished and much pleased, but his mind became only the more avaricious. So he had the Miller's daughter taken to another chamber, larger than the former one, and full of straw, and he ordered her to spin it also in one night, as she valued her life.

The Maiden was at her wit's end, and began to weep. Then again the door sprang open, and the little Mannikin appeared, and said, 'What will you give me if I spin the straw into gold for you?'

'The ring off my finger,' answered the Maiden.

The little man took the ring, began to whir again at the wheel, and had by morning spun all the straw into gold.

The King was delighted at sight of the masses of gold, but was not even yet satisfied. So he had the Miller's daughter taken to a still larger chamber, full of straw, and said, ' This must you to-night spin into gold, but if you succeed you shall become my Queen.' ' Even if she is only a Miller's daughter,' thought he, ' I shan't find a richer woman in the whole world.'

134

RUMPELSTILTSKIN

When the girl was alone the little Man came again, and said for the third time, ' What will you give me if I spin the straw for you this time ? '

' I have nothing more that I can give,' answered the girl.

' Well, promise me your first child if you become Queen.'

' Who knows what may happen,' thought the Miller's daughter ; but she did not see any other way of getting out of the difficulty, so she promised the little Man what he demanded, and in return he spun the straw into gold once more.

When the King came in the morning, and found everything as he had wished, he celebrated his marriage with her, and the Miller's daughter became Queen.

About a year afterwards a beautiful child was born, but the Queen had forgotten all about the little Man. However, he suddenly entered her chamber, and said, ' Now, give me what you promised.'

The Queen was terrified, and offered the little Man all the wealth of the kingdom if he would let her keep the child. But the Mannikin said, ' No ; I would rather have some living thing than all the treasures of the world.' Then the Queen began to moan and weep to such an extent that the little Man felt sorry for her. ' I will give you three days,' said he, ' and if within that time you discover my name you shall keep the child.'

Then during the night the Queen called to mind all the names that she had ever heard, and sent a messenger all over the country to inquire far and wide what other names there were. When the little Man came on the next day, she began with Caspar, Melchoir, Balzer, and mentioned all the names which she knew, one after the other ; but at every one the little Man said : ' No ; that 's not my name.'

The second day she had inquiries made all round the neighbourhood for the names of people living there, and suggested to the little Man all the most unusual and strange names.

Round the fire an indescribably ridiculous little man was leaping, hopping
on one leg, and singing.

RUMPELSTILTSKIN

'Perhaps your name is Cowribs, Spindleshanks, or Spiderlegs ? '

But he answered every time, ' No ; that 's not my name.'

On the third day the messenger came back and said : ' I haven't been able to find any new names, but as I came round the corner of a wood on a lofty mountain, where the Fox says good-night to the Hare, I saw a little house, and in front of the house a fire was burning ; and around the fire an indescribably ridiculous little man was leaping, hopping on one leg, and singing :

> " To-day I bake ; to-morrow I brew my beer ;
> The next day I will bring the Queen's child here.
> Ah ! lucky 'tis that not a soul doth know
> That Rumpelstiltskin is my name, ho ! ho !"'

Then you can imagine how delighted the Queen was when she heard the name, and when presently afterwards the little Man came in and asked, ' Now, your Majesty, what is my name ? ' at first she asked :

' Is your name Tom ? '

' No.'

' Is it Dick ? '

' No.'

' Is it, by chance, Rumpelstiltskin ? '

' The devil told you that ! The devil told you that ! ' shrieked the little Man ; and in his rage stamped his right foot into the ground so deep that he sank up to his waist.

Then, in his passion, he seized his left leg with both hands, and tore himself asunder in the middle.

Clever Grethel

THERE was once a cook called Grethel, who wore shoes with red rosettes; and when she went out in them, she turned and twisted about gaily, and thought, 'How fine I am!'

After her walk she would take a draught of wine, in her light-heartedness; and as wine gives an appetite, she would then taste some of the dishes that she was cooking, saying to herself, 'The cook is bound to know how the food tastes.'

It so happened that one day her master said to her, 'Grethel, I have a guest coming to-night; roast me two fowls in your best style.'

'It shall be done, sir!' answered Grethel. So she killed the chickens, scalded and plucked them, and then put them on the spit; towards evening she put them down to the fire to roast. They got brown and crisp, but still the guest did not come. Then Grethel called to her Master, 'If the guest does not come I must take the fowls from the fire; but it will be a thousand pities if they are not eaten soon while they are juicy.'

Her Master said, 'I will go and hasten the guest myself.'

Hardly had her Master turned his back before Grethel laid the spit with the fowls on it on one side, and said to herself, 'It's thirsty work standing over the fire so long. Who knows when he will come. I'll go down into the cellar in the meantime and take a drop of wine.'

She ran down and held a jug to the tap, then said, 'Here's to your health, Grethel,' and took a good pull. 'Drinking leads to drinking,' she said, 'and it's not easy to give it up,' and again she took a good pull. Then she went upstairs and

138

put the fowls to the fire again, poured some butter over them, and turned the spit round with a will. It smelt so good that she thought, 'There may be something wanting, I must have a taste.' And she passed her finger over the fowls and put it in her mouth. 'Ah, how good they are; it's a sin and a shame that there's nobody to eat them.' She ran to the window to see if her Master was coming with the guest, but she saw nobody. Then she went back to the fowls again, and thought, 'One wing is catching a little, better to eat it—and eat it I will.' So she cut it off and ate it with much enjoyment. When it was finished, she thought, 'The other must follow, or the Master will notice that something is wanting.' When the wings were consumed she went back to the window again to look for her Master, but no one was in sight.

'Who knows,' she thought. 'I dare say they won't come at all; they must have dropped in somewhere else.' Then she said to herself, 'Now, Grethel, don't be afraid, eat it all up: why should the good food be wasted? When it's all gone you can rest; run and have another drink and then finish it up.' So she went down to the cellar, took a good drink, and contentedly ate up the rest of the fowl. When it had all disappeared and still no Master came, Grethel looked at the other fowl and said, 'Where one is gone the other must follow. What is good for one is right for the other. If I have a drink first I shall be none the worse.' So she took another hearty pull at the jug, and then she sent the other fowl after the first one.

In the height of her enjoyment, her Master came back, and cried, 'Hurry, Grethel, the guest is just coming.'

'Very well, sir, I'll soon have it ready,' answered Grethel.

Her Master went to see if the table was properly laid, and took the big carving-knife with which he meant to cut up the fowls, to sharpen it. In the meantime the guest came and knocked politely at the door. Grethel ran to see who was there, and, seeing the guest, she put her finger to her lips and said, 'Be quiet, and get away quickly; if my Master catches you it will be the worse for you. He certainly invited you to supper, but only with the intention of cutting off both your ears. You can hear him sharpening his knife now.'

The guest heard the knife being sharpened, and hurried off down the steps as fast as he could.

Grethel ran with great agility to her Master, shrieking, ' A fine guest you have invited, indeed ! '

' Why, what 's the matter, Grethel ? What do you mean ? '

' Well,' she said, ' he has taken the two fowls that I had just put upon the dish, and run off with them.'

' That 's a clever trick ! ' said her Master, regretting his fine fowls. ' If he had only left me one so that I had something to eat.'

He called out to him to stop, but the guest pretended not to hear. Then he ran after him, still holding the carving-knife, and cried, ' Only one, only one ! '—meaning that the guest should leave him one fowl ; but the guest only thought that he meant he was to give him one ear, and he ran as if he was pursued by fire, and so took both his ears safely home.

The Old Man and his Grandson

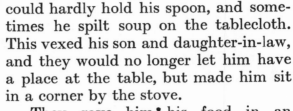

THERE was once a very old Man, so old that his eyes had become dim, and his limbs trembled.

When he sat at table his hands shook so that he could hardly hold his spoon, and sometimes he spilt soup on the tablecloth. This vexed his son and daughter-in-law, and they would no longer let him have a place at the table, but made him sit in a corner by the stove.

They gave him his food in an earthenware bowl, and a very scanty portion too. He sat in his place looking at the others at table, and the tears came into his eyes.

One day his trembling hands could no longer hold the bowl; it fell to the ground and broke to atoms.

The young wife scolded him, but he said nothing; then she bought him a wooden bowl for a few coppers, and he had nothing else to eat from.

As they were sitting together one day, the little Grandson, who was four years old, collected a lot of bits of wood.

'What are you doing there?' asked his Father.

'I am making a little trough,' answered the Child, 'for you and Mother to eat out of when I am big.'

Husband and wife looked at each other for a while till their tears began to fall. Then they led the old Grandfather up to the table to take his meal with them.

And they never again said anything to him when he spilt his food.

The Little Peasant

THERE was once a village in which there was only one poor Peasant; all the others were very well-to-do, so they called him the Little Peasant. He had not even got a single cow, far less money with which to buy one, though he and his Wife would have been so glad to possess one.

One day he said to his Wife, 'Look here, I have a good idea: there is my Godfather, the joiner, he shall make us a wooden calf and paint it brown, so that it looks like a real one, and perhaps some day it will grow into a cow.'

This plan pleased his Wife, so his Godfather, the joiner, cut out and carved the calf and painted it properly, and made its head bent down to look as if it were eating.

Next morning, when the cows were driven out, the Little Peasant called the Cowherd in, and said: 'Look here, I have a little calf, but it is very small and has to be carried.'

The Cowherd said: 'All right,' took it in his arms, carried it to the meadow and put it down in the grass.

The calf stood there all day and appeared to be eating, and the Cowherd said, 'It will soon be able to walk by itself; see how it eats.'

In the evening, when he was going home, he said to the calf, 'If you can stand there all day and eat your fill, you may just walk home on your own legs, I don't mean to carry you!'

But the Little Peasant was standing by his door waiting for the calf, and when the Cowherd came through the village without it, he at once asked where it was.

The Cowherd said, 'It is still standing there; it would not stop eating to come with us.'

142

THE LITTLE PEASANT

The Little Peasant said, ' But I must have my little calf back.'

So they went back together to the field, but some one had stolen the calf in the meantime, and it was gone.

The Cowherd said, ' It must have run away.'

But the Little Peasant said, ' Nothing of the kind,' and he took the Cowherd up before the Bailiff, who condemned him, for his carelessness, to give the Little Peasant a cow, in place of the lost calf.

So at last the Little Peasant and his Wife had the long-wished-for cow; they were delighted, but they had no fodder and could not give it anything to eat, so very soon they had to kill it.

They salted the meat, and the man went to the town to sell the hide, intending to buy another calf with the money he got for it. On the way he came to a mill, on which a raven sat with a broken wing; he took it up out of pity and wrapped it in the hide. Such a storm of wind and rain came on that he could go no further, so he went into the mill to ask for shelter.

Only the Miller's Wife was at home, and she said to the Little Peasant, ' You may lie down in the straw there.' And she gave him some bread and cheese to eat.

The Little Peasant ate it, and then lay down with the hide by his side.

The Miller's Wife thought, ' He is tired, and won't wake up.'

Soon after a Priest came in, and he was made very welcome by the woman, who said, ' My husband is out, so we can have a feast.'

The Little Peasant was listening, and when he heard about the feast he was much annoyed, because bread and cheese had been considered good enough for him.

The Woman then laid the table, and brought out a roast joint, salad, cake and wine. They sat down, but just as they were beginning to eat, somebody knocked at the door.

The Woman said, ' Good heavens, that is my Husband ! '

143

She quickly hid the joint in the oven, the wine under the pillow, the salad on the bed, and the cake under the bed, and, last of all, she hid the Priest in the linen chest. Then she opened the door for her Husband, and said, 'Thank heaven you are back : the world might be coming to an end with such a storm as there is ! '

The Miller saw the Little Peasant lying on the straw, and said, ' What is that fellow doing there ? '

' Oh ! ' said his Wife, ' the poor fellow came in the middle of the storm and asked for shelter, so I gave him some bread and cheese, and told him he might lie on the straw ! '

' He 's welcome as far as I 'm concerned,' said the Man ; ' but get me something to eat, Wife, I 'm very hungry.'

His Wife said, ' I have nothing but bread and cheese.'

' Anything will please me,' said the Man ; ' bread and cheese is good enough.' And his eyes falling on the Little Peasant, he said, ' Come along and have some too.'

The Little Peasant did not wait for a second bidding, but got up at once, and they fell to.

The Miller noticed the hide on the floor in which the Raven was wrapped, and said, ' What have you got there ? '

' I have a soothsayer there,' answered the Little Peasant.

' Can he prophesy something to me ? ' asked the Miller.

' Why not ? ' answered the Little Peasant ; ' but he will only say four things, the fifth he keeps to himself.'

The Miller was inquisitive, and said, ' Let me hear one of his prophecies.'

The Little Peasant squeezed the Raven's head and made him croak.

The Miller asked, ' What did he say ? '

The Little Peasant answered, ' First he said that there was a bottle of wine under the pillow.'

' That 's a bit of luck ! ' said the Miller, going to the pillow and finding the wine. ' What next ? '

The Little Peasant made the Raven croak again, and said, ' Secondly, he says there is a joint in the oven.'

144

THE LITTLE PEASANT

'That 's a bit of luck ! ' said the Miller, going to the oven and finding the joint.

The Little Peasant again squeezed the Raven to make him prophesy, and said, ' Thirdly, he says there is some salad in the bed.'

'That 's a bit of luck ! ' said the Miller, finding the salad.

Again the Little Peasant squeezed the Raven to make him crook, and said, ' Fourthly, he says there is a cake under the bed.'

'That 's a bit of luck ! ' cried the Miller, as he found the cake.

Now the two sat down at the table together ; but the Miller's Wife was in terror. She went to bed, and took all the keys with her.

The Miller would have liked to know what the fifth prophecy could be, but the Little Peasant said, ' We will quietly eat these four things first, the fifth is something dreadful.'

So they went on eating, and then they bargained as to how much the Miller should pay for the fifth prophecy, and at last they agreed upon three hundred thalers.

Then again the Little Peasant squeezed the Raven's head and made him crow very loud.

The Miller said, ' What does he say ? '

The Little Peasant answered, ' He says the devil is hidden in the linen chest.'

The Miller said, ' The devil will have to go out ' ; and he opened the house door and made his Wife give up the keys. The Little Peasant unlocked the linen chest, and the Priest took to his heels as fast as ever he could.

The Miller said, ' I saw the black fellow with my own eyes ; there was no mistake about it.'

The Little Peasant made off at dawn with his three hundred thalers.

After this the Little Peasant began to get on in the world ; he built himself a pretty new house, and the other Peasants said, 'He must have been where the golden snow falls and where one brings home gold in bushels.'

Then he was summoned before the Bailiff to say where he got all his riches.

He answered, 'I sold my cow-hide in the town for three hundred thalers.'

When the other Peasants heard this they all wanted to enjoy the same good luck, so they ran home, killed their cows, and took the hides off to get the same price for them.

The Bailiff said, 'My maid must have the first chance.' When she reached the town the buyer only gave her three thalers for the hide; and he did not even give the others so much, for he said, 'What on earth am I to do with all these hides?'

Now the Peasants were enraged at the Little Peasant for having stolen a march upon them, and to revenge themselves they had him up before the Bailiff and accused him of cheating.

The innocent Little Peasant was unanimously condemned to death; he was to be put into a cask full of holes and rolled into the water. He was led out, and a Priest was brought to read a mass; and all the people had to stand at a distance.

As soon as the Little Peasant looked at the Priest, he knew he was the man who had been at the Miller's. He said to him, 'I saved you out of the chest, now you must save me out of the cask.'

Just then a Shepherd came by driving a flock of sheep, and the Little Peasant knew that he had long wanted to be Bailiff himself; so he called out as loud as he could, 'No, I will not, and if all the world wished it I would not.'

The Shepherd, who heard what he said, came and asked, 'What's the matter, what will you not do?'

The Little Peasant said, 'They want to make me Bailiff if I will sit in this cask, but I won't.'

'If that is all,' said the Shepherd, 'I will get into the cask myself.'

The Little Peasant said, 'If you will get into the cask you shall be made Bailiff.'

146

The Shepherd was delighted, and got in, and the Little Peasant fastened down the cover upon him. The flock of sheep he took for himself, and drove them off.

Then the Priest went back to the Peasants and told them the mass was said; so they went and rolled the cask into the water.

When it began to roll the Shepherd cried out, ' I am quite ready to be Bailiff ! '

The Peasants thought that it was only the Little Peasant crying out, and they said, ' Very likely; but you must go and look about you down below first.' And they rolled the cask straight into the water.

Thereupon they went home, and when they entered the village what was their surprise to meet the Little Peasant calmly driving a flock of sheep before him, as happy as could be. They cried, ' Why, you Little Peasant, how do you come here again ? How did you get out of the water ? '

' Well,' said the Little Peasant, ' I sank deep, deep down till I touched the bottom; then I knocked the head of the cask off, crept out, and found myself in a beautiful meadow in which numbers of lambs were feeding, and I brought this flock back with me.'

The other Peasants said, ' Are there any more ? '

' Oh yes, plenty,' answered the Little Peasant, ' more than we should know what to do with.'

Then the other Peasants planned to fetch some of these sheep for themselves; they would each have a flock.

But the Bailiff said, ' I go first.'

They all ran together to the water; the sky just then was flecked with little fleecy clouds and they were reflected in the water. When the Peasants saw them, they cried, ' Why, there they are ! We can see the sheep below the water ! '

The Bailiff pressed forward, and said, ' I will be the first to go down to look about me; I will call you if it is worth while.' So he sprang into the water with a great splash.

The others thought he cried, 'Come along!' and the whole party plunged in after him.

So all the Peasants perished, and, as the Little Peasant was the sole heir, he became a rich man.

Fred and Kate

FRED and Kate were man and wife. They had not long been married.

One day Fred said, 'I am going into the fields, Kate; I shall be hungry when I come in, so have something good ready for dinner, and a cool draught to quench my thirst.'

'All right, Fred, I will have it ready for you when you come back.'

When dinner-time approached, she took down a sausage from the chimney, put it into a frying-pan with some butter, and placed it on the fire. The sausage began to frizzle and splutter, and Kate stood holding the pan lost in her thoughts.

Suddenly she said : 'While the sausage is cooking, I might go down to the cellar to draw the beer.' So she put the pan firmly on the fire, and took a jug down to the cellar to draw the beer.

Kate watched the beer running into the jug, and suddenly she said : 'I don't believe the dog is tied up ; it might get the sausage out of the frying-pan and run off with it.'

She was up the cellar stairs in a twinkling, but the dog had already got the sausage in his jaws, and was just making off with it. Kate, who was very agile, ran after him, and chased him a good way over the fields. The dog, however, was quicker than she, and without letting go the sausage, he got right away.

'What is gone, is gone !' she said, and being tired out, she turned back and walked slowly home to cool herself.

In the meantime, the beer had been running out of the cask, because Kate had forgotten to turn the tap. As soon as

149

the jug was full, the rest ran all over the cellar floor, till the cask was quite empty.

Kate saw what had happened as soon as she got to the top of the cellar stairs. 'Humph!' she cried, 'what am I to do now, so that Fred shan't discover it?'

She thought a while, and at last she remembered a sack of fine meal they had left over from the last fair. She would

Kate ran after him, and chased him a good way over the fields.

fetch it down and strew it over the beer. 'To be sure,' she said, 'those who save at the right time have something when they need it.'

So she went up to the loft and brought the sack down, but, unfortunately, she threw it right on to the jug full of beer. It was overturned, and away went Fred's drink, flooding the cellar with the rest.

'Oh, that won't matter!' said Kate. 'When part is gone,

150

When Tom had said good-bye to his Father they went away with him.

At last she reached the cellar, and there she found an old, old woman
with a shaking head.

Then he ran after him, still holding the carving-knife, and cried,
'Only one, only one!'

The Old Man had to sit by himself, and ate his food from
a wooden bowl.

the rest may as well follow.' Then she strewed the meal all over the cellar. She was delighted with her handiwork when it was finished, and said : ' How clean and fresh it looks.'

At dinner-time Fred came home. ' Well, wife, what have you got for dinner ? ' he said.

' O Fred ! ' she answered, ' I was frying you a sausage, but while I went down to draw the beer, the dog got it ; and while I ran after the dog, the beer ran out of the cask. Then when I was going to dry up the beer with the meal, I knocked the jug over. But never mind, the cellar is quite dry now.'

Fred said : ' Kate, Kate, what have you been doing ? First you let the sausage be carried off, then you let the beer run out of the cask, and, lastly, you waste our fine meal.'

' Well, Fred, I did not know ; you should have told me what to do.'

The man thought : ' If my wife is like this, I must look after things myself.'

Now, he had saved a nice little sum of money, which he changed into gold, and said to Kate : ' Do you see these yellow counters ? I am going to put them in a pot, and bury them underneath the cow's manger in the stable ; don't you meddle with them, or it will be the worse for you.'

And she said : ' Oh no, Fred, I won't.'

Now, when Fred had gone out, several Pedlars came into the village with earthen pots and pans for sale. They asked the young wife if she had nothing to give in exchange for them.

' Oh, good people,' said Kate, ' I have no money, and I can't buy anything, but if some yellow counters would be any good to you, I might do some business.'

' Yellow counters ! Why not ? You might as well show them to us,' said the men.

' You must go into the stable and dig under the cow's manger, and you will find the yellow counters. I dare not go with you.'

So the rogues went to the stable and dug up the pot of gold.

They seized it and made off with it as fast as they could, leaving their pots and pans behind.

Kate thought she must use the new utensils, but as there was no lack in the kitchen, she knocked the bottom out of every pot and pan, and hung them on the fence round the house as ornaments.

When Fred came home and saw the new decorations, he said : ' Kate, whatever have you been doing now ? '

' I bought them, Fred, with the yellow counters which were hidden in the stable, but I did not get them myself ; the Pedlars dug them up.'

' Alas, wife ! ' said Fred, ' what have you done ? Those were not counters, they were pure gold, and all that we possess. You should not have done it.'

' Well, Fred, I did not know ; you should have told me.'

Kate stood for a while thinking, then she said : ' Listen, Fred, we will run after the thieves and get the money back.'

' Come along then,' said Fred, ' we will try what we can do ; but we must take some butter and cheese with us to eat on the way.'

' All right,' she answered. So they set out, but as Fred was fleeter of foot than Kate he was soon ahead of her.

' I shall be the gainer,' she said ; ' I shall be foremost when we turn.'

Soon they came to a mountain, and on both sides of the road there were deep cart ruts. ' There, just see,' said Kate, ' how the poor earth is torn and scratched and squeezed ; it can never be whole again as long as it lives.'

Then out of the kindness of her heart she took the butter and smeared the ruts right and left, so that they might not be torn by the wheels.

As she was stooping in this compassionate act, one of the cheeses fell out of her pocket, and rolled down the hill.

Kate said : ' I have come up the hill once, and I don't mean to do it again ; I will send another of the cheeses to fetch it. So she took another out of her pocket and rolled it down.

152

As it did not come back she sent a third rolling after it, and thought, ' Perhaps they are waiting for company, and don't like walking alone.'

When all three stayed away, she said : ' I don't know what is the meaning of this ! it may be that the third one lost its way ; I will send the fourth one to call it back.' Nothing was seen of the fourth any more than of the third.

At last Kate got quite angry, and threw down the fifth and sixth, and they were the last.

For a time she stood looking to see if they were coming, but as they did not appear, she said : ' Oh, you would be good folks to send in search of death, you would be a long time coming back. You need not think I am going to wait any longer for you ; I am going on, and you may just come after me, your legs are younger than mine.'

So Kate went on, and caught up Fred, who had stopped because he wanted something to eat. ' Now give me the food you brought with you.'

She handed him some dry bread.

' What has become of the butter and cheese ? ' said the man.

' O Fred ! ' said Kate, ' I smeared the cart ruts with the butter, but the cheese will soon be here. One of them slipped away from me, and then I sent the others to fetch it back.'

Then said Fred : ' You should not have wasted the butter, Kate, or sent the cheeses rolling down the hill.'

' Well, Fred, you ought to have told me so,' said Kate.

So they ate the dry bread together, and Fred said : ' Did you lock up the house, Kate, before you came away ? '

' No, Fred ; you should have told me sooner.'

Her husband said : ' Well, then, go home and lock up the house before we go any further, and bring something else to eat. I will wait for you here.'

So Kate went, and she thought to herself, ' As Fred wants something else to eat, I suppose he does not like bread and cheese, I will take him some dried apples and a jug of vinegar to drink.'

Then she bolted the upper half of the door, but she lifted the lower part from its hinges, and took it with her on her back, thinking that if she had the door in safety the house would be safe. She took plenty of time on her way back, for she thought : ' Fred will have the more time to rest.'

When she reached him again, she said : ' Here you have the house door, Fred, so you can take care of the house yourself.'

' Good heavens,' he said, ' what a clever wife I have. She bolts the upper part of the door, and lifts the lower part off its hinges, so that anything may run in and out. It 's too late to go back to the house now ; but as you have brought the door so far, you may just carry it further.'

' I will carry the door, Fred,' she said. ' But the apples and the jug of vinegar are too heavy ; I will hang them on the door, and it may carry them.'

They now went into the wood to look for the rogues, but they did not find them. As it was dark, they climbed up a tree to spend the night there.

They had hardly settled themselves, before the Pedlars came up. They were the sort of people who take away things which should not be taken, and who find things before they are lost.

They lay down just under the tree in which Fred and Kate were. They lighted a fire, and began to divide their booty.

Fred got down at the other side of the tree, and picked up a lot of stones with which he meant to kill the thieves. The stones did not hit them, however, and the rogues said : ' It will soon be day, the wind is blowing down the pine cones.'

Kate still had the door on her back, and she thought it was the dried apples which made it so heavy, so she said : ' Fred, I must throw down the apples.'

' No, Kate, not now,' he answered ; ' they would betray us.'

' But, Fred, I must, they are so heavy.'

' Well, let them go then, in the name of fortune ! ' he cried, and down rolled the apples.

154

FRED AND KATE

And the Pedlars said : ' The leaves are falling.'

A little later, finding that the door still pressed very heavily, Kate said : ' Fred, I must pour away the vinegar.'

' No, Kate, not now ; it would betray us.'

' But, Fred, I must, it is terribly heavy.'

' Well, do it, then, if you must, in the name of fortune ! '

So she poured out the vinegar, and the Pedlars were sprinkled with it.

They said to each other : ' Why, the dew is falling already.'

At last Kate thought : ' Can it be the door that presses so heavily ? ' And she said : ' Fred, I must throw the door down.'

' No, Kate, not now ; it might betray us.'

' But, Fred, I must ; it weighs me down.'

' No, Kate, hold it fast.'

' Fred, it 's slipping, I must let it fall.'

' Well, let it fall, then, in the devil's name ! '

So down it fell through the branches with such a clatter, that the Pedlars cried : ' The devil 's in this tree.' And they ran away as fast as ever they could go, leaving all their treasure behind them.

In the early morning, when Fred and Kate climbed down, they found all their gold, and took it home with them.

Sweetheart Roland

ONCE upon a time there was a woman who was a real Witch, and she had two daughters; one was ugly and wicked, but she loved her because she was her own daughter. The other was good and lovely, but she hated her for she was only her step-daughter.

Now, this step-daughter had a beautiful apron which the other daughter envied, and she said to her Mother that have it she must and would.

'Just wait quietly, my child,' said her Mother. 'You shall have it; your step-sister has long deserved death, and to-night, when she is asleep, I will go and chop off her head. Only take care to lie on the further side of the bed, against the wall, and push her well to this side.'

Now, all this would certainly have come to pass if the poor girl had not been standing in a corner, and heard what they said. She was not even allowed to go near the door all day, and when bed-time came the Witch's daughter got into bed first, so as to lie at the further side; but when she was asleep the other gently changed places with her, and put herself next the wall.

In the middle of the night the Witch crept up holding an axe in her right hand, while with her left she felt if there was any one there. Then she seized the axe with both hands, struck—and struck off her own child's head.

When she had gone away, the Maiden got up, and went to the house of her Sweetheart Roland, and knocked at his door. When he came out, she said to him, 'Listen, dear Roland; we must quickly fly. My step-mother tried to kill me, but she hit her own child instead. When day comes, and she sees what she has done, we shall be lost.'

The Maiden fetched the magic wand, and then she took her step-sister's head, and dropped three drops of blood from it.

'But,' said Roland, 'you must first steal her magic wand, or we shall not be able to escape if she comes after us.'

The Maiden fetched the magic wand, and then she took her step-sister's head, and dropped three drops of blood from it—one by the bed, one in the kitchen, and one on the stairs. After that, she hurried away with her Sweetheart Roland.

When the old Witch got up in the morning she called her daughter in order to give her the apron, but she did not come. Then she called, 'Where art thou?'

'Here on the stairs,' answered one drop of blood.

The Witch went on to the stairs, but saw nothing, so she called again: 'Where art thou?'

'Here in the kitchen warming myself,' answered the second drop of blood.

The Witch went into the kitchen, but found nothing, then she called again: 'Where art thou?'

'Here in bed, sleeping,' answered the third drop of blood.

So she went into the bedroom, and there she found her own child, whose head she had chopped off herself.

The Witch flew into a violent passion, and sprang out of the window. As she could see for many miles around, she soon discovered her step-daughter hurrying away with Roland.

'That won't be any good,' she cried. 'However far you may go, you won't escape me.'

She put on her seven-league boots, and before long she overtook them. When the Maiden saw her coming, she changed her Sweetheart into a lake, with the magic wand, and herself into a Duck swimming in it. The Witch stood on the shore, and threw bread-crumbs into the water, and did every-thing she could think of to entice the Duck ashore. But it was all to no purpose, and she was obliged to go back at night without having accomplished her object.

When she had gone away, the Maiden and Roland resumed their own shapes, and they walked the whole night till break of day.

Then the Maiden changed herself into a beautiful Rose in

158

the middle of a briar hedge, and Roland into a Fiddler. Before long the Witch came striding along, and said to the Fiddler, ' Good Fiddler, may I pick this beautiful Rose ? '

' By all means,' he said, ' and I will play to you.'

As she crept into the hedge, in great haste to pick the flower (for she knew well who the flower was), Roland began to play, and she had to dance, whether she liked or not, for it was a magic dance. The quicker he played, the higher she had to jump, and the thorns tore her clothes to ribbons, and scratched her till she bled. He would not stop a moment, so she had to dance till she fell down dead.

When the Maiden was freed from the spell, Roland said, ' Now I will go to my father and order the wedding.'

' Then I will stay here in the meantime,' said the Maiden. ' And so that no one shall recognise me while I am waiting, I will change myself into a common red stone.'

So Roland went away, and the Maiden stayed in the field, as a stone, waiting his return.

But when Roland got home, he fell into the snares of another woman, who made him forget all about his love. The poor Maiden waited a long, long time, but when he did not come back, she became very sad, and changed herself into a flower, and thought, ' Somebody at least will tread upon me.'

Now it so happened that a Shepherd was watching his sheep in the field, and saw the flower, and he picked it because he thought it was so pretty. He took it home and put it carefully away in a chest. From that time forward a wonderful change took place in the Shepherd's hut. When he got up in the morning, all the work was done ; the tables and benches were dusted, the fire was lighted, and the water was carried in. At dinner-time, when he came home, the table was laid, and a well-cooked meal stood ready. He could not imagine how it all came about, for he never saw a creature in his house, and nobody could be hidden in the tiny hut. He was much pleased at being so well served, but at last he got rather frightened, and went to a Wise Woman to ask her advice.

159

The Wise Woman said, 'There is magic behind it. You must look carefully about the room, early in the morning, and whatever you see, throw a white cloth over it, and the spell will be broken.'

The Shepherd did what she told him, and next morning, just as the day broke, he saw his chest open, and the flower come out. So he sprang up quickly, and threw a white cloth over it. Immediately the spell was broken, and a lovely Maiden stood before him, who confessed that she had been the flower, and it was she who had done all the work of his hut. She also told him her story, and he was so pleased with her that he asked her to marry him.

But she answered, 'No; I want my Sweetheart Roland, and though he has forsaken me, I will always be true to him.'

She promised not to go away, however, but to go on with the housekeeping for the present.

Now the time came for Roland's marriage to be celebrated. According to old custom, a proclamation was made that every maiden in the land should present herself to sing at the marriage in honour of the bridal pair.

When the faithful Maiden heard this, she grew very sad, so sad that she thought her heart would break. She had no wish to go to the marriage, but the others came and fetched her. But each time as her turn came to sing, she slipped behind the others till she was the only one left, and she could not help herself.

As soon as she began to sing, and her voice reached Roland's ears, he sprang up and cried, ' That is the true Bride, and I will have no other.'

Everything that he had forgotten came back, and his heart was filled with joy. So the faithful Maiden was married to her Sweetheart Roland ; all her grief and pain were over, and only happiness lay before her.

160

Snowdrop

IT was the middle of winter, and the snowflakes were falling from the sky like feathers. Now, a Queen sat sewing at a window framed in black ebony, and as she sewed she looked out upon the snow. Suddenly she pricked her finger and three drops of blood fell on to the snow. And the red looked so lovely on the white that she thought to herself : ' If only I had a child as white as snow and as red as blood, and as black as the wood of the window frame ! ' Soon after, she had a daughter, whose hair was black as ebony, while her cheeks were red as blood, and her skin as white as snow ; so she was called Snowdrop. But when the child was born the Queen died. A year after the King took another wife. She was a handsome woman, but proud and overbearing, and could not endure that any one should surpass her in beauty. She had a magic looking-glass, and when she stood before it and looked at herself she used to say :

> ' Mirror, Mirror on the wall,
> Who is fairest of us all ? '

then the Glass answered,

> ' Queen, thou 'rt fairest of them all.'

Then she was content, for she knew that the Looking-glass spoke the truth.

But Snowdrop grew up and became more and more beautiful, so that when she was seven years old she was as beautiful as the day, and far surpassed the Queen. Once, when she asked her Glass,

'Mirror, Mirror on the wall,
Who is fairest of us all?'

it answered—

'Queen, thou art fairest here, I hold,
But Snowdrop is fairer a thousandfold.'

Then the Queen was horror-struck, and turned green and yellow with jealousy. From the hour that she saw Snowdrop her heart sank, and she hated the little girl.

The pride and envy of her heart grew like a weed, so that she had no rest day nor night. At last she called a Huntsman, and said: 'Take the child out into the wood; I will not set eyes on her again; you must kill her and bring me her lungs and liver as tokens.'

The Huntsman obeyed, and took Snowdrop out into the forest, but when he drew his hunting-knife and was preparing to plunge it into her innocent heart, she began to cry:

'Alas! dear Huntsman, spare my life, and I will run away into the wild forest and never come back again.'

And because of her beauty the Huntsman had pity on her and said, 'Well, run away, poor child.' Wild beasts will soon devour you, he thought, but still he felt as though a weight were lifted from his heart, because he had

'Mirror, Mirror on the wall,
Who is fairest of us all?'

162

not been obliged to kill her. And as just at that moment a young fawn came leaping by, he pierced it and took the lungs and liver as tokens to the Queen. The Cook was ordered to serve them up in pickle, and the wicked Queen ate them thinking that they were Snowdrop's.

Now the poor child was alone in the great wood, with no living soul near, and she was so frightened that she knew not what to do. Then she began to run, and ran over the sharp stones and through the brambles, while the animals passed her by without harming her. She ran as far as her feet could carry her till it was nearly evening, when she saw a little house and went in to rest. Inside, everything was small, but as neat and clean as could be. A small table covered with a white cloth stood ready with seven small plates, and by every plate was a spoon, knife, fork, and cup. Seven little beds were ranged against the walls, covered with snow-white coverlets. As Snowdrop was very hungry and thirsty she ate a little bread and vegetable from each plate, and drank a little wine from each cup, for she did not want to eat up the whole of one portion. Then, being very tired, she lay down in one of the beds. She tried them all but none suited her; one was too short, another too long, all except the seventh, which was just right. She remained in it, said her prayers, and fell asleep.

When it was quite dark the masters of the house came in. They were seven Dwarfs, who used to dig in the mountains for ore. They kindled their lights, and as soon as they could see they noticed that some one had been there, for everything was not in the order in which they had left it.

The first said, ' Who has been sitting in my chair ? '
The second said, ' Who has been eating off my plate ? '
The third said, ' Who has been nibbling my bread ? '
The fourth said, ' Who has been eating my vegetables ? '
The fifth said, ' Who has been using my fork ? '
The sixth said, ' Who has been cutting with my knife ? '
The seventh said, ' Who has been drinking out of my cup ? '

163

Then the first looked and saw a slight impression on his bed, and said, 'Who has been treading on my bed?' The others came running up and said, 'And mine, and mine.'

In the evening the seven Dwarfs came back.

But the seventh, when he looked into his bed, saw Snowdrop, who lay there asleep. He called the others, who came up and cried out with astonishment, as they held their lights and

164

gazed at Snowdrop. 'Heavens! what a beautiful child,' they said, and they were so delighted that they did not wake her up but left her asleep in bed. And the seventh Dwarf slept with his comrades, an hour with each all through the night.

When morning came Snowdrop woke up, and when she saw the seven Dwarfs she was frightened.

But they were very kind and asked her name.

'I am called Snowdrop,' she answered.

'How did you get into our house?' they asked.

Then she told them how her stepmother had wished to get rid of her, how the Huntsman had spared her life, and how she had run all day till she had found the house.

Then the Dwarfs said, 'Will you look after our household, cook, make the beds, wash, sew and knit, and keep everything neat and clean? If so you shall stay with us and want for nothing.'

'Yes,' said Snowdrop, 'with all my heart'; and she stayed with them and kept the house in order.

In the morning they went to the mountain and searched for copper and gold, and in the evening they came back and then their meal had to be ready. All day the maiden was alone, and the good Dwarfs warned her and said, 'Beware of your stepmother, who will soon learn that you are here. Don't let any one in.'

But the Queen, having, as she imagined, eaten Snowdrop's liver and lungs, and feeling certain that she was the fairest of all, stepped in front of her Glass, and asked—

> 'Mirror, Mirror on the wall,
> Who is fairest of us all?'

the Glass answered as usual—

> 'Queen, thou art fairest here, I hold,
> But Snowdrop over the fells,
> Who with the seven Dwarfs dwells,
> Is fairer still a thousandfold.'

165

She was dismayed, for she knew that the Glass told no lies, and she saw that the Hunter had deceived her and that Snowdrop still lived. Accordingly she began to wonder afresh how she might compass her death; for as long as she was not the fairest in the land her jealous heart left her no rest. At last she thought of a plan. She dyed her face and dressed up like an old Pedlar, so that she was quite unrecognisable. In this guise she crossed over the seven mountains to the home of the seven Dwarfs and called out, 'Wares for sale.'

Snowdrop peeped out of the window and said, 'Good-day, mother, what have you got to sell?'

'Good wares, fine wares,' she answered, 'laces of every colour'; and she held out one which was made of gay plaited silk.

'I may let the honest woman in,' thought Snowdrop, and she unbolted the door and bought the pretty lace.

'Child,' said the Old Woman, 'what a sight you are, I will lace you properly for once.'

Snowdrop made no objection, and placed herself before the Old Woman to let her lace her with the new lace. But the Old Woman laced so quickly and tightly that she took away Snowdrop's breath and she fell down as though dead.

'Now I am the fairest,' she said to herself, and hurried away.

Not long after the seven Dwarfs came home, and were horror-struck when they saw their dear little Snowdrop lying on the floor without stirring, like one dead. When they saw she was laced too tight they cut the lace, whereupon she began to breathe and soon came back to life again. When the Dwarfs heard what had happened, they said that the old Pedlar was no other than the wicked Queen. 'Take care not to let any one in when we are not here,' they said.

Now the wicked Queen, as soon as she got home, went to the Glass and asked—

'Mirror, Mirror on the wall,
Who is fairest of us all?'

SNOWDROP

and it answered as usual—

> 'Queen, thou art fairest here, I hold,
> But Snowdrop over the fells,
> Who with the seven Dwarfs dwells,
> Is fairer still a thousandfold.'

When she heard it all her blood flew to her heart, so enraged was she, for she knew that Snowdrop had come back to life again. Then she thought to herself, 'I must plan something which will put an end to her.' By means of witchcraft, in which she was skilled, she made a poisoned comb. Next she disguised herself and took the form of a different Old Woman. She crossed the mountains and came to the home of the seven Dwarfs, and knocked at the door calling out, 'Good wares to sell.'

Snowdrop looked out of the window and said, 'Go away, I must not let any one in.'

'At least you may look,' answered the Old Woman, and she took the poisoned comb and held it up.

The child was so pleased with it that she let herself be beguiled, and opened the door.

When she had made a bargain the Old Woman said, 'Now I will comb your hair properly for once.'

Poor Snowdrop, suspecting no evil, let the Old Woman have her way, but scarcely was the poisoned comb fixed in her hair than the poison took effect, and the maiden fell down unconscious.

'You paragon of beauty,' said the wicked woman, 'now it is all over with you,' and she went away.

Happily it was near the time when the seven Dwarfs came home. When they saw Snowdrop lying on the ground as though dead, they immediately suspected her stepmother, and searched till they found the poisoned comb. No sooner had they removed it than Snowdrop came to herself again and related what had happened. They warned her again to be on her guard, and to open the door to no one.

167

When she got home the Queen stood before her Glass and said—

> ' Mirror, Mirror on the wall,
> Who is fairest of us all ? '

and it answered as usual—

> ' Queen, thou art fairest here, I hold,
> But Snowdrop over the fells,
> Who with the seven Dwarfs dwells,
> Is fairer still a thousandfold.'

When she heard the Glass speak these words she trembled and quivered with rage, ' Snowdrop shall die,' she said, ' even if it cost me my own life.' Thereupon she went into a secret room, which no one ever entered but herself, and made a poisonous apple. Outwardly it was beautiful to look upon, with rosy cheeks, and every one who saw it longed for it, but whoever ate of it was certain to die. When the apple was ready she dyed her face and dressed herself like an old Peasant Woman and so crossed the seven hills to the Dwarfs' home. There she knocked.

Snowdrop put her head out of the window and said, ' I must not let any one in, the seven Dwarfs have forbidden me.'

' It is all the same to me,' said the Peasant Woman. ' I shall soon get rid of my apples. There, I will give you one.'

' No ; I must not take anything.'

' Are you afraid of poison ? ' said the woman. ' See, I will cut the apple in half : you eat the red side and I will keep the other.'

Now the apple was so cunningly painted that the red half alone was poisoned. Snowdrop longed for the apple, and when she saw the Peasant Woman eating she could hold out no longer, stretched out her hand and took the poisoned half. Scarcely had she put a bit into her mouth than she fell dead to the ground.

The Queen looked with a fiendish glance, and laughed aloud and said, ' White as snow, red as blood, and black as ebony,

168

this time the Dwarfs cannot wake you up again.' And when she got home and asked the Looking-glass—

'Mirror, Mirror on the wall,
Who is fairest of us all?'

it answered at last—

'Queen, thou 'rt fairest of them all.'

Then her jealous heart was at rest, as much at rest as a jealous heart can be. The Dwarfs, when they came at evening, found Snowdrop lying on the ground and not a breath escaped her lips, and she was quite dead. They lifted her up and looked to see whether any poison was to be found, unlaced her dress, combed her hair, washed her with wine and water, but it was no use; their dear child was dead. They laid her on a bier, and all seven sat down and bewailed her and lamented over her for three whole days. Then they prepared to bury her, but she looked so fresh and living, and still had such beautiful rosy cheeks, that they said, 'We cannot bury her in the dark earth.' And so they had a transparent glass coffin made, so that she could be seen from every side, laid her inside and wrote on it in letters of gold her name and how she was a King's daughter. Then they set the coffin out on the mountain, and one of them always stayed by and watched it. And the birds came too and mourned for Snowdrop, first an owl, then a raven, and lastly a dove.

Now Snowdrop lay a long, long time in her coffin, looking as though she were asleep. It happened that a Prince was wandering in the wood, and came to the home of the seven Dwarfs to pass the night. He saw the coffin on the mountain and lovely Snowdrop inside, and read what was written in golden letters. Then he said to the Dwarfs, 'Let me have the coffin; I will give you whatever you like for it.'

But they said, 'We will not give it up for all the gold of the world.'

Then he said, 'Then give it to me as a gift, for I cannot

live without Snowdrop to gaze upon; and I will honour and reverence it as my dearest treasure.'

When he had said these words the good Dwarfs pitied him and gave him the coffin.

The Prince bade his servants carry it on their shoulders. Now it happened that they stumbled over some brushwood, and the shock dislodged the piece of apple from Snowdrop's throat. In a short time she opened her eyes, lifted the lid of the coffin, sat up and came back to life again completely.

' O Heaven! where am I?' she asked.

The Prince, full of joy, said, 'You are with me,' and he related what had happened, and then said, 'I love you better than all the world; come with me to my father's castle and be my wife.'

Snowdrop agreed and went with him, and their wedding was celebrated with great magnificence. Snowdrop's wicked stepmother was invited to the feast; and when she had put on her fine clothes she stepped to her Glass and asked—

> ' Mirror, Mirror on the wall,
> Who is fairest of us all ?'

The Glass answered—

> ' Queen, thou art fairest here, I hold,
> The young Queen fairer a thousandfold.'

Then the wicked woman uttered a curse, and was so terribly frightened that she didn't know what to do. Yet she had no rest: she felt obliged to go and see the young Queen. And when she came in she recognised Snowdrop, and stood stock still with fear and terror. But iron slippers were heated over the fire, and were soon brought in with tongs and put before her. And she had to step into the red-hot shoes and dance till she fell down dead.

170

The Pink

THERE was once a Queen, who had not been blessed with children. As she walked in her garden, she prayed every morning that a son or daughter might be given to her. Then one day an Angel came, and said to her : ' Be content : you shall have a son, and he shall be endowed with the power of wishing, so that whatsoever he wishes for shall be granted to him.' She hurried to the King, and told him the joyful news ; and when the time came a son was born to them, and they were filled with delight.

Every morning the Queen used to take her little son into the gardens, where the wild animals were kept, to bathe him in a clear, sparkling fountain. It happened one day, when the child was a little older, that as she sat with him on her lap she fell asleep.

The old Cook, who knew that the child had the power of wishing, came by and stole it ; he also killed a Chicken, and dropped some of its blood on the Queen's garments. Then he took the child away to a secret place, where he placed it out to be nursed. Then he ran back to the King, and accused the Queen of having allowed her child to be carried off by a wild animal.

When the King saw the blood on the Queen's garments he believed the story, and was overwhelmed with anger. He caused a high tower to be built, into which neither the sun nor the moon could penetrate. Then he ordered his wife to be shut up in it, and the door walled up. She was to stay there for seven years, without eating or drinking, so as gradually to pine away. But two Angels from heaven, in the shape of

171

white doves, came to her, bringing food twice a day till the seven years were ended.

Meanwhile the Cook thought, ' If the child really has the power of wishing, and I stay here, I might easily fall into disgrace.' So he left the palace, and went to the boy, who was then old enough to talk, and said to him, ' Wish for a beautiful castle, with a garden, and everything belonging to it.' Hardly had the words passed the boy's lips than all that he had asked for was there.

After a time the Cook said, ' It is not good for you to be so much alone ; wish for a beautiful Maiden to be your companion.'

The Prince uttered the wish, and immediately a Maiden stood before them, more beautiful than any painter could paint. So they grew very fond of each other, and played together, while the old Cook went out hunting like any grand gentleman. But the idea came to him one day that the Prince might wish to go to his father some time, and he would thereby be placed in a very awkward position. So he took the Maiden aside, and said to her, ' To-night, when the boy is asleep, go and drive this knife into his heart. Then bring me his heart and his tongue. If you fail to do it, you will lose your own life.'

Then he went away ; but when the next day came the Maiden had not yet obeyed his command, and she said, ' Why should I shed his innocent blood, when he has never done harm to any creature in his life ? '

The Cook again said, ' If you do not obey me, you will lose your own life.'

When he had gone away, she ordered a young hind to be brought and killed ; then she cut out its heart and its tongue, and put them on a dish. When she saw the old man coming she said to the boy, ' Get into bed, and cover yourself right over.'

The old scoundrel came in and said, ' Where are the tongue and the heart of the boy ? '

172

THE PINK

The scullions brought live coals, which he had to eat till the
flames poured out of his mouth.

The Maiden gave him the dish; but the Prince threw off
the coverings, and said, 'You old sinner, why did you want
to kill me? Now hear your sentence. You shall be turned
into a black Poodle, with a gold chain round your neck, and
you shall be made to eat live coals, so that flames of fire may
come out of your mouth.'

As he said the words, the old man was changed into a
black Poodle, with a gold chain round his neck; and the
scullions brought live coals, which he had to eat till the flames
poured out of his mouth.

The Prince stayed on at the castle for a time, thinking of
his mother, and wondering if she were still alive. At last he
said to the Maiden, 'I am going into my own country. If
you like you can go with me; I will take you.'

173

She answered : ' Alas ! it is so far off, and what should I do in a strange country where I know no one ? '

As she did not wish to go, and yet they could not bear to be parted, he changed her into a beautiful Pink, which he took with him.

Then he set out on his journey, and the Poodle was made to run alongside till the Prince reached his own country.

Arrived there, he went straight to the tower where his mother was imprisoned, and as the tower was so high he wished for a ladder to reach the top. Then he climbed up, looked in, and cried, ' Dearest mother, lady Queen, are you still alive ? '

She, thinking it was the Angels who brought her food come back, said, ' I have just eaten ; I do not want anything more.'

Then he said, ' I am your own dear son whom the wild animals were supposed to have devoured ; but I am still alive, and I shall soon come and rescue you.'

Then he got down and went to his father. He had himself announced as a strange Huntsman, anxious to take service with the King, who said, ' Yes ; if he was skilled in game preserving, and could procure plenty of venison, he would engage him. But there had never before been any game in the whole district.'

The Huntsman promised to procure as much game as the King could possibly require for the royal table.

Then he called the whole Hunt together, and ordered them all to come into the forest with him. He caused a great circle to be enclosed, with only one outlet ; then he took his place in the middle, and began to wish as hard as he could. Immediately over two hundred head of game came running into the enclosure ; these the Huntsmen had to shoot, and then they were piled on to sixty country wagons, and driven home to the King. So for once he was able to load his board with game, after having had none for many years.

The King was much pleased, and commanded his whole court to a banquet on the following day. When they were all assembled, he said to the Huntsman, ' You shall sit by me as you are so clever.'

He answered, ' My lord and King, may it please your Majesty, I am only a poor Huntsman ! '

The King, however, insisted, and said, ' I command you to sit by me.'

As he sat there, his thoughts wandered to his dear mother, and he wished one of the courtiers would speak of her. Hardly had he wished it than the Lord High Marshal said—

' Your Majesty, we are all rejoicing here, how fares it with Her Majesty the Queen ? Is she still alive in the tower, or has she perished ? '

But the King answered, ' She allowed my beloved son to be devoured by wild animals, and I do not wish to hear anything about her.'

Then the Huntsman stood up and said—

' Gracious father, she is still alive, and I am her son. He was not devoured by wild animals ; he was taken away by the scoundrel of a Cook. He stole me while my mother was asleep, and sprinkled her garments with the blood of a chicken.' Then he brought up the black Poodle with the golden chain, and said, ' This is the villain.'

He ordered some live coals to be brought, which he made the dog eat in the sight of all the people till the flames poured out of his mouth. Then he asked the King if he would like to see the Cook in his true shape, and wished him back, and there he stood in his white apron, with his knife at his side.

The King was furious when he saw him, and ordered him to be thrown into the deepest dungeon. Then the Huntsman said further—

' My father would you like to see the Maiden who so tenderly saved my life when she was ordered to kill me, although by so doing she might have lost her own life ? '

The King answered, ' Yes, I will gladly see her.'

Then his son said, ' Gracious father, I will show her to you first in the guise of a beautiful flower.'

He put his hand into his pocket, and brought out the Pink. It was a finer one than the King had ever seen before. Then his son said, ' Now, I will show her to you in her true form.'

The moment his wish was uttered, she stood before them in all her beauty, which was greater than any artist could paint.

The King sent ladies and gentlemen-in-waiting to the tower to bring the Queen back to his royal table. But when they reached the tower they found that she would no longer eat or drink, and she said, ' The merciful God, who has preserved my life so long, will soon release me now.'

Three days after she died. At her burial the two white Doves which had brought her food during her captivity, followed and hovered over her grave.

The old King caused the wicked Cook to be torn into four quarters ; but his own heart was filled with grief and remorse, and he died soon after.

His son married the beautiful Maiden he had brought home with him as a Flower, and, for all I know, they may be living still.

Clever Elsa

THERE was once a Man who had a daughter called Clever Elsa. When she was grown up, her Father said : ' We must get her married.'

' Yes,' said her Mother ; ' if only somebody came who would have her.'

At last a suitor, named Hans, came from a distance. He made an offer for her on condition that she really was as clever as she was said to be.

' Oh ! ' said her Father, ' she is a long-headed lass.'

And her Mother said : ' She can see the wind blowing in the street, and hear the flies coughing.'

' Well,' said Hans, ' if she is not really clever, I won't have her.'

When they were at dinner, her Mother said : ' Elsa, go to the cellar and draw some beer.'

Clever Elsa took the jug from the nail on the wall, and went to the cellar, clattering the lid as she went, to pass the time. When she reached the cellar she placed a chair near the cask so that she need not hurt her back by stooping. Then she put down the jug before her and turned the tap. And while the beer was running, so as not to be idle, she let her eyes rove all over the place, looking this way and that.

Suddenly she discovered a pickaxe just above her head, which a mason had by chance left hanging among the rafters.

Clever Elsa burst into tears, and said : ' If I marry Hans, and we have a child, when it grows big, and we send it down to draw beer, the pickaxe will fall on its head and kill it.' So there she sat crying and lamenting loudly at the impending mishap.

177

The others sat upstairs waiting for the beer, but Clever Elsa never came back.

Then the Mistress said to her Servant: 'Go down to the cellar, and see why Elsa does not come back.'

The Maid went, and found Elsa sitting by the cask, weeping bitterly. 'Why, Elsa, whatever are you crying for?' she asked.

'Alas!' she answered, 'have I not cause to cry? If I marry Hans, and we have a child, when he grows big, and we send him down to draw beer, perhaps that pickaxe will fall on his head and kill him.'

Then the Maid said: 'What a Clever Elsa we have'; and she, too, sat down by Elsa, and began to cry over the misfortune.

After a time, as the Maid did not come back, and they were growing very thirsty, the Master said to the Servingman: 'Go down to the cellar and see what has become of Elsa and the Maid.'

The Man went down, and there sat Elsa and the Maid weeping together. So he said: 'What are you crying for?'

'Alas!' said Elsa, 'have I not enough to cry for? If I marry Hans, and we have a child, and we send it when it is big enough into the cellar to draw beer, the pickaxe will fall on its head and kill it.'

The Man said: 'What a Clever Elsa we have'; and he, too, joined them and howled in company.

The people upstairs waited a long time for the Servingman, but as he did not come back, the Husband said to his Wife: 'Go down to the cellar yourself, and see what has become of Elsa.'

So the Mistress went down and found all three making loud lamentations, and she asked the cause of their grief.

Then Elsa told her that her future child would be killed by the falling of the pickaxe when it was big enough to be sent to draw the beer. Her Mother said with the others: 'Did you ever see such a Clever Elsa as we have?'

178

Her Husband upstairs waited some time, but as his Wife did not return, and his thirst grew greater, he said : 'I must go to the cellar myself to see what has become of Elsa.'

But when he got to the cellar, and found all the others sitting together in tears, caused by the fear that a child which Elsa might one day have, if she married Hans, might be killed by the falling of the pickaxe, when it went to draw beer, he too cried—

'What a Clever Elsa we have !'

Then he, too, sat down and added his lamentations to theirs.

The bridegroom waited alone upstairs for a long time ; then, as nobody came back, he thought : 'They must be waiting for me down there, I must go and see what they are doing.'

So down he went, and when he found them all crying and lamenting in a heart-breaking manner, each one louder than the other, he asked : 'What misfortune can possibly have happened ?'

When she saw the pick-axe just above her head, Clever Elsa burst into tears.

179

' Alas, dear Hans!' said Elsa, ' if we marry and have a child, and we send it to draw beer when it is big enough, it may be killed if that pickaxe left hanging there were to fall on its head. Have we not cause to lament ? '

' Well,' said Hans, ' more wits than this I do not need ; and as you are such a Clever Elsa I will have you for my wife.'

He took her by the hand, led her upstairs, and they celebrated the marriage.

When they had been married for a while, Hans said : ' Wife, I am going to work to earn some money ; do you go into the fields and cut the corn, so that we may have some bread.'

' Yes, my dear Hans ; I will go at once.'

When Hans had gone out, she made some good broth and took it into the field with her.

When she got there, she said to herself : ' What shall I do, reap first, or eat first ? I will eat first.'

So she finished up the bowl of broth, which she found very satisfying, so she said again : ' Which shall I do, sleep first, or reap first ? I will sleep first.' So she lay down among the corn and went to sleep.

Hans had been home a long time, and no Elsa came, so he said : ' What a Clever Elsa I have. She is so industrious, she does not even come home to eat.'

But as she still did not come, and it was getting dusk, Hans went out to see how much corn she had cut. He found that she had not cut any at all, and that she was lying there fast asleep. Hans hurried home to fetch a fowler's net with little bells on it, and this he hung around her without waking her. Then he ran home, shut the house door, and sat down to work.

At last, when it was quite dark, Clever Elsa woke up, and when she got up there was such a jangling, and the bells jingled at every step she took. She was terribly frightened, and wondered whether she really was Clever Elsa or not, and said : ' Is it me, or is it not me ? '

180

But she did not know what to answer, and stood for a time doubtful. At last she thought : ' I will go home, and ask if it is me, or if it is not me ; they will be sure to know.'

She ran to the house, but found the door locked ; so she knocked at the window, and cried : ' Hans, is Elsa at home ? '

' Yes,' answered Hans, ' she is ! '

Then she started and cried : ' Alas ! then it is not me,' and she went to another door ; but when the people heard the jingling of the bells, they would not open the door, and nowhere would they take her in.

So she ran away out of the village, and was never seen again.

The Man among the Thorns

THERE was once a rich Man, and he had a Servant who served him well and faithfully. He was first up in the morning, and last to go to bed at night. If there was any hard work to be done which no one else would do, he was always ready to undertake it. He never made any complaint, but was always merry and content.

When his year of service was over, his Master did not give him any wages, thinking: 'This is my wisest plan. I save by it, and he is not likely to run away.'

The Servant said nothing, and served the second year like the first. And when at the end of the second he again received no wages, he still appeared contented, and stayed on. When the third year had passed, the Master bethought himself, and put his hand into his pocket, but he brought it out empty.

At last the Servant said: 'Master, I have served you well and truly for three years; please pay me my wages. I want to go away and look about the world a bit.'

The Miser answered: 'Yes, my good fellow, you have served me honestly, and you shall be liberally rewarded.'

Again he put his hand into his pocket, and counted three farthings, one by one, into the Servant's hand, and said: 'There, you have a farthing for every year; that is better wages than you would get from most masters.'

The good Servant, who knew little about money, put away his fortune, and thought: 'Now my pocket is well filled, I need no longer trouble myself about work.' Then he left and went singing down the hill, and dancing, in the lightness of his heart.

The quicker he played, the higher she had to jump.

The Dwarfs, when they came in the evening, found Snowdrop
lying on the ground.

THE MAN AMONG THE THORNS

Now it so happened that as he was passing a thicket, that a little Mannikin came out and cried : ' Whither away, my merry fellow ?   I see your troubles are not too heavy to be borne.'

' Why should I be sad ? ' answered the Servant.   ' I have three years' wages in my pocket.'

' And how much is your treasure ? ' asked the Mannikin.

' How much ?   Why, three good farthings.'

' Listen ! ' said the Mannikin.   ' I am a poor needy fellow ; give me your three farthings.   I can't work any more ; but you are young, and can easily earn your bread.'

Now the Servant had a good heart, and he was sorry for the poor little man, so he gave him his three farthings, and said :

' Take them, in the name of heaven !   I shall not miss them.'

' Then,' said the Mannikin, ' I see what a good heart you have.   I will give you three wishes, one for each farthing ; and every wish shall be fulfilled.'

' Aha ! ' said the Servant, ' you are a wonder-worker I see. Very well, then.   First, I wish for a gun which will hit everything I aim at ; secondly, for a fiddle which will make every one dance when I play ; and, thirdly, if I ask anything of any one, that he shall not be able to refuse my request.'

' You shall have them all,' said the Mannikin, diving into the bushes, where, wonderful to relate, lay the gun and the fiddle ready, just as if they had been ordered beforehand. He gave them to the Servant, and said : ' No one will be able to refuse anything you ask.'

' Heart alive ! what more can one desire,' said the Servant to himself, as he went merrily on.

Soon after, he met a Man with a long goat's beard, who was standing still listening to the song of a bird sitting on the top of a tree.   ' Good heavens ! ' he was saying, ' what a tremendous noise such a tiny creature makes.   If only it were mine !   If one could but put some salt upon its tail ! '

' If that is all,' said the Servant, ' the bird shall soon come down.'

183

He took aim, and down fell the bird into a quickset hedge.
' Go, you rogue,' he said to the Man, ' and pick up the bird.'

' Leave out the " rogue," young man.   I will get the bird
sure enough, as you have killed it for me,' said the Man.

He lay down on the ground and began to creep into the
hedge.

When he had got well among the thorns, a spirit of mischief
seized the Servant, and he began to play his fiddle with all

The Man was forced to spring up and begin to dance.

his might.   The Man was forced to spring up and begin to
dance, and the more the Servant played, the faster he had to
dance.   The thorns tore his shabby coat, combed his goat's
beard, and scratched him all over.

' Merciful Heavens ! ' cried the Man.   ' Leave off that
fiddling !   I don't want to dance, my good fellow.'

But the Servant paid no attention to him, but thought :
' You have fleeced plenty of people in your time, my man, and

184

the thorns shan't spare you now ! ' And he played on and on, so that the Man had to jump higher and higher, till his coat hung in ribbons about him.

' I cry " enough ! " ' screamed the Man. ' I will give you anything you like if you will only stop. Take the purse, it is full of gold.'

' Oh, well, if you are so open-handed,' said the Servant, ' I am quite ready to stop my music, but I must say in praise of your dancing, that it has quite a style of its own.' Then he took the purse and went on his way.

The Man stood still looking after him till he was a good way off, then he screamed with all his might : ' You miserable fiddler ! Just you wait till I find you alone ! I will chase you till the soles of your shoes drop off—you rascal ! ' And he went on pouring out a stream of abuse. Having relieved himself by so doing, he hurried off to the Judge in the nearest town.

' Just look here, your worship,' he said, ' look how I have been attacked, and ill-treated, and robbed on the high road by a wretch. My condition might melt the heart of a stone ; my clothes and my body torn and scratched, and my purse with all my poor little savings taken away from me. All my beautiful ducats, each one prettier than the other. Oh dear ! Oh dear ! For heaven's sake, put the wretch in prison.'

The Judge said : ' Was it a soldier who punished you so with his sword ? '

' Heaven preserve us ! ' cried the Man, ' he had no sword, but he had a gun on his shoulder and a fiddle round his neck. The villain is easily to be recognised.'

So the Judge sent out men in pursuit of the honest Servant, who had walked on slowly. They soon overtook him, and the purse of gold was found on him. When he was brought before the Judge, he said—

' I never touched the Man, nor did I take his money away ; he offered it to me of his own free will if I would only stop playing, because he could not bear my music.'

'Heaven defend us!' screamed the Man, 'his lies are as thick as flies on the wall.'

And the Judge did not believe him either, and said: 'That is a very lame excuse; no man ever did such a thing.' So he sentenced the honest Servant to the gallows for having committed a robbery upon the king's highway.

When he was being led away, the Man screamed after him; 'You vagabond, you dog of a fiddler, now you will get your deserts!'

The Servant mounted the ladder to the gallows quite quietly, with the halter round his neck; but at the last rung he turned round and said to the Judge: 'Grant me one favour before I die.'

'Certainly,' said the Judge, 'as long as you don't ask for your life.'

'Not my life,' answered the Servant. 'I only ask to play my fiddle once more.'

Dancing as hard as he could.

The Man raised a tremendous cry. 'Don't allow it, your worship, for heaven's sake, don't allow it!'

But the Judge said: 'Why should I deny him that short

186

pleasure ? His wish is granted, and there's an end of the matter ! '

He could not have refused even if he had wished, because of the Mannikin's gift to the Servant.

The Man screamed, ' Oh dear ! Oh dear ! Tie me tight, tie me tight ! '

The good Servant took his fiddle from his neck, and put it into position, and at the first chord everybody began to wag their heads, the Judge, his Clerk, and all the Officers of Justice, and the rope fell out of the hand of the man about to bind the Man.

At the second scrape, they all lifted their legs, and the Hangman let go his hold of the honest Servant, to make ready to dance.

At the third scrape they one and all leapt into the air, and began to caper about, the Judge and the Man at the head, and they all leapt their best.

Soon, every one who had come to the market-place out of curiosity, old and young, fat and lean, were dancing as hard as they could ; even the dogs got upon their hind legs, and pranced about with the rest. The longer he played, the higher they jumped, till they knocked their heads together, and made each other cry out.

At last the Judge, quite out of breath, cried : ' I will give you your life, if only you will stop playing.'

The honest Servant allowed himself to be prevailed upon, laid his fiddle aside, and came down the ladder. Then he went up to the Man, who lay upon the ground gasping, and said to him :

' You rascal, confess where you got the money, or I will begin to play again.'

' I stole it ! I stole it ! ' he screamed ; ' but you have honestly earned it.'

The Judge then ordered the Man to the gallows to be hanged as a thief.

187

Ashenputtel

THE wife of a rich man fell ill, and when she felt that she was nearing her end, she called her only daughter to her bedside, and said:

'Dear child, continue devout and good, then God will always help you, and I will look down upon you from heaven, and watch over you.'

Thereupon she closed her eyes, and breathed her last.

The maiden went to her mother's grave every day and wept, and she continued to be devout and good. When the winter came, the snow spread a white covering on the grave, and when the sun of spring had unveiled it again, the husband took another wife. The new wife brought home with her two daughters, who were fair and beautiful to look upon, but base and black at heart.

Then began a sad time for the unfortunate step-child.

'Is this stupid goose to sit with us in the parlour?' they said.

'Whoever wants to eat bread must earn it; go and sit with the kitchenmaid.'

They took away her pretty clothes, and made her put on an old grey frock, and gave her wooden clogs.

'Just look at the proud Princess, how well she's dressed,' they laughed, as they led her to the kitchen. There, the girl was obliged to do hard work from morning till night, to get up at daybreak, carry water, light the fire, cook, and wash. Not content with that, the sisters inflicted on her every vexation they could think of; they made fun of her, and tossed the peas and lentils among the ashes, so that she had to

188

sit down and pick them out again. In the evening, when she was worn out with work, she had no bed to go to, but had to lie on the hearth among the cinders. And because, on account of that, she always looked dusty and dirty, they called her Ashenputtel.

It happened one day that the Father had a mind to go to the Fair. So he asked both his step-daughters what he should bring home for them.

' Fine clothes,' said one.

' Pearls and jewels,' said the other.

' But you, Ashenputtel ? ' said he, ' what will you have ? '

' Father, break off for me the first twig which brushes against your hat on your way home.'

Well, for his two step-daughters he brought beautiful clothes, pearls and jewels, and on his way home, as he was riding through a green copse, a hazel twig grazed against him and knocked his hat off. Then he broke off the branch and took it with him.

When he got home he gave his step-daughters what they had asked for, and to Ashenputtel he gave the twig from the hazel bush.

Ashenputtel thanked him, and went to her mother's grave and planted the twig upon it; she wept so much that her tears fell and watered it. And it took root and became a fine tree.

Ashenputtel went to the grave three times every day, wept and prayed, and every time a little white bird came and perched upon the tree, and when she uttered a wish, the little bird threw down to her what she had wished for.

Now it happened that the King proclaimed a festival, which was to last three days, and to which all the beautiful maidens in the country were invited, in order that his son might choose a bride.

When the two step-daughters heard that they were also to be present, they were in high spirits, called Ashenputtel, and said :

'Brush our hair and clean our shoes, and fasten our buckles, for we are going to the feast at the King's palace.'

Ashenputtel obeyed, but wept, for she also would gladly have gone to the ball with them, and begged her step-mother to give her leave to go.

'You, Ashenputtel!' she said. 'Why, you are covered with dust and dirt. You go to the festival! Besides you have no clothes or shoes, and yet you want to go to the ball.'

As she, however, went on asking, her Step-mother said:

'Well, I have thrown a dishful of lentils into the cinders, if you have picked them all out in two hours you shall go with us.'

The girl went through the back door into the garden, and cried, 'Ye gentle doves, ye turtle doves, and all ye little birds under heaven, come and help me,

'The good into a dish to throw,
The bad into your crops can go.'

Then two white doves came in by the kitchen window, and were followed by the turtle doves, and finally all the little birds under heaven flocked in, chirping, and settled down among the ashes. And the doves gave a nod with their little heads, peck, peck, peck; and then the rest began also, peck, peck, peck, and collected all the good beans into the dish. Scarcely had an hour passed before they had finished, and all flown out again.

Then the girl brought the dish to her Step-mother, and was delighted to think that now she would be able to go to the feast with them.

But she said, 'No, Ashenputtel, you have no clothes, and cannot dance; you will only be laughed at.'

But when she began to cry, the Step-mother said:

'If you can pick out two whole dishes of lentils from the ashes in an hour, you shall go with us.'

And she thought, 'She will never be able to do that.'

When her Step-mother had thrown the dishes of lentils

190

among the ashes, the girl went out through the back door, and cried, ' Ye gentle doves, ye turtle doves, and all ye little birds under heaven, come and help me,

> ' The good into a dish to throw,
> The bad into your crops can go.'

Then two white doves came in by the kitchen window, and were followed by the turtle doves, and all the other little birds under heaven, and in less than an hour the whole had been picked up, and they had all flown away.

Then the girl carried the dish to her Step-mother, and was delighted to think that she would now be able to go to the ball.

But she said, ' It 's not a bit of good. You can't go with us, for you 've got no clothes, and you can't dance. We should be quite ashamed of you.'

Thereupon she turned her back upon her, and hurried off with her two proud daughters.

As soon as every one had left the house, Ashenputtel went out to her mother's grave under the hazel-tree, and cried :

> ' Shiver and shake, dear little tree,
> Gold and silver shower on me.'

Then the bird threw down to her a gold and silver robe, and a pair of slippers embroidered with silk and silver. With all speed she put on the robe and went to the feast. But her step-sisters and their mother did not recognise her, and supposed that she was some foreign Princess, so beautiful did she appear in her golden dress. They never gave a thought to Ashenputtel, but imagined that she was sitting at home in the dirt picking the lentils out of the cinders.

The Prince came up to the stranger, took her by the hand, and danced with her. In fact, he would not dance with any one else, and never left go of her hand. If any one came up to ask her to dance, he said, ' This is my partner.'

She danced until nightfall, and then wanted to go home ; but the Prince said, ' I will go with you and escort you.'

For he wanted to see to whom the beautiful maiden belonged. But she slipped out of his way and sprang into the pigeon-house.

Then the Prince waited till her Father came, and told him that the unknown maiden had vanished into the pigeon-house.

The old man thought, ' Could it be Ashenputtel ? ' And he had an axe brought to him, so that he might break down the pigeon-house, but there was no one inside.

When they went home, there lay Ashenputtel in her dirty clothes among the cinders, and a dismal oil lamp was burning in the chimney corner. For Ashenputtel had quietly jumped down out of the pigeon-house and ran back to the hazel-tree. There she had taken off her beautiful clothes and laid them on the grave, and the bird had taken them away again. Then she had settled herself among the ashes on the hearth in her old grey frock.

On the second day, when the festival was renewed, and her parents and step-sisters had started forth again, Ashenputtel went to the hazel-tree, and said :

> ' Shiver and shake, dear little tree,
> Gold and silver shower on me.'

Then the bird threw down a still more gorgeous robe than on the previous day. And when she appeared at the festival in this robe, every one was astounded by her beauty.

The King's son had waited till she came, and at once took her hand, and she danced with no one but him. When others came forward and invited her to dance, he said, ' This is my partner.'

At nightfall she wished to leave ; but the Prince went after her, hoping to see into what house she went, but she sprang out into the garden behind the house. There stood a fine big tree on which the most delicious pears hung. She climbed up among the branches as nimbly as a squirrel, and the Prince could not make out what had become of her.

But he waited till her Father came, and then said to him,

ASHENPUTTEL

'The unknown maiden has slipped away from me, and I think that she has jumped into the pear-tree.'

The Father thought, 'Can it be Ashenputtel?' And he had the axe brought to cut down the tree, but there was no one on it. When they went home and looked into the kitchen, there lay Ashenputtel among the cinders as usual; for she had jumped down on the other side of the tree, taken back the beautiful clothes to the bird on the hazel-tree, and put on her old grey frock.

On the third day, when her parents and sisters had started, Ashenputtel went again to her mother's grave, and said:

> 'Shiver and shake, dear little tree,
> Gold and silver shower on me.'

Then the bird threw down a dress which was so magnificent that no one had ever seen the like before, and the slippers were entirely of gold. When she appeared at the festival in this attire, they were all speechless with astonishment. The Prince danced only with her, and if any one else asked her to dance, he said, 'This is my partner.'

When night fell and she wanted to leave, the Prince was more desirous than ever to accompany her, but she darted away from him so quickly that he could not keep up with her. But the Prince had used a stratagem, and had caused the steps to be covered with cobbler's wax. The consequence was, that as the maiden sprang down them, her left slipper remained sticking there. The Prince took it up. It was small and dainty, and entirely made of gold.

The next morning he went with it to Ashenputtel's Father, and said to him, 'No other shall become my wife but she whose foot this golden slipper fits.'

The two sisters were delighted at that, for they both had beautiful feet. The eldest went into the room intending to try on the slipper, and her Mother stood beside her. But her great toe prevented her getting it on, her foot was too long.

Then her Mother handed her a knife, and said, 'Cut off

the toe; when you are Queen you won't have to walk any more.'

The girl cut off her toe, forced her foot into the slipper, stifled her pain, and went out to the Prince. Then he took her up on his horse as his Bride, and rode away with her.

However, they had to pass the grave on the way, and there sat the two Doves on the hazel-tree, and cried:

> 'Prithee, look back, prithee, look back,
> There's blood on the track,
> The shoe is too small,
> At home the true Bride is waiting thy call.'

Then he looked at her foot and saw how the blood was streaming from it. So he turned his horse round and carried the false Bride back to her home, and said that she was not the right one; the second sister must try the shoe.

Then she went into the room, and succeeded in getting her toes into the shoe, but her heel was too big.

Then her Mother handed her a knife, and said, 'Cut a bit off your heel; when you are Queen you won't have to walk any more.'

The maiden cut a bit off her heel, forced her foot into the shoe, stifled her pain, and went out to the Prince.

Then he took her up on his horse as his Bride, and rode off with her.

As they passed the grave, the two Doves were sitting on the hazel-tree, and crying:

> 'Prithee, look back, prithee, look back,
> There's blood on the track,
> The shoe is too small,
> At home the true Bride is waiting thy call.'

He looked down at her foot and saw that it was streaming with blood, and there were deep red spots on her stockings. Then he turned his horse and brought the false Bride back to her home.

ASHENPUTTEL

'This is not the right one either,' he said. 'Have you no other daughter?'

'No,' said the man. 'There is only a daughter of my late wife's, a puny, stunted drudge, but she cannot possibly be the Bride.'

The Prince said that she must be sent for.

But the Mother answered, 'Oh no, she is much too dirty; she mustn't be seen on any account.'

He was, however, absolutely determined to have his way, and they were obliged to summon Ashenputtel.

When she had washed her hands and face, she went up and curtsied to the Prince, who handed her the golden slipper.

Then she sat down on a bench, pulled off her wooden clog and put on the slipper, which fitted to a nicety.

And when she stood up and the Prince looked into her face, he recognised the beautiful maiden that he had danced with, and cried: 'This is the true Bride!'

The Stepmother and the two sisters were dismayed and turned white with rage; but he took Ashenputtel on his horse and rode off with her.

As they rode past the hazel-tree the two White Doves cried:

> 'Prithee, look back, prithee, look back,
> No blood's on the track,
> The shoe's *not* too small,
> You carry the true Bride home to your hall.'

And when they had said this they both came flying down, and settled on Ashenputtel's shoulders, one on the right, and one on the left, and remained perched there.

When the wedding was going to take place, the two false sisters came and wanted to curry favour with her, and take part in her good fortune. As the bridal party was going to the church, the eldest was on the right side, the youngest on the left, and the Doves picked out one of the eyes of each of them.

195

Afterwards, when they were coming out of the church, the elder was on the left, the younger on the right, and the Doves picked out the other eye of each of them. And so for their wickedness and falseness they were punished with blindness for the rest of their days.

The White Snake

A LONG time ago there lived a King whose wisdom was celebrated far and wide. Nothing was unknown to him, and news of the most secret transactions seemed to reach him through the air.

Now he had one very odd habit. Every day at dinner, when the courtiers had withdrawn, and he was quite alone, a trusted Servant had to bring in another dish. It was always covered, and even the Servant did not know what it contained, nor any one else, for the King never uncovered it till he was alone. This had gone on for a long time, when one day the Servant who carried the dish was overcome by his curiosity, and took the dish to his own room.

When he had carefully locked the door, he took the dish-cover off, and saw a White Snake lying on the dish.

At the sight of it, he could not resist tasting it ; so he cut a piece off, and put it into his mouth.

Hardly had he tasted it, however, when he heard a wonderful whispering of delicate voices.

He went to the window and listened, and he noticed that the whispers came from the sparrows outside. They were chattering away, and telling each other all kinds of things that they had heard in the woods and fields. Eating the Snake had given him the power of understanding the language of birds and animals.

Now it happened on this day that the Queen lost her most precious ring, and suspicion fell upon this trusted Servant who went about everywhere.

The King sent for him, and threatened that if it was not found by the next day, he would be sent to prison.

In vain he protested his innocence ; he was not believed.

In his grief and anxiety he went down into the courtyard and wondered how he should get out of his difficulty.

A number of Ducks were lying peaceably together by a stream, stroking down their feathers with their bills, while they chattered gaily.

The Servant stood still to listen to them. They were telling each other of their morning's walks and experiences.

Then one of them said somewhat fretfully : ' I have something lying heavy on my stomach. In my haste I swallowed the Queen's ring this morning.'

The Servant quickly seized it by the neck, carried it off into the kitchen, and said to the Cook : ' Here 's a fine fat Duck. You had better kill it at once.'

' Yes, indeed,' said the Cook, weighing it in her hand. ' It has spared no pains in stuffing itself; it should have been roasted long ago.'

So she killed it, and cut it open, and there, sure enough, was the Queen's ring.

The Servant had now no difficulty in proving his innocence, and the King, to make up for his injustice, gave the Servant leave to ask any favour he liked, and promised him the highest post about the Court which he might desire.

The Servant, however, declined everything but a horse, and some money to travel with, as he wanted to wander about for a while, to see the world.

His request being granted, he set off on his travels, and one day came to a pond, where he saw three Fishes caught among the reeds, and gasping for breath. Although it is said that fishes are dumb, he understood their complaint at perishing thus miserably. As he had a compassionate heart, he got off his horse and put the three captives back into the water. They wriggled in their joy, stretched up their heads above the water, and cried—

' We will remember that you saved us, and reward you for it.'

He rode on again, and after a time he seemed to hear a voice in the sand at his feet. He listened, and heard an Ant-King complain : ' I wish these human beings and their animals would keep out of our way. A clumsy horse has just put his hoof down upon a number of my people in the most heartless way.'

He turned his horse into a side path, and the Ant-King cried : ' We will remember and reward you.'

The road now ran through a forest, and he saw a pair of Ravens standing by their nest throwing out their young.

' Away with you, you gallows birds,' they were saying. ' We can't feed you any longer. You are old enough to look after yourselves.'

The poor little nestlings lay on the ground, fluttering and flapping their wings, and crying : ' We, poor helpless children, to feed ourselves, and we can't even fly ! We shall die of hunger, there is nothing else for it.'

The good Youth dismounted, killed his horse with his sword, and left the carcase as food for the young Ravens. They hopped along to it, and cried : ' We will remember and reward you.'

Now he had to depend upon his own legs, and after going a long way he came to a large town.

There was much noise and bustle in the streets, where a man on horseback was making a proclamation.

' The King's daughter seeks a husband, but any one who wishes to sue for her hand must accomplish a hard task ; and if he does not bring it to a successful issue, he will forfeit his life.'

Many had already attempted the task, but they had risked their lives in vain.

When the Youth saw the Princess, he was so dazzled by her beauty that he forgot all danger, at once sought an audience of the King, and announced himself as a suitor.

He was immediately led out to the seashore, and a golden ring was thrown into the water before his eyes. Then the

King ordered him to fetch it out from the depths of the sea, and added—

'If you come to land without it, you will be thrown back every time till you perish in the waves.'

Every one pitied the handsome Youth, but they had to go and leave him standing solitary on the seashore.

He was pondering over what he should do, when, all at once, he saw three Fishes swimming towards him. They were no others than the very ones whose lives he had saved.

The middle one carried a mussel-shell in its mouth, which it laid on the sand at the feet of the Youth. When he picked it up, and opened it, there lay the ring.

Full of joy, he took it to the King, expecting that he would give him the promised reward.

The proud Princess, however, when she heard that he was not her equal, despised him, and demanded that he should perform yet another task.

So she went into the garden herself, and strewed ten sacks of millet seeds among the grass.

'He must pick up every one of those before the sun rises to-morrow morning,' said she. 'Not a grain must be missing.'

The Youth sat miserably in the garden, wondering how it could possibly be done. But as he could not think of a plan, he remained sadly waiting for the dawn which would bring death to him.

But when the first sunbeams fell on the garden, he saw the ten sacks full to the top, and not a grain was missing. The Ant-King had come in the night with thousands and thousands of his Ants, and the grateful creatures had picked up the millet and filled the sacks.

The Princess came into the garden herself, and saw with amazement that the Youth had completed the task.

But still she could not control her proud heart, and she said : 'Even if he has accomplished these two tasks, he shall not become my husband till he brings me an apple from the tree of life.'

200

THE WHITE SNAKE

The Youth had no idea where to find the tree of life. However, he started off, meaning to walk as far as his legs would carry him ; but he had no hope of finding it.

When he had travelled through three kingdoms, he was one night passing through a great forest, and he lay down under a tree to sleep.

He heard a rustling among the branches, and a golden apple fell into his hand. At the same time three Ravens flew down and perched on his knee, and said :

' We are the young Ravens you saved from death. When we grew big, and heard that you were looking for the golden apple, we flew across the sea to the end of the world, where the tree of life stands, and brought you the apple.'

The Youth, delighted, started on his homeward journey, and took the golden apple to the beautiful Princess, who had now no further excuse to offer.

They divided the apple of life, and ate it together, and then her heart was filled with love for him, and they lived happily to a great age.

The Wolf and the Seven Kids

THERE was once an old Nanny-goat who had seven Kids, and she was just as fond of them as a mother of her children. One day she was going into the woods to fetch some food for them, so she called them all up to her, and said—

'My dear children, I am going out into the woods. Beware of the Wolf! If once he gets into the house, he will eat you up, skin, and hair, and all. The rascal often disguises himself, but you will know him by his rough voice and his black feet.'

The Kids said, 'Oh, we will be very careful, dear mother. You may be quite happy about us.'

Bleating tenderly, the old Goat went off to her work. Before long, some one knocked at the door, and cried—

'Open the door, dear children! Your mother has come back and brought something for each of you.'

But the Kids knew quite well by the voice that it was the Wolf.

'We won't open the door,' they cried. 'You are not our mother. She has a soft gentle voice; but yours is rough, and we are quite sure that you are the Wolf.'

So he went away to a shop and bought a lump of chalk, which he ate, and it made his voice quite soft. He went back, knocked at the door again, and cried—

'Open the door, dear children. Your mother has come back and brought something for each of you.'

But the Wolf had put one of his paws on the window sill, where the Kids saw it, and cried—

'We won't open the door. Our mother has not got a black foot as you have; you are the Wolf.'

202

Then the Wolf ran to a Baker, and said, ' I have bruised my foot; please put some dough on it.' And when the Baker had put some dough on his foot, he ran to the Miller and said, ' Strew some flour on my foot.'

The Miller thought, ' The old Wolf is going to take somebody in,' and refused.

But the Wolf said, ' If you don't do it, I will eat you up.'

So the Miller was frightened, and whitened his paws. People are like that, you know.

Now the wretch went for the third time to the door, and knocked, and said—

' Open the door, children. Your dear mother has come home, and has brought something for each of you out of the wood.'

The Kids cried, ' Show us your feet first, that we may be sure you are our mother.'

He put his paws on the window sill, and when they saw that they were white, they believed all he said, and opened the door.

Alas! It was the Wolf who walked in. They were terrified, and tried to hide themselves. One ran under the table, the second jumped into bed, the third into the oven, the fourth ran into the kitchen, the fifth got into the cupboard, the sixth into the wash-tub, and the seventh hid in the tall clock-case. But the Wolf found them all but one, and made short work of them. He swallowed one after the other, except the youngest one in the clock-case, whom he did not find. When he had satisfied his appetite, he took himself off, and lay down in a meadow outside, where he soon fell asleep.

Not long after the old Nanny-goat came back from the woods. Oh! what a terrible sight met her eyes! The house door was wide open, table, chairs, and benches were over-turned, the washing bowl was smashed to atoms, the covers and pillows torn from the bed. She searched all over the house for her children, but nowhere were they to be found. She called them by name, one by one, but no one answered.

At last, when she came to the youngest, a tiny voice cried :

'I am here, dear mother, hidden in the clock-case.'

She brought him out, and he told her that the Wolf had come and devoured all the others.

You may imagine how she wept over her children.

At last, in her grief, she went out, and the youngest Kid ran by her side. When they went into the meadow, there lay the Wolf under a tree, making the branches shake with his snores. They examined him from every side, and they could plainly see movements within his distended body.

'Ah, heavens !' thought the Goat, 'is it possible that my poor children whom he ate for his supper, should be still alive ?'

She sent the Kid running to the house to fetch scissors, needles, and thread. Then she cut a hole in the monster's side, and, hardly had she begun, when a Kid popped out its head, and as soon as the hole was big enough, all six jumped out, one after the other, all alive, and without having suffered the least injury, for, in his greed, the monster had swallowed them whole. You may imagine the mother's joy. She hugged them, and skipped about like a tailor on his wedding day. At last she said :

'Go and fetch some big stones, children, and we will fill up the brute's body while he is asleep.'

Then the seven Kids brought a lot of stones, as fast as they could carry them, and stuffed the Wolf with them till he could hold no more. The old mother quickly sewed him up, without his having noticed anything, or even moved.

At last, when the Wolf had had his sleep out, he got up, and, as the stones made him feel very thirsty, he wanted to go to a spring to drink. But as soon as he moved the stones began to roll about and rattle inside him. Then he cried—

'What 's the rumbling and tumbling
That sets my stomach grumbling ?
I thought 'twas six Kids, flesh and bones,
Now find it 's nought but rolling stones.'

THE WOLF AND THE SEVEN KIDS

When he reached the spring, and stooped over the water to drink, the heavy stones dragged him down, and he was drowned miserably.

When the seven Kids saw what had happened, they came running up, and cried aloud—'The Wolf is dead, the Wolf is dead!' and they and their mother capered and danced round the spring in their joy.

The Queen Bee

ONCE upon a time two Princes started off in search of adventure, and, falling into a wild, free mode of life, did not come home again.

The third Brother, who was called the Blockhead, set out to look for the other two. But when at last he found them, they mocked him for thinking of making his way in the world with his simplicity, while they, who were so much cleverer, could not get on.

They all three went on together till they came to an antheap. The two elder Princes wanted to disturb it, to see how the little ants crept away, carrying their eggs.

But the Blockhead said : ' Leave the little creatures alone ; I will not allow you to disturb them.'

Then they went on further till they came to a lake, in which a great many ducks were swimming about. The two wanted to catch and roast a pair.

But the Blockhead would not allow it, and said : ' Leave the creatures alone. You shall not kill them.'

At last they came to a bee's nest, containing such a quantity of honey that it flowed round the trunk of the tree.

The two Princes wanted to set fire to the tree, and suffocate the bees, so as to remove the honey.

But the Blockhead stopped them again, and said : ' Leave the creatures alone. I will not let you burn them.'

At last the three Brothers came to a castle, where the stables were full of stone horses, but not a soul was to be seen. They went through all the rooms till they came to a door quite at the end, fastened with three bolts. In the middle of the door was a lattice, through which one could see into the room.

206

THE QUEEN BEE

There they saw a little grey Man sitting at a table. They called to him once—twice—but he did not hear them. Finally, when they had called him the third time, he stood up and opened the door, and came out. He said not a word, but led them to a richly-spread table, and when they had eaten and drunk, he took them each to a bedroom.

The next morning the little grey Man came to the eldest Prince, beckoned, and led him to a stone tablet whereon were inscribed three tasks by means of which the castle should be freed from enchantment.

This was the first task: In the wood, under the moss, lay the Princesses' pearls, a thousand in number. These had all to be found, and if at sunset a single one were missing, the seeker was turned to stone.

The eldest went away, and searched all day, but when evening came, he had only found the first hundred, and it happened as the inscription foretold. He was turned to stone.

The next day the second Brother undertook the quest; but he fared no better than the first, for he only found two hundred pearls, and he too was turned to stone.

At last came the Blockhead's turn; he searched in the moss, but the pearls were hard to find, and he got on but slowly.

Then he sat down on a rock and cried, and as he was sitting there, the Ant-King, whose life he had saved, came up with five thousand ants, and it was not long before the little creatures had found all the pearls and laid them in a heap.

Now the second task was to get the key of the Princesses' room out of the lake.

When the Blockhead came to the lake, the ducks he had once saved, swam up, dived, and brought up the key from the depths.

But the third task was the hardest. The Prince had to find out which was the youngest and most charming of the Princesses while they were asleep.

They were exactly alike, and could not be distinguished in any way, except that before going to sleep each had eaten a different kind of sweet. The eldest a piece of sugar, the second a little syrup, and the third a spoonful of honey.

Then the Queen of the Bees, whom the Blockhead had saved from burning, came and tried the lips of all three. Finally, she settled on the mouth of the one who had eaten the honey, and so the Prince recognised the right one.

Then the charm was broken and everything in the castle was set free, and those who had been turned to stone took human form again.

And the Blockhead married the youngest and sweetest Princess, and became King after her father's death, while his two Brothers married the other sisters.

The Three Sleeping Princesses.

The Elves and the Shoemaker

THERE was once a Shoemaker who, through no fault of his own, had become so poor that at last he had only leather enough left for one pair of shoes. At evening he cut out the shoes which he intended to begin upon the next morning, and since he had a good conscience, he lay down quietly, said his prayers, and fell asleep.

In the morning when he had said his prayers, and was preparing to sit down to work, he found the pair of shoes standing finished on his table. He was amazed, and could not understand it in the least.

He took the shoes in his hand to examine them more closely. They were so neatly sewn that not a stitch was out of place, and were as good as the work of a master-hand.

Soon after a purchaser came in, and as he was much pleased with the shoes, he paid more than the ordinary price for them, so that the Shoemaker was able to buy leather for two pairs of shoes with the money.

He cut them out in the evening, and next day, with fresh courage, was about to go to work; but he had no need to, for when he got up, the shoes were finished, and buyers were not lacking. These gave him so much money that he was able to buy leather for four pairs of shoes.

Early next morning he found the four pairs finished, and so it went on; what he cut out at evening was finished in the morning, so that he was soon again in comfortable circumstances, and became a well-to-do man.

Now it happened one evening, not long before Christmas, when he had cut out some shoes as usual, that he said to his

Wife : ' How would it be if we were to sit up to-night to see who it is that lends us such a helping hand ? '

The Wife agreed, lighted a candle, and they hid themselves in the corner of the room behind the clothes which were hanging there.

At midnight came two little naked men who sat down at the Shoemaker's table, took up the cut-out work, and began with their tiny fingers to stitch, sew, and hammer so neatly and quickly, that the Shoemaker could not believe his eyes. They did not stop till everything was quite finished, and stood complete on the table ; then they ran swiftly away.

The next day the Wife said : ' The little men have made us rich, and we ought to show our gratitude. They were running about with nothing on, and must freeze with cold. Now I will make them little shirts, coats, waistcoats, and hose, and will even knit them a pair of stockings, and you shall make them each a pair of shoes.'

The Husband agreed, and at evening, when they had everything ready, they laid out the presents on the table, and hid themselves to see how the little men would behave.

At midnight they came skipping in, and were about to set to work ; but, instead of the leather ready cut out, they found the charming little clothes.

At first they were surprised, then excessively delighted. With the greatest speed they put on and smoothed down the pretty clothes, singing :

> ' Now we 're boys so fine and neat,
> Why cobble more for other's feet ? '

Then they hopped and danced about, and leapt over chairs and tables and out at the door. Henceforward, they came back no more, but the Shoemaker fared well as long as he lived, and had good luck in all his undertakings.

The Wolf and the Man

A FOX was one day talking to a Wolf about the strength of man.

'No animals,' he said, 'could withstand man, and they were obliged to use cunning to hold their own against him.'

The Wolf answered, 'If ever I happened to see a man, I should attack him all the same.'

'Well, I can help you to that,' said the Fox. 'Come to me early to-morrow, and I will show you one!'

The Wolf was early astir, and the Fox took him out to a road in the forest, traversed daily by a Huntsman.

First came an old discharged soldier.

'Is that a Man?' asked the Wolf.

'No,' answered the Fox. 'He has been a Man.'

After that, a little boy appeared on his way to school.

'Is that a Man?'

'No; he is going to be a Man.'

At last the Huntsman made his appearance, his gun on his back, and his hunting-knife at his side. The Fox said to the Wolf,—

'Look! There comes a Man. You may attack him, but I will make off to my hole!'

The Wolf set on the Man, who said to himself when he saw him, 'What a pity my gun isn't loaded with ball,' and fired a charge of shot in the Wolf's face. The Wolf made a wry face, but he was not to be so easily frightened, and attacked him again. Then the Huntsman gave him the second charge. The Wolf swallowed the pain, and rushed at the Huntsman; but he drew his bright hunting-knife, and hit out right and left

211

with it, so that, streaming with blood, the Wolf ran back to the Fox.

'Well, brother Wolf,' said the Fox, 'and how did you get on with the Man?'

'Alas!' said the Wolf. 'I never thought the strength of man would be what it is. First, he took a stick from his shoulder, and blew into it, and something flew into my face, which tickled frightfully. Then he blew into it again, and it flew into my eyes and nose like lightning and hail. Then he drew a shining rib out of his body, and struck at me with it till I was more dead than alive.'

'Now, you see,' said the Fox, 'what a braggart you are. You throw your hatchet so far that you can't get it back again.'

The Turnip

THERE were once two Brothers who both served as soldiers, and one was rich and the other was poor.

The poor one, wishing to better himself, discarded his uniform and worked like a Peasant. Then he dug and hoed his little field and sowed Turnips.

The seed came up, and one of the Turnips grew to such an enormous size, that it seemed as though it would never have finished; and it might have been called the Queen of Turnips, for its like had never been seen before, nor ever will be again.

At last it was so big that it filled a cart, and needed two oxen to draw it; and the Peasant could not imagine what would come of it, whether it would bring good luck or bad.

At last he said to himself: 'If I sell it what shall I gain? I might eat it, but the little Turnips would do as well for that. The best thing will be to take it to the King and offer it to him.'

So he loaded a cart, harnessed two oxen, and took it to the Court to present it to the King.

'What is that extraordinary object?' said the King. 'I have seen many marvels in my time, but never anything so remarkable as this. What seed did it spring from? Perhaps it belongs to you, especially if you are a child of good luck?'

'Oh no,' said the Peasant, 'lucky I certainly am not, for I am a poor Soldier, who, since he could keep himself no longer, has hung up his uniform on a nail, and tills the earth. Further, I have a Brother who is rich, and well known to you, my Lord King; but I, because I have nothing, am forgotten by all the world.'

Then the King pitied him and said: 'Your poverty shall

213

be at an end, and you shall receive such rich presents from me that your wealth will equal that of your Brother.'

Thereupon he gave him plenty of gold, lands, fields, and flocks, and enriched him with precious stones, so that the other Brother's wealth could not be compared with his.

Now, when the rich Brother heard what his Brother with the single Turnip had acquired, he envied him, and pondered how he might gain a like treasure for himself.

But he wanted to show himself much cleverer, so he took

So the rich Brother had to put his Brother's Turnip into
a cart, and have it taken home.

gold and horses and presented them to the King, feeling certain that he would give him a far handsomer gift; for if his Brother got so much for a Turnip, what would not he get for his beautiful things.

The King took the present, saying that he could give him in return nothing rarer or better than the huge Turnip.

So the rich Brother had to put his Brother's Turnip into a cart, and have it taken home.

Then he did not know on whom to expend his wrath and bitterness, till evil thoughts came to him, and he determined to kill his Brother.

He hired Murderers, who were to place themselves in

Ashenputtel goes to the ball.

The Fishes, in their joy, stretched up their heads above the water, and promised to reward him.

ambush, and then he went to his Brother, and said : 'Dear Brother, I know of a secret treasure which we will carry off and divide.'

The other agreed, and went without suspicion. But when they got out, the Murderers sprang upon him, bound him, and prepared to hang him on a tree.

While they were about it, they heard in the distance the clatter of hoofs and the sound of singing, which frightened them so much that they stuck their Prisoner into a sack, head foremost, slung it up on a branch, and took to flight.

But the Man up in the sack worked a hole in it, and stuck his head through.

Now the traveller turned out to be nothing more than a Student, a young fellow who was riding through the wood, singing cheerily.

When the Man up in the sack saw some one down below, he called out : 'Good-day. You come in the nick of time.'

The Student looked all round, but could not make out where the voice came from.

At last he said : 'Who calls ? '

A voice from above answered : 'Raise your eyes, I am sitting up here in the Sack of Wisdom, and in a short time I have learnt so much that the wisdom of the schools is as air compared to mine. Soon I shall be quite perfect, and shall come down and be the wisest of all mankind. I understand the stars and signs of the heavens, the blowing of the winds, the sand of the sea, the healing of sickness, the power of herbs, birds, and stones. If you were once inside, you would feel what wonders flow from the Sack of Knowledge.'

When the Student heard this he was astonished, and said : 'Blessed be the hour when I met you, if only I too might get into the sack for a little.'

The other answered, as though unwillingly : 'I will let you in for a little while for payment and kind words, but you must wait an hour, as there is something rather difficult which I must learn first.'

215

But when the Student had waited a little, he grew impatient and entreated permission to get in, so great was his thirst for knowledge. Then the Man in the sack pretended to give in, and said : ' In order that I may get out of the sack you must let it down, then you can get in.'

So the Student let it down, undid the sack and released the Prisoner, and said : ' Now pull me up as fast as possible ' ; and he tried to get into the sack and stand upright in it.

' Stop,' said the other. ' That won't do.' And he packed him in head first, tied it up, and slung up the Disciple of Wisdom, dangling him in the air, and said : ' How are you, my dear fellow ? You will soon feel wisdom coming upon you, and will have a most interesting experience. Sit still till you are wiser.'

Thereupon he mounted the Student's horse, and rode off, but sent some one in an hour to let him down again.

Clever Hans

'WHERE are you going, Hans?' asked his Mother.
'To see Grettel,' answered Hans.
'Behave well, Hans!'
'All right, Mother. Good-bye.'
'Good-bye, Hans.'
Hans comes to Grettel.
'Good morning, Grettel.'
'Good morning, Hans. What have you brought me?'
'I've not brought you anything. I want a present.'
Grettel gives him a needle. Hans takes the needle, and sticks it in a load of hay, and walks home behind the cart.
'Good evening, Mother.'
'Good evening, Hans. Where have you been?'
'I've been to Grettel's.'
'What did you give her?'
'I gave her nothing. But she made me a present.'
'What did she give you?'
'She gave me a needle.'
'What did you do with it?'
'Stuck it in the hay-cart.'
'That was stupid, Hans. You should have stuck it in your sleeve.'
'Never mind, Mother; I'll do better next time.'
'Where are you going, Hans?'
'To see Grettel, Mother.'
'Behave well.'
'All right, Mother. Good-bye.'
'Good-bye, Hans.'
Hans comes to Grettel.

217

'Good morning, Grettel.'

'Good morning, Hans. What have you brought me?'

'I've brought nothing. But I want something.'

Grettel gives him a knife.

'Good-bye, Grettel.'

'Good-bye, Hans.'

Hans takes the knife, and sticks it in his sleeve, and goes home.

'Good evening, Mother.'

'Good evening, Hans. Where have you been?'

'Been to see Grettel.'

'What did you give her?'

'I gave her nothing. But she gave me something.'

'What did she give you?'

'She gave me a knife.'

'Where is the knife, Hans?'

'I stuck it in my sleeve.'

'That's a stupid place, Hans. You should have put it in your pocket.'

'Never mind, Mother; I'll do better next time.'

'Where are you going, Hans?'

'To see Grettel, Mother.'

'Behave well, then.'

'All right, Mother. Good-bye.'

'Good-bye, Hans.'

Hans comes to Grettel.

'Good morning, Grettel.'

'Good morning, Hans. Have you brought me anything nice?'

'I've brought nothing. What have you got for me?'

Grettel gives him a young kid.

'Good-bye, Grettel.'

'Good-bye, Hans.'

Hans takes the kid, ties its legs together, and puts it in his pocket.

When he got home, it was suffocated.

218

'Good evening, Mother.'

'Good evening, Hans. Where have you been?'

'Been to see Grettel, Mother.'

'What did you give her?'

'I gave her nothing. But I brought away something.'

'What did Grettel give you?'

'She gave me a young kid.'

'What did you do with the kid?'

'Put it in my pocket, Mother.'

'That was very stupid. You should have led it by a rope.'

'Never mind, Mother; I'll manage better next time.'

'Where are you going, Hans?'

'To see Grettel, Mother.'

'Manage well, then.'

'All right, Mother. Good-bye.'

'Good-bye, Hans.'

Hans comes to Grettel.

'Good morning, Grettel.'

'Good morning, Hans. What have you brought me?'

'I've brought you nothing. What have you got for me?'

Grettel gives him a piece of bacon.

'Good-bye, Grettel.'

'Good-bye, Hans.'

Hans takes the bacon, ties a rope round it, and drags it along behind him. The dogs come after him, and eat it up. When he got home he had the rope in his hand, but there was nothing at the end of it.

'Good evening, Mother.'

'Good evening, Hans. Where have you been?'

'To see Grettel, Mother.'

'What did you take her?'

'I took nothing. But I brought something away.'

'What did she give you?'

'She gave me a piece of bacon.'

'What did you do with the bacon, Hans?'

'I tied it to a rope, and dragged it home. But the dogs ate it.'

'That was a stupid business, Hans. You should have carried it on your head.'

'Never mind, Mother; I'll do better next time.'

'Where are you going, Hans?'

'To see Grettel, Mother.'

'Behave properly, then.'

'All right, Mother. Good-bye.'

'Good-bye, Hans.'

Hans comes to Grettel.

'Good morning, Grettel.'

'Good morning, Hans. What have you brought me?'

'I've brought nothing. What have you got for me?'

Grettel gives Hans a calf.

'Good-bye, Grettel.'

'Good-bye, Hans.'

Hans takes the calf, and puts it on his head. It kicks his face.

'Good evening, Mother.'

'Good evening, Hans. Where have you been?'

'Been to see Grettel, Mother.'

'What did you take her?'

'I took her nothing, Mother.   She gave me something.'

'What did she give you, Hans?'

'She gave me a calf, Mother.'

'What did you do with the calf?'

'Put it on my head, Mother, and it kicked my face.'

'That was very stupid, Hans.   You should have led it by a rope, and put it in the cow-stall.'

'Never mind, Mother; I 'll do better next time.'

'Where are you going, Hans?'

'To see Grettel, Mother.'

'Mind how you behave, Hans.'

'All right, Mother. Good-bye.'

Hans goes to Grettel.

When he got home he had the rope in his hand, but there was nothing at the end of it.

'Good morning, Grettel.'

'Good morning, Hans.   What have you brought me?'

' I 've brought you nothing. I want to take away something.'

' I 'll go with you myself, Hans.'

Hans ties Grettel to a rope, and leads her home, where he puts her in a stall, and ties her up.   Then he goes into the house to his Mother.

' Good evening, Mother.'

' Good evening, Hans.   Where have you been ? '

' To see Grettel, Mother.'

' What did you take her ? '

' I took nothing.'

' What did Grettel give you ? '

' She gave me nothing.   She came with me.'

' Where did you leave Grettel ? '

' Tied up in the stable with a rope.'

' That was stupid.   You should have cast sheep's eyes at her.'

' Never mind ; I 'll do better next time.'

Hans went into the stable, plucked the eyes out of the cows and calves, and threw them in Grettel's face.

Grettel got angry, broke the rope, and ran away.

Yet she became Hans' wife.

The Three Languages

THERE once lived in Switzerland an old Count, who had an only son; but he was very stupid, and could learn nothing. So his father said to him: ' Listen to me, my son. I can get nothing into your head, try as hard as I may. You must go away from here, and I will hand you over to a renowned Professor for a whole year.' At the end of the year he came home again, and his father asked: ' Now, my son, what have you learnt ? '

' Father, I have learnt the language of dogs.'

' Mercy on us ! ' cried his father, ' is that all you have learnt ? I will send you away again to another Professor in a different town.' The youth was taken there, and remained with this Professor also for another year. When he came back his father asked him again: ' My son, what have you learnt ? '

He answered : ' I have learnt bird language.'

Then the father flew into a rage, and said : ' Oh, you hopeless creature, have you been spending all this precious time and learnt nothing ? Aren't you ashamed to come into my presence ? I will send you to a third Professor, but if you learn nothing this time, I won't be your father any longer.'

The son stopped with the third Professor in the same way for a whole year, and when he came home again and his father asked, ' My son, what have you learnt ? ' he answered—

' My dear father, this year I have learnt frog language.'

Thereupon his father flew into a fearful passion, and said : ' This creature is my son no longer. I turn him out of the house and command you to lead him into the forest and take his life.'

They led him forth, but when they were about to kill him, for pity's sake they could not do it, and let him go. Then they

On the way he passed a swamp, in which a number of Frogs were croaking.

cut out the eyes and tongue of a Fawn, in order that they might take back proofs to the old Count.

The youth wandered about, and at length came to a castle, where he begged a night's lodging.

'Very well,' said the Lord of the castle. 'If you like to pass the night down there in the old tower, you may; but I warn you that it will be at the risk of your life, for it is full of savage dogs. They bark and howl without ceasing, and at certain hours they must have a man thrown to them, and they devour him at once.'

The whole neighbourhood was distressed by the scourge, but no one could do anything to remedy it. But the youth was not a bit afraid, and said: 'Just let me go down to these barking dogs, and give me something that I can throw to them; they won't do me any harm.'

As he would not have anything else, they gave him some food for the savage dogs, and took him down to the tower.

The dogs did not bark at him when he entered, but ran round him wagging their tails in a most friendly manner, ate the food he gave them, and did not so much as touch a hair of his head.

The next morning, to the surprise of every one, he made his appearance again, and said to the Lord of the castle, 'The Dogs have revealed to me in their own language why they live there and bring mischief to the country. They are enchanted, and obliged to guard a great treasure which is hidden under the tower, and will get no rest till it has been dug up; and how that has to be done I have also learnt from them.'

Every one who heard this was delighted, and the Lord of the castle said he would adopt him as a son if he accomplished the task successfully. He went down to the tower again, and as he knew how to set to work he accomplished his task, and brought out a chest full of gold. The howling of the savage Dogs was from that time forward heard no more. They entirely disappeared, and the country was delivered from the scourge.

After a time, he took it into his head to go to Rome. On

the way he passed a swamp, in which a number of Frogs were croaking. He listened, and when he heard what they were saying he became quite pensive and sad.

At last he reached Rome, at a moment when the Pope had just died, and there was great doubt among the Cardinals whom they ought to name as his successor. They agreed at last that the man to whom some divine miracle should be manifested ought to be chosen as Pope. Just as they had come to this decision, the young Count entered the church, and suddenly two snow-white doves flew down and alighted on his shoulders.

The clergy recognised in this the sign from Heaven, and asked him on the spot whether he would be Pope.

He was undecided, and knew not whether he was worthy of the post; but the Doves told him that he might accept, and at last he said ' Yes.'

Thereupon he was anointed and consecrated, and so was fulfilled what he had heard from the Frogs on the way, which had disturbed him so much—namely, that he should become Pope.

Then he had to chant mass, and did not know one word of it. But the two Doves sat upon his shoulders and whispered it to him.

The Fox and the Cat

IT happened once that the Cat met Mr. Fox in the wood, and because she thought : ' He is clever and experienced in all the ways of the world,' she addressed him in a friendly manner.

' Good morning, dear Mr. Fox ! how are you and how do you get along in these hard times ? '

The Fox, full of pride, looked at the Cat from head to foot for some time hardly knowing whether he would deign to answer or not.   At last he said—

' Oh, you poor whisker-wiper, you piebald fool, you starveling mouse-hunter ! what has come into your head ?   How dare you ask me how I am getting on ? What sort of education have you had?   How many arts are you master of ? '

' Only one,' said the Cat, meekly.

' And what might that one be ? ' asked the Fox.

The Cat crept stealthily up to the topmost branch.

' When the hounds run after me, I can jump into a tree and save myself.'

' Is that all ? ' said the Fox.   ' I am master of a hundred arts, and I have a sack full of cunning tricks in addition.   But

227

I pity you. Come with me, and I will teach you how to escape the hounds.'

Just then, a huntsman came along with four hounds. The Cat sprang trembling into a tree, and crept stealthily up to the topmost branch, where she was entirely hidden by twigs and leaves.

'Open your sack, Mr. Fox! open your sack!' cried the Cat; but the hounds had gripped him, and held him fast.

'O Mr. Fox!' cried the Cat, 'you with your hundred arts, and your sack full of tricks, are caught, while I, with my one, am safe. Had you been able to climb up here, you would not have lost your life.'

The Four Clever Brothers

THERE was once a poor man who had four sons, and when they were grown up, he said to them : 'Dear children, you must go out into the world now, for I have nothing to give you. You must each learn a trade and make your own way in the world.'

So the four Brothers took their sticks in their hands, bid their father good-bye, and passed out of the town gate.

When they had walked some distance, they came to four cross roads, which led into four different districts. Then the eldest one said : ' We must part here, but this day four years, we will meet here again, having in the meantime done our best to make our fortunes.'

Then each one went his own way. The eldest met an old man, who asked him where he came from, and what he was going to do.

' I want to learn a trade,' he answered.

Then the Man said : ' Come with me and learn to be a Thief.'

' No,' answered he, ' that is no longer considered an honest trade ; and the end of that song would be that I should swing as the clapper in a bell.'

' Oh,' said the Man, ' you need not be afraid of the gallows. I will only teach you how to take things no one else wants, or knows how to get hold of, and where no one can find you out.'

So he allowed himself to be persuaded, and under the Man's instructions he became such an expert thief that nothing was safe from him which he had once made up his mind to have.

The second Brother met a Man who put the same question to him, as to what he was going to do in the world.

' I don't know yet,' he answered.

' Then come with me and be a Star-gazer. It is the grandest thing in the world, nothing is hidden from you.'

He was pleased with the idea, and became such a clever Star-gazer, that when he had learnt everything and wanted to go away, his master gave him a telescope, and said—

' With this you can see everything that happens in the sky and on earth, and nothing can remain hidden from you.'

The third Brother was taken in hand by a Huntsman, who taught him everything connected with sport so well, that he became a first-rate Huntsman.

On his departure his master presented him with a gun, and said : ' This gun will never miss : whatever you aim at you will hit without fail.'

The youngest Brother also met a Man who asked him what he was going to do.

' Wouldn't you like to be a Tailor ? ' he asked.

' I don't know about that,' said the young man. ' I don't much fancy sitting cross-legged from morning till night, and everlastingly pulling a needle in and out, and pushing a flat iron.'

' Dear, dear ! ' said the Man, ' what are you talking about ? If you come to me you will learn quite a different sort of tailoring. It is a most pleasant and agreeable trade, not to say most honourable.'

So he allowed himself to be talked over, and went with the Man, who taught him his trade thoroughly.

On his departure, he gave him a needle, and said : ' With this needle you will be able to stitch anything together, be it as soft as an egg, or as hard as steel ; and it will become like a whole piece of stuff with no seam visible.'

When the four years, which the Brothers had agreed upon, had passed, they met at the cross-roads. They embraced one another and hurried home to their Father.

' Well ! ' said he, quite pleased to see them, ' has the wind wafted you back to me again ? '

230

THE FOUR CLEVER BROTHERS

They told him all that had happened to them, and that each had mastered a trade. They were sitting in front of the house under a big tree, and their Father said—

'Now, I will put you to the test, and see what you can do.'

Then he looked up and said to his second son—

'There is a chaffinch's nest in the topmost branch of this tree; tell me how many eggs there are in it?'

The Star-gazer took his glass and said: 'There are five.'

His Father said to the eldest: 'Bring the eggs down without disturbing the bird sitting on them.'

The cunning Thief climbed up and took the five eggs from under the bird so cleverly that it never noticed they were gone, and he gave them to his Father. His Father took them, and put them one on each corner of the table, and one in the middle, and said to the Sportsman—

'You must shoot the five eggs through the middle at one shot.'

The Sportsman levelled his gun, and divided each egg in half at one shot, as his Father desired. He certainly must have had some of the powder which shoots round the corner.

'Now it is your turn,' said his Father to the fourth son. 'You will sew the eggs together again, the shells and the young birds inside them; and you will do it in such a manner that they will be none the worse for the shot.'

The Tailor produced his needle, and stitched away as his Father ordered. When he had finished, the Thief had to climb up the tree again, and put the eggs back under the bird without her noticing it. The bird spread herself over the eggs, and a few days later the fledglings crept out of the shell, and they all had a red line round their throats where the Tailor had sewn them together.

'Yes,' said the old man to his sons; 'I can certainly praise your skill. You have learnt something worth knowing, and made the most of your time. I don't know which of you to give the palm to. I only hope you may soon have a chance of showing your skill so that it may be settled.'

231

Not long after this there was a great alarm raised in the country : the King's only daughter had been carried off by a Dragon. The King sorrowed for her day and night, and proclaimed that whoever brought her back should marry her.

The four Brothers said to one another : ' This would be an opportunity for us to prove what we can do.' And they decided to go out together to deliver the Princess.

' I shall soon know where she is,' said the Star-gazer, as he looked through his telescope ; and then he said—

' I see her already. She is a long way from here, she is sitting on a rock in the middle of the sea, and the Dragon is near, watching her.'

Then he went to the King and asked for a ship for himself and his Brothers to cross the sea in search of the rock.

They found the Princess still on the rock, but the Dragon was asleep with his head on her lap.

The Sportsman said : ' I dare not shoot. I should kill the beautiful maiden.'

' Then I will try my luck,' said the Thief, and he stole her away from beneath the Dragon. He did it so gently and skilfully, that the monster never discovered it, but went snoring on.

Full of joy, they hurried away with her to the ship, and steered for the open sea. But the Dragon on waking had missed the Princess, and now came after them through the air, foaming with rage.

Just as he was hovering over the ship and about to drop on them, the Sportsman took aim with his gun and shot him through the heart. The monster fell down dead, but he was so huge, that in falling, he dragged the whole ship down with him. They managed to seize a few boards, on which they kept themselves afloat.

They were now in great straits, but the Tailor, not to be outdone, produced his wonderful needle, and put some great stitches into the boards, seated himself on them, and collected all the floating bits of the ship. Then he stitched them all

232

They found the Princess still on the rock, but the Dragon was asleep
with his head on her lap.

together so cleverly, that in a very short time the ship was seaworthy again, and they sailed happily home.

The King was overjoyed when he saw his daughter again, and he said to the four Brothers : ' One of you shall marry her, but which one, you must decide among yourselves.'

An excited discussion then took place among them, for each one made a claim.

The Star-gazer said : ' Had I not discovered the Princess, all your arts would have been in vain, therefore she is mine ! '

The Thief said : ' What would have been the good of discovering her if I had not taken her from under the Dragon ? So she is mine.'

The Sportsman said : ' You, as well as the Princess, would have been destroyed by the monster if my shot had not hit him. So she is mine.'

The Tailor said : ' And if I had not sewn the ship together with my skill, you would all have been drowned miserably. Therefore she is mine.'

The King said : ' Each of you has an equal right ; but, as you can't all have her, none of you shall have her. I will give every one of you half a kingdom as a reward.'

The Brothers were quite satisfied with this decision, and they said : ' It is better so than that we should quarrel over it.'

So each of them received half a kingdom, and they lived happily with their Father for the rest of their days.

The Lady and the Lion

THERE was once a Man who had to take a long journey, and when he was saying good-bye to his daughters he asked what he should bring back to them.

The eldest wanted pearls, the second diamonds, but the third said, ' Dear father, I should like a singing, soaring lark.'

The father said, ' Very well, if I can manage it, you shall have it ' ; and he kissed all three and set off. He bought pearls and diamonds for the two eldest, but he had searched everywhere in vain for the singing, soaring lark, and this worried him, for his youngest daughter was his favourite child.

Once his way led through a wood, in the midst of which was a splendid castle ; near it stood a tree, and right up at the top he saw a lark singing and soaring.   ' Ah,' he said, ' I have come across you in the nick of time ' ; and he called to his Servant to dismount and catch the little creature.   But as he approached the tree a Lion sprang out from underneath, and shook himself, and roared so that the leaves on the tree trembled.

' Who dares to steal my lark ? ' said he.   ' I will eat up the thief ! '

Then the Man said, ' I didn't know that the bird was yours. I will make up for my fault by paying a heavy ransom.   Only spare my life.'

But the Lion said, ' Nothing can save you, unless you promise to give me whatever first meets you when you get home.   If you consent, I will give you your life and the bird into the bargain.'

But the Man hesitated, and said, ' Suppose my youngest and favourite daughter were to come running to meet me when I go home ! '

But the Servant was afraid, and said, ' Your daughter will not necessarily be the first to come to meet you ; it might just as well be a cat or a dog.'

So the Man let himself be persuaded, took the lark, and promised to the Lion for his own whatever first met him on his return home. When he reached home, and entered his house, the first person who met him was none other than his youngest daughter ; she came running up and kissed and caressed him, and when she saw that he had brought the singing, soaring lark, she was beside herself with joy. But her father could not rejoice ; he began to cry, and said, ' My dear child, it has cost me dear, for I have had to promise you to a Lion who will tear you in pieces when he has you in his power.' And he told her all that had happened, and begged her not to go, come what might.

But she consoled him, saying, ' Dear father, what you have promised must be performed. I will go and will soon soften the Lion's heart, so that I shall come back safe and sound.' The next morning the way was shown to her, and she said good-bye and went confidently into the forest.

Now the Lion was an enchanted Prince, who was a Lion by day, and all his followers were Lions too ; but by night they reassumed their human form. On her arrival she was kindly received, and conducted to the castle. When night fell, the Lion turned into a handsome man, and their wedding was celebrated with due magnificence. And they lived happily together, sitting up at night and sleeping by day. One day he came to her and said, ' To-morrow there is a festival at your father's house to celebrate your eldest sister's wedding ; if you would like to go my Lions shall escort you.'

She answered that she was very eager to see her father again, so she went away accompanied by the Lions.

There was great rejoicing on her coming, for they all thought that she had been torn to pieces and had long been dead.

But she told them what a handsome husband she had and how well she fared ; and she stayed with them as long as the

236

wedding festivities lasted. Then she went back again into the wood.

When the second daughter married, and the youngest was again invited to the wedding, she said to the Lion, ' This time I will not go alone, you must come too.'

But the Lion said it would be too dangerous, for if a gleam of light touched him he would be changed into a Dove and would have to fly about for seven years.

' Ah,' said she, ' only go with me, and I will protect you and keep off every ray of light.'

So they went away together, and took their little child with them too. They had a hall built with such thick walls that no ray could penetrate, and thither the Lion was to retire when the wedding torches were kindled. But the door was made of fresh wood which split and caused a little crack which no one noticed.

Now the wedding was celebrated with great splendour. But when the procession came back from church with a large number of torches and lights, a ray of light no broader than a hair fell upon the Prince, and the minute this ray touched him he was changed ; and when his wife came in and looked for him, she saw nothing but a White Dove sitting there. The Dove said to her, ' For seven years I must fly about the world ; every seventh step I will let fall a drop of blood and a white feather which will show you the way, and if you will follow the track you can free me.'

Thereupon the Dove flew out of the door, and she followed it, and every seventh step it let fall a drop of blood and a little white feather to show her the way. So she wandered about the world, and never rested till the seven years were nearly passed. Then she rejoiced, thinking that she would soon be free of her troubles ; but she was still far from release. One day as they were journeying on in the accustomed way, the feather and the drop of blood ceased falling, and when she looked up the Dove had vanished.

' Man cannot help me,' she thought. So she climbed up to

the Sun and said to it, ' You shine upon all the valleys and mountain peaks, have you not seen a White Dove flying by ? '

' No,' said the Sun, ' I have not seen one ; but I will give you a little casket. Open it when you are in dire need.'

She thanked the Sun, and went on till night, when the Moon shone out. ' You shine all night,' she said, ' over field and forest, have you seen a White Dove flying by ? '

' No,' answered the Moon, ' I have seen none ; but here is an egg. Break it when you are in great need.'

She thanked the Moon, and went on till the Night Wind blew upon her. ' You blow among all the trees and leaves, have not you seen a White Dove ? ' she asked.

' No,' said the Night Wind, ' I have not seen one ; but I will ask the other three Winds, who may, perhaps, have seen it.'

The East Wind and the West Wind came, but they had seen no Dove. Only the South Wind said, ' I have seen the White Dove. It has flown away to the Red Sea, where it has again become a Lion, since the seven years are over ; and the Lion is ever fighting with a Dragon who is an enchanted Princess.'

Then the Night Wind said, ' I will advise you. Go to the Red Sea, you will find tall reeds growing on the right bank ; count them, and cut down the eleventh, strike the Dragon with it and then the Lion will be able to master it, and both will regain human shape. Next, look round, and you will see the winged Griffin, who dwells by the Red Sea, leap upon its back with your beloved, and it will carry you across the sea. Here is a nut. Drop it when you come to mid-ocean ; it will open immediately and a tall nut-tree will grow up out of the water, on which the Griffin will settle. Could it not rest, it would not be strong enough to carry you across, and if you forget to drop the nut, it will let you fall into the sea.'

Then she journeyed on, and found everything as the Night Wind had said. She counted the reeds by the sea and cut off the eleventh, struck the Dragon with it, and the Lion mastered it ; immediately both regained human form. But when the

238

Princess who had been a Dragon was free from enchantment, she took the Prince in her arms, seated herself on the Griffin's back, and carried him off. And the poor wanderer, again forsaken, sat down and cried. At last she took courage and said to herself : ' Wherever the winds blow, I will go, and as long as cocks crow, I will search till I find him.'

So she went on a long, long way, till she came to the castle where the Prince and Princess were living. There she heard that there was to be a festival to celebrate their wedding. Then she said to herself, ' Heaven help me,' and she opened the casket which the Sun had given her ; inside it was a dress, as brilliant as the Sun itself. She took it out, put it on, and went into the castle, where every one, including the Bride, looked at her with amazement. The dress pleased the Bride so much that she asked if it was to be bought.

' Not with gold or goods,' she answered ; ' but with flesh and blood.'

The Bride asked what she meant, and she answered, ' Let me speak with the Bridegroom in his chamber to-night.'

The Bride refused. However, she wanted the dress so much that at last she consented ; but the Chamberlain was ordered to give the Prince a sleeping draught.

At night, when the Prince was asleep, she was taken to his room. She sat down and said : ' For seven years I have followed you. I have been to the Sun, and the Moon, and the Four Winds to look for you. I have helped you against the Dragon, and will you now quite forget me ? '

But the Prince slept so soundly that he thought it was only the rustling of the wind among the pine-trees. When morning came she was taken away, and had to give up the dress ; and as it had not helped her she was very sad, and went out into a meadow and cried. As she was sitting there, she remembered the egg which the Moon had given her ; she broke it open, and out came a hen and twelve chickens, all of gold, who ran about chirping, and then crept back under their mother's wings. A prettier sight could not be seen. She got up and drove them

239

about the meadow, till the Bride saw them from the window. The chickens pleased her so much that she asked if they were for sale. 'Not for gold and goods, but for flesh and blood. Let me speak with the Bridegroom in his chamber once more.'

The Bride said 'Yes,' intending to deceive her as before; but when the Prince went to his room he asked the Chamberlain what all the murmuring and rustling in the night meant. Then the Chamberlain told him how he had been ordered to give him a sleeping draught because a poor girl had been concealed in his room, and that night he was to do the same again. 'Pour out the drink, and put it near my bed,' said the Prince. At night she was brought in again, and when she began to relate her sad fortunes he recognised the voice of his dear wife, sprang up, and said, 'Now I am really free for the first time. All has been as a dream, for the foreign Princess cast a spell over me so that I was forced to forget you; but heaven in a happy hour has taken away my blindness.'

Then they both stole out of the castle, for they feared the Princess's father, because he was a sorcerer. They mounted the Griffin, who bore them over the Red Sea, and when they got to mid-ocean, she dropped the nut. On the spot a fine nut-tree sprang up, on which the bird rested; then it took them home, where they found their child grown tall and beautiful, and they lived happily till the end.

The Fox and the Horse

A PEASANT once had a faithful Horse, but it had grown old and could no longer do its work. Its master grudged it food, and said : ' I can't use you any more, but I still feel kindly towards you, and if you show yourself strong enough to bring me a Lion I will keep you to the end of your days. But away with you now, out of my stable'; and he drove it out into the open country.

The poor Horse was very sad, and went into the forest to get a little shelter from the wind and weather. There he met a Fox, who said: 'Why do you hang your head, and wander about in this solitary fashion?'

'Alas!' answered the Horse, 'avarice and honesty cannot live together. My master has forgotten all the service I have done him for these many years, and because I can no longer plough he will no longer feed me, and he has driven me away.'

'Without any consideration?' asked the Fox.

'Only the poor consolation of telling me that if I was strong enough to bring him a Lion he would keep me, but he knows well enough that the task is beyond me.'

The Fox said: 'But I will help you. Just you lie down here, and stretch your legs out as if you were dead.' The Horse did as he was told, and the Fox went to the Lion's den, not far off, and said: 'There is a dead Horse out there. Come along with me, and you will have a rare meal.' The Lion went with him, and when they got up to the Horse, the Fox said: 'You can't eat it in comfort here. I'll tell you what. I will tie it to you, and you can drag it away to your den, and enjoy it at your leisure.'

The plan pleased the Lion, and he stood quite still, close to the Horse, so that the Fox should fasten them together. But the Fox tied the Lion's legs together with the Horse's tail, and twisted and knotted it so that it would be quite impossible for it to come undone.

When he had finished his work he patted the Horse on the shoulder, and said: 'Pull, old Grey! Pull!'

Then the Horse sprang up, and dragged the Lion away behind him. The Lion in his rage roared, so that all the birds in the forest were terrified, and flew away. But the Horse let him roar, and never stopped till he stood before his master's door.

242

THE FOX AND THE HORSE

When the master saw him he was delighted, and said to him : ' You shall stay with me, and have a good time as long as you live.'

And he fed him well till he died.

Then the Horse sprang up, and dragged the Lion away behind him.

The Blue Light

THERE was once a Soldier who had served his King well and faithfully for many years. But, on account of his many wounds, he could serve no longer.

The King said : 'You can go home now. I have no further need for you. I can only pay those who serve me.'

The Soldier did not know what to do for a living, and he went sadly away.

He walked all day, till he reached a wood, where, in the distance, he saw a light. On approaching it, he found a house inhabited by a Witch.

'Pray give me shelter for the night, and something to eat and drink,' he said, ' or I shall perish.'

'Oh ho!' she said. 'Who gives anything to a runaway Soldier, I should like to know. But I will be merciful and take you in, if you will do something for me.'

'What is it?' asked the Soldier.

'I want you to dig up my garden to-morrow.'

The Soldier agreed to this, and next day he worked as hard as he could, but he could not finish before evening.

'I see,' said the Witch, 'that you can do no more this evening. I will keep you one night more, and to-morrow you shall split up some logs for firewood.

The Soldier took the whole day over this task, and in the evening the Witch proposed that he should again stay another night.

'You shall only have a very light task to-morrow,' she said. 'There is an old, dry well behind my house. My light, which burns blue, and never goes out, has fallen into it, and I want you to bring it back.'

244

Next day the Witch led him to the well, and let him down in a basket.

He found the light, and made a sign to be pulled up ; but when he was near the top, the Witch put out her hand, and wanted to take it from him.

But he, seeing her evil designs, said : ' No ; I will not give you the light till I have both feet safe on dry land again.'

The Witch flew into a passion, let him fall back into the well again, and went away.

The poor Soldier fell on to the damp ground without taking any harm, and the Blue Light burnt as brightly as ever. But what was the good of that ? He saw that he could not escape death.

He sat for some time feeling very sad, then happening to put his hand into his pocket, he found his pipe still half full.

' This will be my last pleasure,' he thought, as he lighted it at the Blue Light, and began to smoke.

When the cloud of smoke he made cleared off a little, a tiny black Man appeared before him, and asked : ' What orders, Master ? '

' What do you mean ? ' the Soldier asked in amazement.

' I must do anything that you command,' said the Little Man.

' Oh, if that is so,' said the Soldier, ' get me out of this well first.'

The Little Man took him by the hand, and led him through an underground passage ; but the Soldier did not forget to take the Blue Light with him.

On the way he showed the Soldier all the treasures the Witch had amassed there, and he took as much gold as he could carry.

When they reached the top he said to the Little Man : ' Now go, bind the Witch and take her before the Judge.'

Before long she came by riding at a furious pace on a tom cat, and screaming at the top of her voice.

The Little Man soon after appeared, and said : ' Everything

is done as you commanded, and the Witch hangs on the gallows. What further orders have you, Master ? '

'Nothing at this moment,' answered the Soldier. 'You can go home ; only be at hand when I call.'

'You only have to light your pipe at the Blue Light, and I will be there,' said the Little Man, and then he vanished.

The Soldier went back to the town that he had left, and ordered some new clothes, then he went to the best inn and told the landlord to give him the best rooms.

Before long the Witch came by riding at a furious pace on a tom cat.

When he had taken possession, he summoned the little black Man, and said : 'I served my King faithfully, but he sent me away to die of hunger. Now I will have my revenge.'

'What do you wish me to do ? ' asked the Little Man.

'Late at night, when the Princess is asleep in her bed, bring her, sleeping, to me, and I will make her do menial service for me.'

'It is an easy enough thing for me to do,' said the Little

The Seven Kids and their mother capered and danced
round the spring in their joy.

The Ducks which he had once saved, dived and brought up
the key from the depths.

So the four Brothers took their sticks in their hands, bade their Father good-bye, and passed out of the town gate.

The King's only daughter had been carried off by a Dragon.

THE BLUE LIGHT

Man. 'But it will be a bad business for you if it comes out.'

As the clock struck twelve, the door sprang open, and the Little Man bore the Maiden in.

'Ah ha! There you are!' cried the Soldier. 'Set about your work at once. Fetch the broom and sweep the floor.'

When she had finished, he sat down and ordered her to take his boots off. Then he threw them at her, and made her pick them up and clean them. She did everything he ordered without resistance, silently, and with half-shut eyes.

At the first cock-crow, the Little Man carried her away to the royal palace, and put her back in bed.

In the morning when the Princess got up, she went to her Father, and told him that she had had an extraordinary dream.

'I was carried through the streets at lightning speed, and taken to the room of a Soldier, whom I had to serve as a maid, and do all kinds of menial work. I had to sweep the room, and clean his boots. Of course, it was only a dream, and yet I am as tired this morning as if I had done it all.'

'The dream could not have been true,' said the King. 'But I will give you a piece of advice. Fill your pocket with peas, and cut a little hole in it, then if you are carried away again, they will drop out and leave a track on the road.'

When the King said this, the Little Man was standing by, invisible, and heard it all.

At night, when he again carried off the Princess, the peas certainly fell out of her pocket, but they were useless to trace her by, for the cunning Little Man had scattered peas all over the streets. Again the Princess had to perform her menial duties till cock-crow.

The next morning the King sent out people who were to find the track; but they were unable to do so, because in every street the poor children were picking up peas, and saying: 'It must have rained peas in the night.'

'We must devise a better plan,' said the King. 'Keep your shoes on when you go to bed, and before you come away from the place where you are taken, hide one of them. I shall be sure to find it.'

The Little Man heard this plan also; and when the Soldier told him to bring the Princess again, he advised him to put it off. He said he knew no further means against their craftiness; and if the shoe were found, it would be very dangerous for his master.

'Do what I tell you,' answered the Soldier; and for the third time the Princess was brought and made to work like a servant. But before leaving she hid one of her shoes under the bed.

Next morning the King ordered the whole town to be searched for his Daughter's shoe, and it was soon found in the Soldier's room. He himself, at the request of the Little Man, had gone outside the gates; but before long he was seized and thrown into prison.

In his flight he had forgotten his greatest treasures, the Blue Light and his gold. He had but one ducat in his pocket.

As he stood at his window in the prison, loaded with chains, he saw one of his comrades going by. He tapped on the pane, and said:

'Be so good as to fetch me the little bundle I left behind at the inn, and I will give you a ducat.'

His comrade hurried off and brought him the bundle. As soon as the Soldier was alone, he lighted his pipe and summoned the Little Man.

'Don't be afraid,' he said to his Master. 'Go where they take you, and let what will happen, only take the Blue Light with you.'

Next day a trial was held, and although the Soldier had done no harm, the Judge sentenced him to death.

When he was led out to execution he asked a last favour of the King.

'What is your wish?' asked the King.

'That I may smoke a last pipe.'

248

' You may smoke three,' answered the King. ' But don't imagine that I will therefore grant you your life.'

Then the Soldier drew out his pipe, and lighted it at the Blue Light.

As soon as a few rings of smoke arose, the Little Man appeared with a little cudgel in his hand, and said : ' What is my Master's command ? '

' Strike the false Judge and his minions to the ground, and do not spare the King either for all his cruelty to me.'

Then the Little Man flew about like lightning, zig-zag, hither and thither, and whomever he touched with his cudgel fell to the ground, and dared not move.

The King was now seized with alarm, and, begging on his knees that his life might be spared, he rendered up his kingdom and gave his Daughter to the Soldier to be his wife.

The Raven

THERE was once a Queen who had a little daughter still in arms.

One day the child was naughty, and would not be quiet, whatever her mother might say.

So she grew impatient, and as the Ravens were flying round the castle, she opened the window, and said : ' I wish you were a Raven, that you might fly away, and then I should have peace.'

She had hardly said the words, when the child was changed into a Raven, and flew out of the window.

She flew straight into a dark wood, and her parents did not know what had become of her.

One day a Man was passing through this wood and heard the Raven calling.

When he was near enough, the Raven said : ' I am a Princess by birth, and I am bewitched, but you can deliver me from the spell.'

' What must I do ? ' asked he.

' Go further into the wood,' she said, ' and you will come to a house with an old Woman in it, who will offer you food and drink. But you must not take any. If you eat or drink what she offers you, you will fall into a deep sleep, and then you will never be able to deliver me. There is a great heap of tan in the garden behind the house ; you must stand on it and wait for me. I will come for three days in a coach drawn by four horses which, on the first day, will be white, on the second, chestnut, and on the last, black. If you are not awake, I shall not be delivered.'

250

THE RAVEN

The Man promised to do everything that she asked.

But the Raven said : 'Alas ! I know that you will not deliver me. You will take what the Woman offers you, and I shall never be freed from the spell.'

He promised once more not to touch either the food or the drink. But when he reached the house, the Old Woman said to him : 'Poor man ! How tired you are. Come and refresh yourself. Eat and drink.'

'No,' said the Man ; 'I will neither eat nor drink.'

But she persisted, and said : 'Well, if you won't eat, take a sip out of the glass. One sip is nothing.'

Then he yielded, and took a little sip.

About two o'clock he went down into the garden, and stood on the tan-heap to wait for the Raven. All at once he became so tired that he could not keep on his feet, and lay down for a moment, not meaning to go to sleep. But he had hardly stretched himself out, before his eyelids closed, and he fell fast asleep. He slept so soundly, that nothing in the world could have awakened him.

At two o'clock the Raven came, drawn by her four white horses. But she was already very sad, for she said : 'I know he is asleep.'

She alighted from the carriage, went to him, shook him, and called him, but he did not wake.

Next day at dinner-time the Old Woman came again, and brought him food and drink ; but again he refused to touch it. But she left him no peace, till at last she induced him to take a sip from the glass.

Towards two o'clock he again went into the garden, and stood on the tan-heap, meaning to wait for the Raven. But he suddenly became so tired, that he sank down and fell into a deep sleep.

When the Raven drove up with her chestnut horses, she was very mournful, and said : 'I know he is asleep.'

She went to him, but he was fast asleep, and she could not wake him.

Next day the Old Woman said : ' What is the meaning of this ? If you don't eat or drink you will die.'

He said : ' I must not, and I will not either eat or drink.'

She put the dish of food and the glass of wine before him, and when the scent of the wine reached him, he could withstand it no longer, and took a good draught.

When the time came he went into the garden and stood on the tan-heap and waited for the Raven. But he was more tired than ever, lay down and slept like a log.

At two o'clock the Raven came, drawn by four black horses, the coach and everything about it was black. She herself was in the deepest mourning, and said : ' Alas ! I know he is asleep.'

She shook him, and called him, but she could not wake him.

Finding her efforts in vain, she placed a loaf beside him, a piece of meat, and a bottle of wine. Then she took a golden ring on which her name was engraved, and put it on his finger. Lastly, she laid a letter by him, saying that the bread, the meat, and the wine were inexhaustible. She also said—

' I see that you cannot deliver me here, but if you still wish to do so, come to the Golden Castle of Stromberg. I know that it is still in your power.'

Then she seated herself in her coach again, and drove to the Golden Castle of Stromberg.

When the Man woke and found that he had been asleep, his heart grew heavy, and he said : ' She certainly must have passed, and I have not delivered her.'

Then his eyes fell on the things lying by him, and he read the letter which told him all that had occurred.

So he got up and went away to find the Golden Castle of Stromberg, but he had no idea where to find it.

When he had wandered about for a long time he came to a dark wood whence he could not find his way out.

After walking about in it for a fortnight, he lay down one night under a bush to sleep, for he was very tired. But he

252

heard such lamentations and howling that he could not go to sleep.

Then he saw a light glimmering in the distance and went towards it. When he reached it, he found that it came from

The Golden Castle of Stromberg.

a house which looked very tiny because a huge Giant was standing at the door.

He thought: 'If I go in and the Giant sees me, I shan't escape with my life.'

253

But at last he ventured to go forward.

When the Giant saw him, he said : ' It 's a good thing you have appeared. I have had nothing to eat for an age. I will just swallow you for my supper.'

' You had better let me alone,' said the Man. ' I shan't let myself be swallowed in a hurry. If you only want something to eat, I have plenty here to satisfy you.'

' If you are speaking the truth,' said the Giant, ' you may be quite easy. I was only going to eat you because I had nothing else.'

Then they went in and sat down at the table, and the Man produced the bread, the meat, and the wine, which were inexhaustible.

' This just suits me,' said the Giant. And he ate as much as ever he could.

The Man said to him : ' Can't you tell me where to find the Golden Castle ? '

The Giant said : ' I will look at my map. Every town, village, and house is marked upon it.'

He fetched the map, but the castle was not to be found.

' It doesn't matter,' he said. ' I have a bigger map upstairs in my chest ; we will look for it there.'

At last the Golden Castle was discovered, but it was many thousands of miles away.

' How am I ever to get there ? ' asked the Man.

The Giant said : ' I have a couple of hours to spare. I will carry you near it. But then I must come back to look after my wife and child.'

Then the Giant transported him to within a hundred miles of the Castle, and said : ' You will be able to find your way from here alone.' Then he went back ; and the Man went on, till at last he came to the Golden Castle.

It stood on a mountain of glass, and the bewitched Maiden drove round and round it every day in her coach.

He was delighted to see her again, and wanted to go to her

at once. But when he tried to climb the mountain, he found it was so slippery, that he slid back at every step.

When he found he could not reach her, he grew very sad, and said to himself: ' I will stay down here and wait for her.'

So he built himself a little hut, and lived in it for a whole year. He could see the Princess above, driving round the castle every day, but he could never get to her.

Then one day he saw three Robbers fighting, and called out to them: ' God be with you!'

They stopped at the sound of his voice, but, seeing nothing, they began to fight again.

Then he cried again: ' God be with you!'

They stopped and looked about, but, seeing no one, went on fighting.

Then he cried for the third time: ' God be with you!'

Again they stopped and looked about, but, as there was no one visible, they fell to more savagely than ever.

One day he saw three Robbers fighting.

He said to himself: ' I must go and see what it is all about.'

He went up and asked them why they were fighting

One of them said he had found a stick which made any door fly open which it touched.

The second said he had found a cloak which made him invisible when he wore it.

The third said he had caught a horse which could go any-where, even up the mountain of glass.

They could not decide whether these things should be common property or whether they should divide them.

Then said the Man : ' I will exchange them with you if you like. I have no money, but I have something more valuable. First, however, I must test your things to see if you are speaking the truth.'

They let him get on to the horse, put on the cloak, and take the stick in his hand. When he had got them all, he was nowhere to be seen.

Then he gave them each a sound drubbing, and said : ' There, you have your deserts, you bears. You may be satisfied with that.'

Then he rode up the glass mountain, and when he reached the castle he found the gate was shut. He touched it with his stick and it flew open.

He went in and straight up the stairs into the gallery where the Maiden sat with a golden cup of wine before her.

But she could not see him because he had the cloak on.

He took the ring she had given him, and dropped it into the cup, where it fell with a clink.

She cried : ' That is my ring. The Man who is to deliver me must be here.'

They searched for him all over the castle, but could not find him, for he had gone outside, taken off the cloak, and mounted his horse.

When the people came to the gate and saw him, they raised cries of joy.

He dismounted and took the Princess in his arms. She kissed him, and said : ' Now you have delivered me, and to-morrow we will celebrate our marriage.'

The Golden Goose

THERE was once a man who had three sons. The youngest of them was called Simpleton; he was scorned and despised by the others, and kept in the background.

The eldest son was going into the forest to cut wood, and before he started, his mother gave him a nice sweet cake and a bottle of wine to take with him, so that he might not suffer from hunger or thirst. In the wood he met a little, old, grey Man, who bade him good-day, and said, ' Give me a bit of the cake in your pocket, and let me have a drop of your wine. I am so hungry and thirsty.'

But the clever son said : ' If I give you my cake and wine, I shan't have enough for myself. Be off with you.'

He left the little Man standing there, and went on his way. But he had not been long at work, cutting down a tree, before he made a false stroke, and dug the axe into his own arm, and he was obliged to go home to have it bound up.

Now, this was no accident ; it was brought about by the little grey Man.

The second son now had to go into the forest to cut wood, and, like the eldest, his mother gave him a sweet cake and a bottle of wine. In the same way the little grey Man met him, and asked for a piece of his cake and a drop of his wine. But the second son made the same sensible answer, ' If I give you any, I shall have the less for myself. Be off out of my way,' and he went on.

His punishment, however, was not long delayed. **After a** few blows at the tree, he hit his own leg, and had to be **carried** home.

Then Simpleton said, ' Let me go to cut the wood, father.'

But his father said, ' Your brothers have only come to **harm** by it; you had better leave it alone. You know nothing

There stands an old tree; cut it down, and you will find
something at the roots.

about it.' But Simpleton begged so hard to be allowed to go that at last his father said, ' Well, off you go then. You will be wiser when you have hurt yourself.'

His mother gave him a cake which was only mixed with water and baked in the ashes, and a bottle of sour beer. When he reached the forest, like the others, he met the little **grey**

258

Man, who greeted him, and said, ' Give me a bit of your cake and a drop of your wine. I am so hungry and thirsty.'

Simpleton answered, ' I only have a cake baked in the ashes, and some sour beer ; but, if you like such fare, we will sit down and eat it together.'

So they sat down ; but when Simpleton pulled out his cake it was a sweet, nice cake, and his sour beer was turned into good wine. So they ate and drank, and the little Man said, ' As you have such a good heart, and are willing to share your goods, I

So now there were seven people running behind Simpleton and his Goose.

will give you good luck. There stands an old tree ; cut it down, and you will find something at the roots.'

So saying he disappeared.

Simpleton cut down the tree, and when it fell, lo, and behold ! a Goose was sitting among the roots, and its feathers were of pure gold. He picked it up, and taking it with him, went to an inn, where he meant to stay the night. The land-lord had three daughters, who saw the Goose, and were very curious as to what kind of bird it could be, and wanted to get one of its golden feathers.

The eldest thought, 'There will soon be some opportunity for me to pull out one of the feathers,' and when Simpleton went outside, she took hold of its wing to pluck out a feather; but her hand stuck fast, and she could not get away.

Soon after, the second sister came up, meaning also to pluck out one of the golden feathers; but she had hardly touched her sister when she found herself held fast.

Lastly, the third one came, with the same intention, but the others screamed out, 'Keep away! For goodness sake, keep away!'

But she, not knowing why she was to keep away, thought, 'Why should I not be there, if they are there?'

So she ran up, but as soon as she touched her sisters she had to stay hanging on to them, and they all had to pass the night like this.

And so they followed up hill and down dale after Simpleton and his Goose.

In the morning, Simpleton took up the Goose under his arm, without noticing the three girls hanging on behind. They had to keep running behind, dodging his legs right and left.

In the middle of the fields they met the Parson, who, when

he saw the procession, cried out : ' For shame, you bold girls ! Why do you run after the lad like that ? Do you call that proper behaviour ? '

Then he took hold of the hand of the youngest girl to pull her away ; but no sooner had he touched her than he felt himself held fast, and he, too, had to run behind.

Soon after the Sexton came up, and, seeing his master the Parson treading on the heels of the three girls, cried out in amazement, 'Hullo, your

Reverence! Whither away so fast? Don't forget that we have a christening ! '

So saying, he plucked the Parson by the sleeve, and soon found that he could not get away.

As this party of five, one behind the other, tramped on, two Peasants came along the road, carrying their hoes. The Parson called them, and asked them to set the Sexton and himself free. But as soon as ever they touched the Sexton they were held fast, so now there were seven people running behind Simpleton and his Goose.

By-and-by they reached a town, where a King ruled whose only daughter was so solemn that nothing and nobody could make her laugh. So the King had proclaimed that whoever could make her laugh should marry her.

When Simpleton heard this he took his Goose, with all his following, before her, and when she saw these seven people running, one behind another, she burst into fits of laughter, and seemed as if she could never stop.

Thereupon Simpleton asked her in marriage. But the King did not like him for a son-in-law, and he made all sorts of conditions. First, he said Simpleton must bring him a man who could drink up a cellar full of wine.

Then Simpleton at once thought of the little grey Man who might be able to help him, and he went out to the forest to look for him. On the very spot where the tree that he had cut down had stood, he saw a man sitting with a very sad face. Simpleton asked him what was the matter, and he answered—

' I am so thirsty, and I can't quench my thirst. I hate cold water, and I have already emptied a cask of wine ; but what is a drop like that on a burning stone ? '

' Well, there I can help you,' said Simpleton. ' Come with me, and you shall soon have enough to drink and to spare.'

He led him to the King's cellar, and the Man set to upon the great casks, and he drank and drank till his sides ached, and by the end of the day the cellar was empty.

Then again Simpleton demanded his bride. But the King was annoyed that a wretched fellow called ' Simpleton ' should have his daughter, and he made new conditions. He was now to find a man who could eat up a mountain of bread.

Simpleton did not reflect long, but went straight to the forest, and there in the self-same place sat a man tightening a strap round his body, and making a very miserable face. He said : ' I have eaten up a whole ovenful of rolls, but what is the good of that when any one is as hungry as I am. I am never satisfied. I have to tighten my belt every day if I am not to die of hunger.'

Simpleton was delighted, and said : ' Get up and come with me.   You shall have enough to eat.'

And he took him to the Court, where the King had caused all the flour in the kingdom to be brought together, and a huge mountain of bread to be baked.   The Man from the forest sat down before it and began to eat, and at the end of the day the whole mountain had disappeared.

Now, for the third time, Simpleton asked for his bride. But again the King tried to find an excuse, and demanded a ship which could sail on land as well as at sea.

' As soon as you sail up in it, you shall have my daughter,' he said.

Simpleton went straight to the forest, and there sat the little grey Man to whom he had given his cake.   The little Man said : ' I have eaten and drunk for you, and now I will give you the ship, too.   I do it all because you were merciful to me.'

Then he gave him the ship which could sail on land as well as at sea, and when the King saw it he could no longer withhold his daughter.   The marriage was celebrated, and, at the King's death, the Simpleton inherited the kingdom, and lived long and happily with his wife.

The King could no longer withhold his daughter.

The Water of Life

THERE was once a King who was so ill that it was thought impossible his life could be saved. He had three sons, and they were all in great distress on his account, and they went into the castle gardens and wept at the thought that he must die. An old man came up to them and asked the cause of their grief. They told him that their father was dying, and nothing could save him. The old man said, 'There is only one remedy which I know; it is the Water of Life. If he drinks of it, he will recover, but it is very difficult to find.'

The eldest son said, 'I will soon find it'; and he went to the sick man to ask permission to go in search of the Water of Life, as that was the only thing to cure him.

'No,' said the King. 'The danger is too great. I would rather die.'

But he persisted so long that at last the King gave his permission.

The Prince thought, 'If I bring this water I shall be the favourite, and I shall inherit the kingdom.'

So he set off, and when he had ridden some distance he came upon a Dwarf standing in the road, who cried, 'Whither away so fast?'

'Stupid little fellow,' said the Prince, proudly; 'what business is it of yours?' and rode on.

The little man was very angry, and made an evil vow.

Soon after, the Prince came to a gorge in the mountains, and the further he rode the narrower it became, till he could go no further. His horse could neither go forward nor turn round for him to dismount; so there he sat, jammed in.

264

The sick King waited a long time for him, but he never came back. Then the second son said, 'Father, let me go and find the Water of Life,' thinking, 'if my brother is dead I shall have the kingdom.'

The King at first refused to let him go, but at last he gave his consent. So the Prince started on the same road as his brother, and met the same Dwarf, who stopped him and asked where he was going in such a hurry.

'Little Snippet, what does it matter to you?' he said, and rode away without looking back.

But the Dwarf cast a spell over him, and he, too, got into a narrow gorge like his brother, where he could neither go backwards nor forwards.

This is what happens to the haughty.

As the second son also stayed away, the youngest one offered to go and fetch the Water of Life, and at last the King was obliged to let him go.

When he met the Dwarf, and he asked him where he was hurrying to, he stopped and said, 'I am searching for the Water of Life, because my father is dying.'

'Do you know where it is to be found?'

'No,' said the Prince.

'As you have spoken pleasantly to me, and not been haughty like your false brothers, I will help you and tell you how to find the Water of Life. It flows from a fountain in the courtyard of an enchanted castle; but you will never get in unless I give you an iron rod and two loaves of bread. With the rod strike three times on the iron gate of the castle, and it will spring open. Inside you will find two Lions with wide-open jaws, but if you throw a loaf to each they will be quiet. Then you must make haste to fetch the Water of Life before it strikes twelve, or the gates of the castle will close and you will be shut in.'

The Prince thanked him, took the rod and the loaves, and set off. When he reached the castle all was just as the Dwarf had said. At the third knock the gate flew open, and when he had pacified the Lions with the loaves, he walked into the castle. In the great hall he found several enchanted Princes, and he took the rings from their fingers. He also took a sword and a loaf, which were lying by them. On passing into the next room he found a beautiful Maiden, who rejoiced at his coming. She embraced him, and said that he had saved her, and should have the whole of her kingdom; and if he would come back in a year she would marry him. She also told him where to find the fountain with the enchanted water; but, she said, he must make haste to get out of the castle before the clock struck twelve.

Then he went on, and came to a room where there was a beautiful bed freshly made, and as he was very tired he thought he would take a little rest; so he lay down and fell asleep. When he woke it was striking a quarter to twelve. He sprang up in a fright, and ran to the fountain, and took some of the water in a cup which was lying near, and then hurried away. The clock struck just as he reached the iron gate, and it banged so quickly that it took off a bit of his heel.

He was rejoiced at having got some of the Water of Life, and hastened on his homeward journey. He again passed the Dwarf, who said, when he saw the sword and the loaf, ' Those things will be of much service to you. You will be able to strike down whole armies with the sword, and the loaf will never come to an end.'

The Prince did not want to go home without his brothers, and he said, ' Good Dwarf, can you not tell me where my brothers are? They went in search of the Water of Life before I did, but they never came back.'

' They are both stuck fast in a narrow mountain gorge. I cast a spell over them because of their pride.'

Then the Prince begged so hard that they might be released that at last the Dwarf yielded; but he warned him against them, and said, ' Beware of them; they have bad hearts.'

He was delighted to see his brothers when they came back, and told them all that had happened to him; how he had found the Water of Life, and brought a goblet full with him. How he had released a beautiful Princess, who would wait a year for him and then marry him, and he would become a great Prince.

Then they rode away together, and came to a land where famine and war were raging. The King thought he would be utterly ruined, so great was the destitution.

The Prince went to him and gave him the loaf, and with it he fed and satisfied his whole kingdom. The Prince also gave him his sword, and he smote the whole army of his enemies with it, and then he was able to live in peace and quiet. Then the Prince took back his sword and his loaf, and the three brothers rode on. But they had to pass through two more countries where war and famine were raging, and each time the Prince gave his sword and his loaf to the King, and in this way he saved three kingdoms.

After that they took a ship and crossed the sea. During the passage the two elder brothers said to each other, ' Our youngest brother found the Water of Life, and we did not, so our father will give him the kingdom which we ought to have, and he will take away our fortune from us.'

This thought made them very vindictive, and they made up their minds to get rid of him. They waited till he was asleep, and then they emptied the Water of Life from his goblet and took it themselves, and filled up his cup with salt sea water.

As soon as they got home the youngest Prince took his goblet to the King, so that he might drink of the water which was to make him well ; but after drinking only a few drops of the sea water he became more ill than ever. As he was bewailing himself, his two elder sons came to him and accused the youngest of trying to poison him, and said that they had the real Water of Life, and gave him some. No sooner had he drunk it than he felt better, and he soon became as strong and well as he had been in his youth.

Then the two went to their youngest brother, and mocked him, saying, ' It was you who found the Water of Life ; you had all the trouble, while we have the reward. You should have been wiser, and kept your eyes open; we stole it from you while you were asleep on the ship. When the end of the year comes, one of us will go and bring away the beautiful Princess. But don't dare to betray us. Our father will certainly not believe you, and if you say a single word you will lose your life; your only chance is to keep silence.'

The old King was very angry with his youngest son, thinking that he had tried to take his life. So he had the Court assembled to give judgment upon him, and it was decided that he must be secretly got out of the way.

One day when the Prince was going out hunting, thinking no evil, the King's Huntsman was ordered to go with him. Seeing the Huntsman look sad, the Prince said to him, 'My good Huntsman, what is the matter with you?'

The Huntsman answered, 'I can't bear to tell you, and yet I must.'

The Prince said, 'Say it out; whatever it is I will forgive you.'

'Alas!' said the Huntsman, 'I am to shoot you dead; it is the King's command.'

The Prince was horror-stricken, and said, 'Dear Huntsman, do not kill me, give me my life. Let me have your dress, and you shall have my royal robes.'

The Huntsman said, 'I will gladly do so; I could never have shot you.' So they changed clothes, and the Huntsman went home, but the Prince wandered away into the forest.

After a time three wagon loads of gold and precious stones came to the King for his youngest son. They were sent by the Kings who had been saved by the Prince's sword and his miraculous loaf, and who now wished to show their gratitude.

Then the old King thought, 'What if my son really was innocent?' and said to his people, 'If only he were still alive! How sorry I am that I ordered him to be killed.'

'He is still alive,' said the Huntsman. 'I could not find

it in my heart to carry out your commands,' and he told the King what had taken place.

A load fell from the King's heart on hearing the good news, and he sent out a proclamation to all parts of his kingdom that his son was to come home, where he would be received with great favour.

In the meantime, the Princess had caused a road to be made of pure shining gold leading to her castle, and told her people that whoever came riding straight along it would be the true bridegroom, and they were to admit him. But any one who came either on one side of the road or the other would not be the right one, and he was not to be let in.

When the year had almost passed, the eldest Prince thought that he would hurry to the Princess, and by giving himself out as her deliverer would gain a wife and a kingdom as well. So he rode away, and when he saw the beautiful golden road he thought it would be a thousand pities to ride upon it; so he turned aside, and rode to the right of it. But when he reached the gate the people told him that he was not the true bridegroom, and he had to go away.

Soon after the second Prince came, and when he saw the golden road he thought it would be a thousand pities for his horse to tread upon it; so he turned aside, and rode up on the left of it. But when he reached the gate he was also told that he was not the true bridegroom, and, like his brother, was turned away.

When the year had quite come to an end, the third Prince came out of the wood to ride to his beloved, and through her to forget all his past sorrows. So on he went, thinking only of her, and wishing to be with her; and he never even saw the golden road. His horse cantered right along the middle of it, and when he reached the gate it was flung open and the Princess received him joyfully, and called him her Deliverer, and the Lord of her Kingdom. Their marriage was celebrated without delay, and with much rejoicing. When it was over, she told him that his father had called him back and forgiven him. So he went to him and told him everything; how his brothers had deceived him, and how they had forced him to keep silence. The old King wanted to punish them, but they had taken a ship and sailed away over the sea, and they never came back as long as they lived.

The Twelve Huntsmen

THERE was once a Prince, who was betrothed to a Maiden, the daughter of a King, whom he loved very much. One day when they were together, and very happy, a messenger came from the Prince's father, who was lying ill, to summon him home as he wished to see him before he died. He said to his beloved, ' I must go away, and leave you now ; but I give you this ring as a keepsake. When I am King, I will come and fetch you away.'

Then he rode off, and when he got home he found his father on his death-bed. His father said, ' My dear son, I wanted to see you once more before I die. Promise to marry the bride I have chosen for you,' and he named a certain Princess.

His son was very sad, and without reflecting promised to do what his father wished, and thereupon the King closed his eyes and died.

Now, when the Prince had been proclaimed King, and the period of mourning was past, the time came when he had to keep his promise to his father. He made his offer to the Princess, and it was accepted. His betrothed heard of this, and grieved so much over his faithlessness that she very nearly died. The King her father asked, ' Dear child, why are you so sad ? You shall have whatever you desire.'

She thought for a moment, then said, ' Dear father, I want eleven maidens all exactly like me in face, figure, and height.'

The King said, ' If it is possible, your wish shall be fulfilled.'

Then he caused a search to be made all over his kingdom, till the eleven maidens were found, all exactly like his daughter. The Princess ordered twelve huntsmen's dresses to be made, which she commanded the maidens to wear, putting on the

271

twelfth herself. Then she took leave of her father, and rode away with the maidens to the court of her former bridegroom whom she loved so dearly. She asked him if he wanted any Huntsmen, and whether he would take them all into his service. The King did not recognise her, but, as they were all so handsome, he said Yes, he would engage them. So they all entered the King's service.

Now, the King had a Lion which was a wonderful creature, for he knew all secret and hidden things. He said to the King one evening, 'You fancy you have twelve Huntsmen there, don't you?'

'Yes,' said the King.

'You are mistaken,' said the Lion. 'They are twelve maidens.'

The King answered, 'That can't be true! How can you prove it?'

'Oh, have some peas strewn in your ante-room to-morrow, and you will soon see. Men have a firm tread, and when they walk on peas they don't move; but maidens trip and trot and slide, and make the peas roll about.'

The King was pleased with the Lion's advice, and ordered the peas to be strewn on the floor.

There was, however, a servant of the King who favoured the Huntsmen, and when he heard that they were to be put to this test, he went and told them all about it, and said, 'The Lion is going to prove to the King that you are maidens.'

The Princess thanked him, and said afterwards to her maidens, 'Do your utmost to tread firmly on the peas.'

Next morning, when the King ordered them to be called, they walked into the ante-chamber with so firm a tread that not a pea moved When they had gone away, the King said to the Lion, 'You lied; they walked just like men.'

But the Lion answered, 'They had been warned of the test, and were prepared for it. Just let twelve spinning-wheels be brought into the ante-chamber, and they will be delighted at the sight, as no man would be.'

This plan also pleased the King, and he ordered the spinning wheels. But again the kind servant warned the Huntsmen of the plan. When they were alone, the Princess said to her maidens, ' Control yourselves, and don't so much as look at the spinning-wheels.'

When the King next morning sent for the Huntsmen, they walked through the ante-chamber without even glancing at the spinning-wheels.

Then the King said to the Lion, ' You lied to me. They *are* men ; they never looked at the spinning-wheels.'

The Lion answered, ' They knew that they were on their trial, and restrained themselves.'

But the King would not believe him any more.

The twelve Huntsmen always went with the King on his hunting expeditions, and the longer he had them, the better he liked them. Now, it happened one day when they were out hunting, that the news came of the royal bride's approach.

When the true bride heard it, the shock was so great that her heart nearly stopped, and she fell down in a dead faint. The King, thinking something had happened to his favourite Huntsman, ran to help him, and pulled off his glove. Then he saw the ring which he had given to his first betrothed, and when he looked her in the face he recognised her. He was so moved that he kissed her, and when she opened her eyes he said, ' Thou art mine, and I am thine, and nobody in the world shall separate us.'

Then he sent a messenger to the other bride, and begged her to go home, as he already had a wife, and he who has an old dish does not need a new one. Their marriage was then celebrated, and the Lion was taken into favour again, as, after all, he had spoken the truth.

The King of the Golden Mountain

THERE was once a Merchant who had two children, a boy and a girl. They were both small, and not old enough to run about. He had also two richly-laden ships at sea, and just as he was expecting to make a great deal of money by the merchandise, news came that they had both been lost. So now instead of being a rich man he was quite poor, and had nothing left but one field near the town.

To turn his thoughts from his misfortune, he went out into this field, and as he was walking up and down a little black Mannikin suddenly appeared before him, and asked why he was so sad. The Merchant said, ' I would tell you at once, if you could help me.'

' Who knows,' answered the little Mannikin. ' Perhaps I could help you.'

Then the Merchant told him that all his wealth had been lost in a wreck, and that now he had nothing left but this field.

' Don't worry yourself,' said the Mannikin. ' If you will promise to bring me in twelve years' time the first thing which rubs against your legs when you go home, you shall have as much gold as you want.'

The Merchant thought, ' What could it be but my dog ? ' He never thought of his boy, but said Yes, and gave the Mannikin his bond signed and sealed, and went home.

When he reached the house his little son, delighted to hold on to the benches and totter towards his father, seized him by the leg to steady himself.

The Merchant was horror-stricken, for his vow came into his head, and now he knew what he had promised to give away. But as he still found no gold in his chests, he thought it must only have been a joke of the Mannikin's. A month later he went up into the loft to gather together some old tin to sell it, and there he found a great heap of gold on the floor. So he was soon up in the world again, bought and sold, became a richer merchant than ever, and was altogether contented.

In the meantime the boy had grown up, and he was both clever and wise. But the nearer the end of the twelve years came, the more sorrowful the Merchant grew ; you could even see his misery in his face. One day his son asked him what was the matter, but his father would not tell him. The boy, however, persisted so long that at last he told him that, without knowing what he was doing, he had promised to give him up at the end of twelve years to a little black Mannikin, in return for a quantity of gold. He had given his hand and seal on it, and the time was now near for him to go.

Then his son said, ' O father, don't be frightened, it will be all right. The little black Mannikin has no power over me.'

When the time came, the son asked a blessing of the Priest, and he and his father went to the field together ; and the son made a circle within which they took their places.

When the little black Mannikin appeared, he said to the father, ' Have you brought what you promised me ? '

The man was silent, but his son said, ' What do you want ? '

The Mannikin said, ' My business is with your father, and not with you.'

The son answered, ' You deceived and cheated my father. Give me back his bond.'

' Oh no ! ' said the little man ; ' I won't give up my rights.'

They talked to each other for a long time, and at last they decided that, as the son no longer belonged to his father, and declined to belong to his foe, he should get into a boat on a flowing stream, and his father should push it off himself, thus giving him up to the stream.

So the youth took leave of his father, got into the boat, and his father pushed it off. Then, thinking that his son was lost to him for ever, he went home and sorrowed for him. The little boat, however, did not sink, it drifted quietly down the stream, and the youth sat in it in perfect safety. It drifted for a long time, till at last it stuck fast on an unknown shore. The youth landed, and seeing a beautiful castle near, walked towards it. As he passed under the doorway, however, a spell fell upon him. He went through all the rooms, but found them empty, till he came to the very last one, where a Serpent lay coiling and uncoiling itself. The Serpent was really an enchanted maiden, who was delighted when she saw the youth, and said, ' Have you come at last, my preserver ? I have been waiting twelve years for you. This whole kingdom is bewitched, and you must break the spell.'

' How am I to do that ? ' he asked.

She said, ' To-night, twelve black men hung with chains will appear, and they will ask what you are doing here. But do not speak a word, whatever they do or say to you. They will torment you, strike, and pinch you, but don't say a word. At twelve o'clock they will have to go away. On the second night twelve more will come, and on the third twenty-four. These will cut off your head. But at twelve o'clock their power goes, and if you have borne it, and not spoken a word, I shall be saved. Then I will come to you, and bring a little flask containing the Water of Life, with which I will sprinkle you, and you will be brought to life again, as sound and well as ever you were.'

Then he said, ' I will gladly save you ! '

Everything happened just as she had said. The black men could not force a word out of him ; and on the third night the Serpent became a beautiful Princess, who brought the Water of Life as she had promised, and restored the youth to life. Then she fell on his neck and kissed him, and there were great rejoicings all over the castle.

Their marriage was celebrated, and he became King of the Golden Mountain.

276

They lived happily together, and in course of time a beautiful boy was born to them.

When eight years had passed, the King's heart grew tender within him as he thought of his father, and he wanted to go home to see him. But the Queen did not want him to go. She said, ' I know it will be to my misfortune.' However, he gave her no peace till she agreed to let him go. On his departure she gave him a wishing-ring, and said, ' Take this ring, and put it on your finger, and you will at once be at the place where you wish to be. Only, you must promise never to use it to wish me away from here to be with you at your father's.'

He made the promise, and put the ring on his finger ; he then wished himself before the town where his father lived, and at the same moment found himself at the gate. But the sentry would not let him in because his clothes, though of rich material, were of such strange cut. So he went up a mountain, where a Shepherd lived, and, exchanging clothing with him, put on his old smock, and passed into the town unnoticed.

When he reached his father he began making himself known ; but his father, never thinking that it was his son, said that it was true he had once had a son, but he had long been dead. But, he added, seeing that he was a poor Shepherd, he would give him a plate of food.

The supposed Shepherd said to his parents, ' I am indeed your son. Is there no mark on my body by which you may know me ? '

His mother said, ' Yes, our son has a strawberry mark under his right arm.'

He pushed up his shirt sleeve, and there was the strawberry mark ; so they no longer doubted that he was their son. He told them that he was the King of the Golden Mountain, his wife was a Princess, and they had a little son seven years old.

' That can't be true,' said his father. ' You are a fine sort of King to come home in a tattered Shepherd's smock.'

His son grew angry, and, without stopping to reflect, turned his ring round and wished his wife and son to appear.

In a moment they both stood before him ; but his wife did nothing but weep and lament, and said that he had broken his promise, and by so doing had made her very unhappy. He said, ' I have acted incautiously, but from no bad motive,' and he tried to soothe her.

She appeared to be calmed, but really she nourished evil intentions towards him in her heart.

Shortly after he took her outside the town to the field, and showed her the stream down which he had drifted in the little boat. Then he said, ' I am tired ; I want to rest a little.'

So she sat down, and he rested his head upon her lap, and soon fell fast asleep. As soon as he was asleep, she drew the ring from his finger, and drew herself gently away from him, leaving only her slipper behind. Last of all, taking her child in her arms, she wished herself back in her own kingdom. When he woke up, he found himself quite deserted ; wife and child were gone, the ring had disappeared from his finger, and only her slipper remained as a token.

' I can certainly never go home to my parents,' he said. ' They would say I was a sorcerer. I must go away and walk till I reach my own kingdom again.'

So he went away, and at last he came to a mountain, where three Giants were quarrelling about the division of their father's property. When they saw him passing, they called him up, and said, ' Little people have sharp wits,' and asked him to divide their inheritance for them.

It consisted, first, of a sword, with which in one's hand, if one said, ' All heads off, mine alone remain,' every head fell to the ground. Secondly, of a mantle which rendered any one putting it on invisible. Thirdly, of a pair of boots which transported the wearer to whatever place he wished.

He said, ' Give me the three articles so that I may see if they are all in good condition.'

So they gave him the mantle, and he at once became invisible. He took his own shape again, and said, ' The mantle is good ; now give me the sword.'

278

She went away accompanied by the Lions.

Good Dwarf, can you not tell me where my brothers are?

The Son made a circle, and his Father and he took their places within
it, and the little black Mannikin appeared.

Once upon a time a poor Peasant, named Crabb, was taking a load of wood drawn by two oxen to the town for sale.

But they said, ' No, we can't give you the sword. If you were to say, " All heads off, mine alone remain," all our heads would fall, and yours would be the only one left.'

At last, however, they gave it to him, on condition that he was to try it on a tree. He did as they wished, and the sword went through the tree trunk as if it had been a straw. Then he wanted the boots, but they said, ' No, we won't give them away. If you were to put them on and wish yourself on the top of the mountain, we should be left standing here without anything.'

' No,' said he ; ' I won't do that.'

So they gave him the boots too ; but when he had all three he could think of nothing but his wife and child, and said to himself, ' Oh, if only I were on the Golden Mountain again ! ' and immediately he disappeared from the sight of the Giants, and there was an end of their inheritance.

When he approached his castle he heard sounds of music, fiddles and flutes, and shouts of joy. People told him that his wife was celebrating her marriage with another husband. He was filled with rage, and said, ' The false creature ! She deceived me, and deserted me when I was asleep.'

Then he put on his mantle, and went to the castle, invisible to all. When he went into the hall, where a great feast was spread with the richest foods and the costliest wines, the guests were joking and laughing while they ate and drank. The Queen sat on her throne in their midst in gorgeous clothing, with the crown on her head. He placed himself behind her, and no one saw him. Whenever the Queen put a piece of meat on her plate, he took it away and ate it, and when her glass was filled he took it away and drank it. Her plate and her glass were constantly refilled, but she never had anything, for it disappeared at once. At last she grew frightened, got up, and went to her room in tears, but he followed her there too. She said to herself, ' Am I still in the power of the demon ? Did my preserver never come ? '

He struck her in the face, and said, ' Did your preserver

never come? He is with you now, deceiver that you are. Did I deserve such treatment at your hands?' Then he made himself visible, and went into the hall, and cried, 'The wedding is stopped, the real King has come.'

The Kings, Princes, and Nobles who were present laughed him to scorn. But he only said, 'Will you go, or will you not?' They tried to seize him, but he drew his sword and said,

'All heads off, mine alone remain.'

Then all their heads fell to the ground, and he remained sole King and Lord of the Golden Mountain.

Doctor Know-All

ONCE upon a time a poor Peasant, named Crabb, was taking a load of wood drawn by two oxen to the town for sale. He sold it to a Doctor for four thalers. When the money was being paid to him, it so happened that the Doctor was sitting at dinner. When the Peasant saw how daintily the Doctor was eating and drinking, he felt a great desire to become a Doctor too. He remained standing and looking on for a time, and then asked if he could not be a Doctor.

' Oh yes ! ' said the Doctor ; ' that is easily managed.'

' What must I do ? ' asked the Peasant.

' First buy an ABC book ; you can get one with a cock as a frontispiece. Secondly, turn your wagon and oxen into money, and buy with it clothes and other things suitable for a Doctor. Thirdly, have a sign painted with the words, " I am Doctor Know-all," and have it nailed over your door.'

The Peasant did everything that he was told to do.

Now when he had been doctoring for a while, not very long though, a rich nobleman had some money stolen from him. He was told about Doctor Know-all, who lived in such and such a village, who would be sure to know what had become of it. So the gentleman ordered his carriage and drove to the village.

He stopped at the Doctor's house, and asked Crabb if he were Doctor Know-all.

' Yes, I am.'

' Then you must go with me to get my stolen money back.'

' Yes, certainly ; but Grethe, my wife, must come too.'

The nobleman agreed, and gave both of them seats in his carriage, and they all drove off together.

When they reached the nobleman's castle the dinner was ready, and Crabb was invited to sit down to table.

'Yes; but Grethe, my wife, must dine too'; and he seated himself with her.

When the first Servant brought in a dish of choice food, the Peasant nudged his wife, and said: 'Grethe, that was the first,'—meaning that the servant was handing the first dish. But the servant thought he meant, 'That was the first thief.' As he really was the thief, he became much alarmed, and said to his comrades outside—

'That Doctor knows everything, we shan't get out of this hole; he said I was the first.'

The second Servant did not want to go in at all, but he had to go, and when he offered his dish to the Peasant he nudged his wife, and said—'Grethe, that is the second.'

This Servant also was frightened and hurried out.

The third one fared no better. The Peasant said again: 'Grethe, that is the third.'

The fourth one brought in a covered dish, and the master told the Doctor that he must show his powers and guess what was under the cover. Now it was a dish of crabs.

The Peasant looked at the dish and did not know what to do, so he said: 'Wretched Crabb that I am.'

When the Master heard him he cried: 'There, he knows it! Then he knows where the money is too.'

Then the Servant grew terribly frightened, and signed to the Doctor to come outside.

When he went out, they all four confessed to him that they had stolen the money; they would gladly give it to him and a large sum in addition, if only he would not betray them to their Master, or their necks would be in peril. They also showed him where the money was hidden. Then the Doctor was satisfied, went back to the table, and said—

'Now, Sir, I will look in my book to see where the money is hidden.'

The fifth, in the meantime, had crept into the stove to hear if the Doctor knew still more. But he sat there turning over the pages of his ABC book looking for the cock, and as he could not find it at once, he said : 'I know you are there, and out you must come.'

The man in the stove thought it was meant for him, and sprang out in a fright, crying : 'The man knows everything.'

Then Doctor Know-all showed the nobleman where the money was hidden, but he did not betray the servants ; and he received much money from both sides as a reward, and became a very celebrated man.

The Seven Ravens

THERE was once a Man who had seven sons, but never a daughter, however much he wished for one.

At last, however, he had a daughter.

His joy was great, but the child was small and delicate, and, on account of its weakness, it was to be christened at home.

The Father sent one of his sons in haste to the spring to fetch some water; the other six ran with him, and because each of them wanted to be the first to draw the water, between them the pitcher fell into the brook.

There they stood and didn't know what to do, and not one of them ventured to go home.

As they did not come back, their Father became impatient, and said: 'Perhaps the young rascals are playing about, and have forgotten it altogether.'

He became anxious lest his little girl should die unbaptized, and in hot vexation, he cried: 'I wish the youngsters would all turn into Ravens!'

Scarcely were the words uttered, when he heard a whirring in the air above his head, and, looking upwards, he saw seven coal-black Ravens flying away.

The parents could not undo the spell, and were very sad about the loss of their seven sons, but they consoled themselves in some measure with their dear little daughter, who soon became strong, and every day more beautiful.

For a long time she was unaware that she had had any brothers, for her parents took care not to mention it.

However, one day by chance she heard some people saying about her: 'Oh yes, the girl's pretty enough; but you know she is really to blame for the misfortune to her seven brothers.'

284

Then she became very sad, and went to her father and mother and asked if she had ever had any brothers, and what had become of them.

The parents could no longer conceal the secret. They said, however, that what had happened was by the decree of heaven, and that her birth was merely the innocent occasion.

But the little girl could not get the matter off her conscience for a single day, and thought that she was bound to release her brothers again. She had no peace or quiet until she had secretly set out, and gone forth into the wide world to trace her brothers, wherever they might be, and to free them, let it cost what it might.

She took nothing with her but a little ring as a remembrance of her parents, a loaf of bread against hunger, a pitcher of water against thirst, and a little chair in case of fatigue. She kept ever going on and on until she came to the end of the world.

Then she came to the Sun, but it was hot and terrible, it devoured little children. She ran hastily away to the Moon, but it was too cold, and, moreover, dismal and dreary. And when the child was looking at it, it said : ' I smell, I smell man's flesh ! '

Then she quickly made off, and came to the Stars, and they were kind and good, and every one sat on his own special seat.

But the Morning Star stood up, and gave her a little bone, and said : ' Unless you have this bone, you cannot open the glass mountain, and in the glass mountain are your brothers.'

The girl took the bone, and wrapped it up carefully in a little kerchief, and went on again until she came to the glass mountain.

The gate was closed, and she meant to get out the little bone. But when she undid the kerchief it was empty, and she had lost the good Star's present.

How, now, was she to set to work ? She was determined to rescue her brothers, but had no key to open the glass mountain.

The good little sister took a knife and cut off her own tiny finger, fitted it into the keyhole, and succeeded in opening the lock.

When she had entered, she met a Dwarf, who said : 'My child, what are you looking for ? '

'I am looking for my brothers, the Seven Ravens,' she answered.

The Dwarf said : 'My masters, the Ravens, are not at home ; but if you like to wait until they come, please to walk in.'

Thereupon the Dwarf brought in the Ravens' supper, on seven little plates, and in seven little cups, and the little sister ate a crumb or two from each of the little plates, and took a sip from each of the little cups, but she let the ring she had brought with her fall into the last little cup.

All at once a whirring and crying were heard in the air ; then the Dwarf said : 'Now my masters the Ravens are coming home.'

Then they came in, and wanted to eat and drink, and began to look about for their little plates and cups.

But they said one after another : 'Halloa ! who has been eating off my plate ? Who has been drinking out of my cup ? There has been some human mouth here.'

When she entered she met a Dwarf.

And when the seventh drank to the bottom of his cup, the ring rolled up against his lips.

He looked at it, and recognised it as a ring belonging to his father and mother, and said : 'God grant that our sister may be here, and that we may be delivered.'

286

THE SEVEN RAVENS

As the maiden was standing behind the door listening, she heard the wish and came forward, and then all the Ravens got back their human form again.

And they embraced and kissed one another, and went joyfully home.

The Ravens coming home.

The Marriage of Mrs. Reynard

THERE was once an old Fox who thought that his wife was not true to him, and determined to put her to the test. He stretched himself under the bank, lay motionless, and pretended to be as dead as a door nail. Mrs. Reynard went to her chamber, and shut herself in; and her servant, Mistress Cat, sat by the fire, and cooked the dinner.

Now, when it became known that the old Fox was dead, suitors began to announce themselves. Soon afterwards, the servant heard some one knocking at the front door. She went and opened the door, and there stood a young Fox, who said—

> 'What are ye doing, pray, Mistress Cat?
> Sleeping or waking? or what are ye at?'

She answered—

> 'I'm not asleep; I'm wide awake.
> D'ye want to know what now I make?
> I'm warming beer, with butter in it;
> I beg ye'll taste it in a minute.'

'I'm much obliged, Mistress,' said the Fox. 'What is Mrs. Reynard doing?'
The Maid answered—

> 'In chamber sad she sits alone,
> And ceases not with grief to moan.
> She weeps until her eyes are red,
> Because the dear old Fox is dead.'

'Well, just tell her, Mistress, that there's a young Fox here, who would be glad to woo her.'
'Very well, young gentleman.'

288

THE MARRIAGE OF MRS. REYNARD

'Then went the Cat with pit-a-pat
And smote the door, rat-tata-tat!
"Pray, Mrs. Reynard, are you in?
Outside a wooer waits below!"'

'Well, what 's he like? I want to know. Has he got nine such beautiful tails as the late lamented Mr. Reynard?'

'Oh dear no,' answered the Cat. 'He has only got one.'

'Then I won't have him.'

Mistress Cat went down, and sent the wooer away.

Soon after this there was knocking again, and another Fox appeared at the door, who wished to pay his addresses to Mrs. Reynard. He had two tails, but he came off no better than the first. Afterwards others came, each with one tail more; but they were all rejected, till at last one came that had nine tails like old Mr. Reynard.

When the widow heard this, full of joy, she said to the Cat—

'Open the gates and doors; be swift.
Old Mr. Reynard turn adrift.'

But when the wedding was about to be celebrated, then old Mr. Reynard under the bank roused himself, and gave the whole crew a good drubbing, and sent them, Mrs. Reynard and all, helter-skelter out of the house.

SECOND TALE

WHEN old Mr. Reynard really died, the Wolf came as a suitor, and knocked at the door, and the Cat who acted as servant to Mrs. Reynard, opened it.

The Wolf greeted her, and said—

'Good-day, Miss Cat, of sprightly wit,
How comes it that alone you sit?
What are you making there, so good?'

The Cat answered—

'Tumbling milk and butter up.
Will your Lordship have a sup?'

' Thank you kindly, Mistress Cat.   Mistress Reynard is not at home, I suppose.'

> ' Upstairs in her chamber she sits,
> And weeps as her sorrow befits.
> Her sad case she doth much deplore,
> Because Mr. Reynard's no more.'

The Wolf answered— .

> ' " If now she wants to wed again,
> She must come down the stairs, 'tis plain."
> The Cat ran up without delay,
> Nor did her claws their clatter stay
> Until she reached the long saloon.
> There, tapping with her five gold rings,
> " Is Mrs. Reynard in ? " she sings.
> " If now she wants to wed again,
> She must come down the stairs, 'tis plain." '

Mrs. Reynard asked : ' Does the gentleman wear red breeches, and has he a pointed muzzle ? '

' No,' answered the Cat.

' Then he is no use to me.'

When the Wolf was rejected, there came a Dog, a Stag, a Hare, a Bear, and one after another every sort of wild animal. But in every one there was wanting some of the good qualities which old Mr. Reynard had possessed, and the Cat was obliged to dismiss the suitors every time.   At last there came a young Fox.   Then Mrs. Reynard asked : ' Does the gentleman wear red breeches, and has he got a pointed muzzle ? '

' Yes,' said the Cat.   ' He has both.'

' Then let him come up,' said Mrs. Reynard, and ordered the maid to make ready the wedding feast.

> ' Now, Cat, set to and sweep the room.
> Then fling the old Fox from the house ;
> Bring in many a good fat mouse,
> But eat them all yourself alone,
> Nor give your mistress e'er a one.'

THE MARRIAGE OF MRS. REYNARD

Then the wedding with young Mr. Fox was held, and there was merry-making and dancing, and if they haven't stopped, they are dancing still.

Does the gentleman wear red breeches,
and has he a pointed muzzle?

The Salad

THERE was once a merry young Huntsman, who went into the forest to hunt. He was gay and light-hearted, and whistled a tune upon a leaf as he went along.

Suddenly an ugly old Crone spoke to him, and said: ' Good morning, dear Huntsman ; you are merry and happy enough, while I am hungry and thirsty. Pray give me an alms.'

The Huntsman pitied the poor Old Woman, put his hand in his pocket, and made her a present according to his means.

Then he wanted to go on. But the Old Woman held him back, and said : ' Hark ye, dear Huntsman, I will make you a present because of your good heart. Go on your way, and you will come to a tree, on which nine birds are sitting. They will have a cloak in their claws, over which they are fighting. Take aim with your gun, and shoot into the middle of them. They will drop the cloak, and one of the birds will fall down dead. Take the cloak with you, it is a wishing-cloak. When you throw it round your shoulders you only have to wish your-self at a place to be there at once. Take the heart out of the dead bird and swallow it whole, then you will find a gold coin under your pillow every single morning when you wake.'

The Huntsman thanked the Wise Woman, and thought : ' She promises fine things, if only they turn out as well.'

When he had gone about a hundred paces, he heard above him, in the branches of a tree, such a chattering and screaming that he looked up.

There he saw a flock of birds tearing a garment with their

292

beaks and claws; snatching and tearing at it as if each one wanted to have it for himself.

'Well,' said the Huntsman, 'this is extraordinary, it is exactly what the Old Woman said.'

He put his gun to his shoulder, took aim and fired right into the middle of them, making the feathers fly about.

The birds took flight with a great noise, all except one, which fell down dead, and the cloak dropped at his feet.

He did as the Old Woman had told him, cut the heart out of the bird and swallowed it whole. Then he took the cloak home with him.

When he woke in the morning, he remembered the Old Woman's promise, and looked under his pillow to see if it was true.

There, sure enough, lay the golden coin shining before him, and the next morning he found another, and the same every morning when he got up.

He collected quite a heap of gold, and at last he thought : ' What is the good of all my gold if I stay at home here ? I will go and look about me in the world.'

So he took leave of his parents, shouldered his gun, and started off into the world.

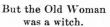

But the Old Woman was a witch.

It so happened that one day he came to a thick forest, and when he got through it, he saw a fine castle lying in the plain beyond.

He saw an Old Woman standing in one of the windows looking out, with a beautiful Maiden beside her.

But the Old Woman was a witch, and she said to the Maiden : ' Here comes some one out of the forest. He has a wonderful treasure inside him ; we must try to get it from him, my darling, it will suit us better than him. He has a bird's heart about him, and therefore he finds a gold coin every morning under his pillow when he wakes.'

She told the girl how he had got it, and at last said : ' If you don't get it from him, it will be the worse for you.'

When the Huntsman got nearer, he saw the Maiden, and said : ' I have been wandering about for a long time, I will go into this castle and take a rest. I have plenty of money.'

But the real reason was that he had caught sight of the pretty picture at the window. He went in, and he was kindly received and hospitably treated.

Before long, he was so enamoured of the Witch-Maiden that he thought of nothing else, and cared for nothing but pleasing her.

The Old Woman said to the Maiden : ' Now we must get the bird's heart, he will never miss it.'

They concocted a potion, and when it was ready they put it into a goblet.

And the Maiden took it to him, and said : ' Now, my beloved, you must drink to me.'

He took the cup and drank the potion, and when he was overpowered by it the bird's heart came out of his mouth.

The Maiden took it away secretly and swallowed it herself, for the Old Woman wanted to have it.

From this time the Huntsman found no more gold under his pillow ; but the coin was always under the Maiden's instead, and the Old Woman used to fetch it away every morning.

But he was so much in love, that he thought of nothing but enjoying himself in the Maiden's company.

Then the Old Woman said : ' We have got the bird's heart, but we must have his wishing-cloak too.'

The Maiden said : ' Let us leave him that ; we have taken away his wealth.'

The Old Woman was very angry, and said : ' A cloak like that is a very wonderful thing, and not often to be got. Have it I must, and will ! '

So she obeyed the Witch's orders, placed herself at the window, and looked sadly out at the distant hills.

The Huntsman said : ' Why are you so sad ? '

294

THE SALAD

' Alas ! my love,' was her answer, ' over there are the garnet mountains, where the precious stones are found. I long for them so much that I grow sad whenever I think of them. But who could ever get them ? The birds which fly, perhaps ; no mortal could ever reach them.'

' If that is all your trouble,' said the Huntsman, ' I can soon lift that load from your heart.'

Then he drew her under his cloak, and in a moment they were both sitting on the mountain. The precious stones were glittering around them ; their hearts rejoiced at the sight of them, and they soon gathered together some of the finest and largest.

Now the Witch had so managed that the Huntsman began to feel his eyes grow very heavy.

So he said to the Maiden : ' We will sit down to rest a while, I am so tired I can hardly stand.'

So they sat down, and he laid his head on her lap and was soon fast asleep.

As soon as he was asleep, the Maiden slipped the cloak from his shoulders and put it on her own, loaded herself with the precious garnets, and wished herself at home.

When the Huntsman had had his sleep out, he woke up and saw that his beloved had betrayed him, and left him alone on the wild mountain.

' Oh, what treachery there is in the world ! ' he exclaimed, as he sat down in grief, and did not know what to do.

Now the mountain belonged to some wild and savage Giants who lived on it, and before long he saw three of them striding along.

He quickly lay down again and pretended to be fast asleep.

The first one, as he came along, stumbled against him, and said : ' What kind of earthworm is this ? '

The second said : ' Tread on him and kill him.'

But the third said : ' It isn't worth the trouble. Let him alone,—he can't live here ; and when he climbs higher up the mountain, the clouds will roll down and carry him off.'

Then they passed on, and as soon as they were gone, the Huntsman, who had heard all they said, got up and climbed up to the top of the mountain.

After he had sat there for a time, a cloud floated over him, and carried him away.

At first he was swept through the air, but then he was gently lowered and deposited within a large walled garden, upon a soft bed of lettuces and other herbs.

He looked around him and said : ' If only I had something to eat ; I am so hungry. And it will be difficult to get away from here. I see neither apples nor pears, nor any other fruit, nothing but salad and herbs.'

At last, however, he thought : ' At the worst, I can eat some of this salad ; it does not taste very good, but it will, at least, be refreshing.'

He picked out a fine head of lettuce, and began eating it. But he had hardly swallowed a little piece, when he began to feel very odd, and quite changed. He felt four legs growing, a big head, and two long ears, and he saw to his horror that he was changed into an ass.

As he at the same time felt as hungry as ever, and the juicy salad was now very much to his taste, he went on eating greedily.

At last he reached another kind of salad, which he had hardly tasted when he felt a new change taking place, and found himself back in his human shape.

After this he lay down and slept off his fatigue.

When he woke next morning he broke off a head of the bad salad, and a head of the good, and thought : ' These will help me to regain my own, and also to punish the traitors.'

He put the salad into his wallet, climbed over the wall, and went off to find the castle of his beloved.

After wandering about for a few days, he was fortunate enough to find it. Then he stained his face, and disguised himself so that his own mother would not have known him, and went to the castle to ask for shelter.

296

THE SALAD

' I am so tired,' he said ; ' I cannot go any further.'

The Witch said : ' Who are you, countryman, and what do you want ? '

He answered : ' I am a messenger from the King. He sent me to find the rarest salad which grows under the sun. I have been lucky enough to find it, and I carry it with me. But the sun is so burning, that I am afraid the tender plant will be withered, and I don't know if I shall be able to take it any further.'

When the Old Witch heard about the rare salad, she felt a great desire to have some, and said : ' Good countryman, let me try the wonderful salad ! '

' By all means,' he answered. ' I have two heads with me, and you shall have one.' So saying, he opened his sack, and handed her the bad one.

The Witch had no suspicions, and her mouth so watered for the new dish, that she went to the kitchen herself to prepare it.

When it was ready, she could not wait till it was put upon the table, but put a few leaves into her mouth at once.

Hardly had she swallowed them, when she lost her human shape, and ran out into the courtyard, as an old she-ass.

Then the Maid came into the kitchen, saw the salad standing ready, and was about to put it on the table. But on the way the fancy seized her to taste it, according to her usual habit, and she ate a few leaves.

The power of the salad at once became apparent, because she also turned into an ass, and ran out into the yard to join the Old Witch, while the dish of salad fell to the ground.

In the meantime the messenger was sitting with the beautiful Maiden, and as no one appeared with the salad, she also was seized with a desire to taste it, and said : ' I don't know what has become of the salad.'

But the Huntsman thought : ' The plant must have done its work,' and said : ' I will go into the kitchen and see.'

As soon as he got downstairs he saw the two asses running about, and the salad lying on the ground.

'This is all right!' he said; 'two of them are done for.'

Then he picked up the leaves, put them on a dish, and took them to the Maiden.

'I am bringing the precious food to you myself,' said he, 'so that you may not have to wait any longer.'

She ate some, and, like the others, was immediately changed into an ass, and ran out to them in the yard.

He tied them all together and drove them along till he came to a mill.

When the Huntsman had washed his face so that the transformed creatures might know him, he went into the court-yard, and said: 'Now, you shall be paid for your treachery.'

He tied them all together with a rope, and drove them along till he came to a mill. He tapped at the window, and the Miller put his head out and asked what he wanted.

298

THE SALAD

' I have three bad animals here,' he said, ' that I want to get rid of. If you will take them and feed them, and treat them as I wish, I will pay you what you like to ask.'

' Why not ? ' said the Miller. ' How do you want them treated ? '

The Huntsman said he wanted the old she-ass (the Witch) to be well beaten three times a day and fed once. The younger one, which was the Maid, beaten once and fed three times. The youngest of all, who was the beautiful Maiden, was to be fed three times, and not beaten at all ; he could not find it in his heart to have her beaten.

Then he went back to the castle and found everything he wanted in it.

A few days later the Miller came and told him that the old ass which was to be beaten three times and fed once, was dead. ' The other two,' he said, ' which are to be fed three times, are not dead, but they are pining away, and won't last long.'

The Huntsman's heart was stirred with pity, and he told the Miller to bring them back to him.

When they came he gave them some of the other salad to eat, so that they took their human shapes again.

The beautiful Maiden fell on her knees before him, and said : ' O my beloved, forgive me all the wrong I have done you. My mother forced me to do it. It was against my own will, for I love you dearly. Your wishing-cloak is hanging in the cupboard, and you shall have the bird's heart back too.'

But he said : ' Keep it ; it will be all the same, as I will take you to be my own true wife.'

Their marriage was soon after celebrated, and they lived happily together till they died.

The Youth who could not Shudder

THERE was once a Father who had two sons. One was clever and sensible, and always knew how to get on. But the younger one was stupid, and could not learn anything, and he had no imagination.

When people saw him, they said : ' His Father will have plenty of trouble with him.'

Whenever there was anything to be done, the eldest one always had to do it. But if his Father sent him to fetch anything late in the evening, or at night, and the way lay through the churchyard, or any other dreary place, he would answer : ' Oh no, Father, not there ; it makes me shudder ! ' For he was afraid.

In the evening, when stories were being told round the fire which made one's flesh creep, and the listeners said : ' Oh, you make me shudder ! ' the youngest son, sitting in the corner listening, could not imagine what they meant. ' They always say " It makes me shudder ! It makes me shudder ! " And it doesn't make me shudder a bit. It must be some art which I can't understand.'

Now it happened one day that his Father said to him : ' I say, you in the corner there, you are growing big and strong. You must learn something by which you can make a living. See what pains your brother takes, but you are not worth your salt.'

' Well, Father,' he answered, ' I am quite ready to learn something ; nay, I should very much like to learn how to shudder, for I know nothing about that.'

The elder son laughed when he heard him, and thought :
300

' Good heavens ! what a fool my brother is ; he will never do any good as long as he lives.'

But his Father sighed, and answered : ' You will easily enough learn how to shudder, but you won't make your bread by it.'

Soon after, the Sexton came to the house on a visit, and the Father confided his troubles about his son to him. He told him how stupid he was, and how he never could learn anything. ' Would you believe that when I asked him how he was going to make his living, he said he would like to learn how to shudder ? '

' If that 's all,' said the Sexton, ' he may learn that from me. Just let me have him, and I 'll soon put the polish on him.'

The Father was pleased, for he thought : ' Anyhow, the Lad will gain something by it.'

So the Sexton took him home with him, and he had to ring the church bells.

A few days after, the Sexton woke him at midnight, and told him to get up and ring the bells. ' You shall soon be taught how to shudder ! ' he thought, as he crept stealthily up the stairs beforehand.

When the Lad got up into the tower, and turned round to catch hold of the bell rope, he saw a white figure standing on the steps opposite the belfry window.

' Who is there ? ' he cried ; but the figure neither moved nor answered.

' Answer,' cried the Lad, ' or get out of the way. You have no business here in the night.'

But so that the Lad should think he was a ghost, the Sexton did not stir.

The Lad cried for the second time : ' What do you want here ? Speak if you are an honest fellow, or I 'll throw you down the stairs.'

The Sexton did not think he would go to such lengths, so he made no sound, and stood as still as if he were made of stone.

Then the Lad called to him the third time, and, as he had

no answer, he took a run and threw the ghost down the stairs. It fell down ten steps, and remained lying in a corner.

Then he rang the bells, went home, and, without saying a word to anybody, went to bed and was soon fast asleep.

The Sexton's wife waited a long time for her husband, but, as he never came back, she got frightened, and woke up the Lad.

'Don't you know what has become of my husband?' she asked. 'He went up into the church tower before you.'

'No,' answered the Lad. 'There was somebody standing on the stairs opposite the belfry window, and, as he would neither answer me nor go away, I took him to be a rogue and threw him downstairs. Go and see if it was your husband; I should be sorry if it were.'

The woman hurried away and found her husband lying in the corner, moaning, with a broken leg. She carried him down, and then hastened with loud cries to the Lad's father.

'Your son has brought about a great misfortune; he has thrown my husband downstairs and broken his leg. Take the good-for-nothing fellow away, out of our house.'

The Father was horrified, and, going back with her, gave the Lad a good scolding.

'What is the meaning of this inhuman prank? The evil one must have put it into your head.'

'Father,' answered the Lad, 'just listen to me. I am quite innocent. He stood there in the dark, like a man with some wicked design. I did not know who it was, and I warned him three times to speak, or to go away!'

'Alas!' said his Father, 'you bring me nothing but disaster. Go away out of my sight. I will have nothing more to do with you.'

'Gladly, Father. Only wait till daylight; then I will go away, and learn to shudder. Then, at least, I shall have one art to make my living by.'

'Learn what you like,' said his Father. 'It's all the same to me. Here are fifty thalers for you. Go out into the world, and don't tell a creature where you come from, or who your Father is, for you will only bring me to shame.'

' Just as you please, Father. If that is all you want, I can easily fulfil your desire.'

At daybreak, the Lad put his fifty thalers into his pocket, and went out along the high road, repeating over and over to himself as he went : ' If only I could shudder, if only I could shudder.'

A Man came by and overheard the words the Lad was saying to himself, and when they had gone a little further, and came within sight of the gallows, he said : ' See, there is the tree where those seven have been wedded to the ropemaker's daughter, and are now learning to fly. Sit down below them, and when night comes you will soon learn to shudder.'

' If nothing more than that is needed,' said the Lad, ' it is easily done. And if I learn to shudder as easily as that, you shall have my fifty thalers. Come back to me early to-morrow morning.'

Then the Lad went up to the gallows, and sat down under them to wait till night came.

As he was cold he lighted a fire, but at midnight the wind grew so cold that he did not know how to keep himself warm.

The wind blew the men on the gallows backwards and forwards, and swung them against each other, so he thought : ' Here am I freezing by the fire, how much colder they must be up there.'

And as he was very compassionate, he mounted the ladder, undid them, and brought all seven down one by one.

Then he blew up the fire, and placed them round it to warm themselves.

They sat there and never moved, even when the fire caught their clothing.

' Take care, or I will hang you all up again.'

The dead men, of course, could not hear, and remained silent while their few rags were burnt up.

Then he grew angry, and said : ' If you won't take care of

yourselves, I can't help you, and I won't be burnt with you.'

So he hung them all up again in a row, and sat down by the fire and went to sleep again.

Next morning, the Man, wanting to get his fifty thalers, came to him and said : ' Now do you know what shuddering means ? '

' No,' he said ; ' how should I have learnt it ? Those fellows up there never opened their mouths, and they were so stupid that they let the few poor rags they had about them burn.'

Then the Man saw that no thalers would be his that day, and he went away, saying : ' Never in my life have I seen such a fellow as this.'

The Lad also went on his way, and again began saying to himself : ' Oh, if only I could learn to shudder, if only I could learn to shudder.'

A Carter, walking behind him, heard this, and asked : ' Who are you ? '

' I don't know,' answered the Youth.

' Who is your Father ? '

' That I must not say.'

' What are you always mumbling in your beard ? '

' Ah,' answered the Youth, ' I want to learn to shudder, but no one can teach me.'

' Stop your silly chatter,' said the Carter. ' Just you come with me, and I 'll see that you have what you want.'

The Youth went with the Carter, and in the evening they reached an inn, where they meant to pass the night. He said quite loud, as they entered : ' Oh, if only I could learn to shudder, if only I could learn to shudder.'

The Landlord, who heard him, laughed, and said : ' If that 's what you want, there should be plenty of opportunity for you here.'

' I will have nothing to say to it,' said the Landlady. ' So many a prying fellow has already paid the penalty with his life.

THE YOUTH WHO COULD NOT SHUDDER

It would be a sin and a shame if those bright eyes should not see the light of day again.'

But the Youth said : ' I will learn it somehow, however hard it may be. I have been driven out for not knowing it.'

He gave the Landlord no peace till he told him that there was an enchanted castle a little way off, where any one could be made to shudder, if he would pass three nights in it.

The King had promised his daughter to wife to any one who dared do it, and she was the prettiest maiden the sun had ever shone on.

There were also great treasures hidden in the castle, watched over by evil spirits, enough to make any poor man rich who could break the spell.

Already many had gone in, but none had ever come out.

Next morning the Youth went to the King, and said : ' By your leave, I should like to pass three nights in the enchanted castle.'

The King looked at him, and, as he took a fancy to him, he said : ' You may ask three things to take into the castle with you, but they must be lifeless things.'

He answered : ' Then I ask for a fire, a turning-lathe, and a cooper's bench with the knife.'

The King had all three carried into the castle for him.

When night fell, the Youth went up to the castle and made a bright fire in one of the rooms. He put the cooper's bench with the knife near the fire, and seated himself on the turning-lathe.

' Oh, if only I could shudder,' he said ; ' but I shan't learn it here either.'

Towards midnight he wanted to make up the fire, and, as he was blowing it up, something in one corner began to shriek : ' Miau, miau, how cold we are ! '

' You fools ! ' he cried. ' What do you shriek for ? If you are cold, come and warm yourselves by the fire.'

As he spoke, two big black cats bounded up and sat down, one on each side of him, and stared at him with wild, fiery eyes.

305

After a time, when they had warmed themselves, they said : ' Comrade, shall we have a game of cards ? '

' Why not ? ' he answered ; ' but show me your paws first.'

Then they stretched out their claws.

' Why,' he said, ' what long nails you 've got. Wait a bit ; I must cut them for you.'

He seized them by the scruff of their necks, lifted them on to the cooper's bench, and screwed their paws firmly to it.

Crowds of black cats and dogs swarmed out of every corner.

' I have looked at your fingers, and the desire to play cards with you has passed.'

Then he killed them and threw them out into the moat.

306

But no sooner had he got rid of these two cats, and was about to sit down by his fire again, than crowds of black cats and dogs swarmed out of every corner, more and more of them.

They howled horribly, and trampled on his fire, and tried to put it out.

For a time he looked quietly on, but when it grew too bad he seized his cooper's knife, and cried: 'Away with you, you rascally pack,' and let fly among them right and left. Some of them sprang away, the others he killed, and threw them out into the water.

When he came back he scraped the embers of his fire together again, and warmed himself. He could hardly keep his eyes open, and felt the greatest desire to go to sleep. He looked round, and in one corner he saw a big bed.

'That's the very thing,' he said, and lay down in it. As soon as he closed his eyes, the bed began to move, and soon it was tearing round and round the castle. 'Very good!' he said. 'The faster the better!' The bed rolled on as if it were dragged by six horses; over thresholds and stairs, up and down.

Suddenly it went hop, hop, hop, and turned topsy-turvy, so that it lay upon him like a mountain. But he pitched the pillows and blankets into the air, slipped out of it, and said: 'Now any one may ride who likes.'

Then he lay down by his fire and slept till daylight.

In the morning the King came, and when he saw him lying on the floor, he thought the ghosts had killed him, and he was dead. So he said: 'It's a sad pity, for such a handsome fellow.'

But the Youth heard him, and sat up, saying: 'It has not come to that yet.'

The King was surprised and delighted, and asked him how he had got on.

'Pretty well!' he answered. 'One night is gone, I suppose I shall get through the others too.'

When the Landlord saw him he opened his eyes, and said:

'I never thought I should see you alive again. Have you learnt how to shudder now?'

'No,' he answered; 'it's all in vain. If only some one would tell me how.'

The second night came, and up he went again and sat down by the fire, and began his old song: 'Oh, if only I could learn to shudder.'

In the middle of the night a great noise and uproar began, first soft, and then growing louder; then for a short time there would be silence.

At last, with a loud scream, half the body of a man fell down the chimney in front of him.

'Hullo!' he said, 'another half is wanting here; this is too little.'

The noise began again, and, amidst shrieks and howls, the other half fell down.

'Wait a bit,' he said; 'I'll blow up the fire.'

When this was done, and he looked round, the two halves had come together, and a hideous man sat in his place.

'We didn't bargain for that,' said the Youth. 'The bench is mine.'

The man wanted to push him out of the way, but the Youth would not have it, flung him aside, and took his own seat.

Then more men fell down the chimney, one after the other, and they fetched nine human shin bones and two skulls, and began to play skittles.

The Youth felt inclined to join them, and cried: 'I say, can I play too?'

'Yes, if you've got any money.'

'Money enough,' he answered, 'but your balls aren't quite round.'

Then he took the skulls and turned them on the lathe till they were quite round. 'Now they will roll better,' he said. 'Here goes! The more, the merrier!'

So he played with them, and lost some money, but when it

struck twelve everything disappeared. He lay down, and was soon fast asleep.

Next morning the King came again to look after him, and said : ' Well, how did you get on this time ? '

' I played skittles,' he answered, ' and lost a few coins.'

' Didn't you learn to shudder ? '

' Not I. I only made merry. Oh, if I could but find out how to shudder.'

On the third night he again sat down on his bench, and said quite savagely : ' If only I could shudder ! '

When it grew late, six tall men came in, carrying a bier, and he said : ' Hullo there ! That must be my cousin who died a few days ago.' And he beckoned and said : ' Come along, cousin, come along.'

The men put the coffin on the floor, and he went up and took the lid off, and there lay a dead man. He felt the face, and it was as cold as ice. ' Wait,' he said ; ' I will warm him.'

Then he went to the fire and warmed his hand, and laid it on his face, but the dead man remained cold. He took him out of the coffin, sat down by the fire, and took him on his knees, and rubbed his arms to make the blood circulate.

But it was all no good. Next, it came into his head that if two people were in bed together, they warmed each other. So he put the dead man in the bed, covered him up, and lay down beside him.

After a time the dead man grew warm, and began to move.

Then the Youth said : ' There, you see, cousin mine, have I not warmed you ? '

But the Man rose up, and cried : ' Now, I will strangle you ! '

' What ! ' said he, ' are those all the thanks I get. Back you go into your coffin then.' So saying, he lifted him up, threw him in, and fastened down the lid. Then the six men came back and carried the coffin away.

' I cannot shudder,' he said ; ' and I shall never learn it here.'

Just then a huge Man appeared. He was frightful to look at, old, and with a long white beard.

'Oh, you miserable wight!' he cried. 'You shall soon learn what shuddering is, for you shall die.'

'Not so fast,' said the Youth. 'If I am to die, I must be present.'

'I will make short work of you,' said the old monster.

'Softly! softly! don't you boast. I am as strong as you, and very likely much stronger.'

'We shall see about that,' said the Old Man. 'If you are the stronger, I will let you go. Come; we will try.'

Then he led him through numberless dark passages to a smithy, took an axe, and with one blow struck one of the anvils into the earth.

'I can better that,' said the Youth, and went to the other anvil. The Old Man placed himself near to see, and his white beard hung over.

Then the Youth took the axe and split the anvil with one blow, catching in the Old Man's beard at the same time.

'Now, I have you fast,' said the Youth, 'and you will be the one to die.'

Then he seized an iron rod, and belaboured the Old Man with it, till he shrieked for mercy, and promised him great riches if he would stop.

Then the Youth pulled out the axe and released him, and the Old Man led him back into the castle, and showed him three chests of gold in a cellar.

'One is for the poor,' he said, 'one for the King, and one for you.'

The clock struck twelve, and the ghost disappeared, leaving the Youth in the dark.

'I must manage to get out somehow,' he said, and groped about till he found his way back to his room, where he lay down by the fire and went to sleep.

Next morning the King came and said: 'Now you must have learnt how to shudder.'

The good little Sister cut off her own tiny finger, fitted it into
the lock, and succeeded in opening it.

But they said one after another: 'Halloa! who has been eating off my
plate?   Who has been drinking out of my cup?'

Then the Youth took the axe and split the anvil with one blow,
catching in the Old Man's beard at the same time.

The Beggar took her by the hand and led her away.

'No,' said he. 'What can it be? My dead cousin was there, and an Old Man with a beard came and showed me a lot of gold. But what shuddering is, that no man can tell me.'

Then said the King: 'You have broken the spell on the castle, and you shall marry my daughter.'

'That is all very well,' he said; 'but still I don't know what shuddering is.'

The gold was got out of the castle, and the marriage was celebrated, but, happy as the young King was, and much as he loved his wife, he was always saying: 'Oh, if only I could learn to shudder, if only I could learn to shudder.'

At last his wife was vexed by it, and her waiting-woman said: 'I can help you; he shall be taught the meaning of shuddering.'

And she went out to the brook which ran through the garden and got a pail full of cold water and little fishes.

At night, when the young King was asleep, his wife took the coverings off and poured the cold water over him, and all the little fishes flopped about him.

Then he woke up, and cried: 'Oh, how I am shuddering, dear wife, how I am shuddering! Now I know what shuddering is!'

King Thrushbeard

THERE was once a King who had a Daughter. She was more beautiful than words can tell, but at the same time so proud and haughty that no man who came to woo her was good enough for her. She turned away one after another, and even mocked them.

One day her father ordered a great feast to be given, and invited to it all the marriageable young men from far and near.

They were all placed in a row, according to their rank and position. First came Kings, then Princes, then Dukes, Earls, and Barons.

The Princess was led through the ranks, but she had some fault to find with all of them.

One was too stout. 'That barrel!' she said. The next was too tall. 'Long and lean is no good!' The third was too short. 'Short and stout, can't turn about!' The fourth was too white. 'Pale as death!' The fifth was too red. 'Turkey-cock!' The sixth was not straight. 'Oven-dried!'

So there was something against each of them. But she made specially merry over one good King, who stood quite at the head of the row, and whose chin was a little hooked.

'Why!' she cried, 'he has a chin like the beak of a thrush.'

After that, he was always called 'King Thrushbeard.'

When the old King saw that his Daughter only made fun of them, and despised all the suitors who were assembled, he was very angry, and swore that the first beggar who came to the door should be her husband.

A few days after, a wandering Musician began to sing at the window, hoping to receive charity.

When the King heard him, he said : 'Let him be brought in.'

312

KING THRUSHBEARD

The Musician came in, dressed in dirty rags, and sang to the King and his Daughter, and when he had finished, he begged alms of them.

The King said : ' Your song has pleased me so much, that I will give you my Daughter to be your wife.'

The Princess was horror-stricken. But the King said : ' I have sworn an oath to give you to the first beggar who came ; and I will keep my word.'

No entreaties were of any avail. A Parson was brought, and she had to marry the Musician there and then.

When the marriage was completed, the King said : ' Now you are a beggar-woman, you can't stay in my castle any longer. You must go away with your Husband.'

The Beggar took her by the hand and led her away, and she was obliged to go with him on foot.

When they came to a big wood, she asked :

> ' Ah ! who is the Lord of this forest so fine ? '
> ' It belongs to King Thrushbeard. It might have been thine,
> If his Queen you had been.'
> ' Ah ! sad must I sing !
> I would I 'd accepted the hand of the King.'

After that they reached a great meadow, and she asked again :

> ' Ah ! who is the Lord of these meadows so fine ? '
> ' They belong to King Thrushbeard, and would have been thine,
> If his Queen you had been.'
> ' Ah ! sad must I sing !
> I would I 'd accepted the love of the King.'

Then they passed through a large town, and again she asked :

> ' Ah ! who is the Lord of this city so fine ? '
> ' It belongs to King Thrushbeard, and it might have been thine,
> If his Queen you had been.'
> ' Ah ! sad must I sing !
> I would I 'd accepted the heart of the King.'

'It doesn't please me at all,' said the Musician, 'that you are always wishing for another husband. Am I not good enough for you?'

At last they came to a miserable little hovel, and she said:

> 'Ah, heavens! what's this house, so mean and small?
> This wretched little hut's no house at all.'

The Musician answered: 'This is my house, and yours; where we are to live together.'

The door was so low that she had to stoop to get in.

'Where are the servants?' asked the Princess.

'Servants indeed!' answered the Beggar. 'Whatever you want done, you must do for yourself. Light the fire, and put the kettle on to make my supper. I am very tired.'

But the Princess knew nothing about lighting fires or cooking, and to get it done at all, the Beggar had to do it himself.

When they had finished their humble fare, they went to bed. But in the morning the Man made her get up very early to do the housework.

They lived like this for a few days, till they had eaten up all their store of food.

Then the Man said: 'Wife, this won't do any longer; we can't live here without working. You shall make baskets.'

So he went out and cut some osiers, and brought them home. She began to weave them, but the hard osiers bruised her tender hands.

'I see that won't do,' said the Beggar. 'You had better spin; perhaps you can manage that.'

So she sat down and tried to spin, but the harsh yarn soon cut her delicate fingers and made them bleed.

'Now you see,' said the Man, 'what a good-for-nothing you are. I have made a bad bargain in you. But I will try to start a trade in earthenware. You must sit in the market and offer your goods for sale.'

'Alas!' she thought, 'if any of the people from my father's kingdom come and see me sitting in the market-place, offering

314

goods for sale, they will scoff at me.' But it was no good. She had to obey, unless she meant to die of hunger.

All went well the first time. The people willingly bought her wares because she was so handsome, and they paid what she asked them—nay, some even gave her the money and left her the pots as well.

They lived on the gains as long as they lasted, and then the Man laid in a new stock of wares.

She took her seat in a corner of the market, set out her crockery about her, and began to cry her wares.

Suddenly, a drunken Hussar came galloping up, and rode right in among the pots, breaking them into thousands of bits.

She began to cry, and was so frightened that she did not know what to do. 'Oh! what will become of me?' she cried. 'What will my Husband say to me?' She ran home, and told him her misfortune.

'Who would ever think of sitting at the corner of the market with crockery?' he said. 'Stop that crying. I see you are no manner of use for any decent kind of work. I have been to our King's palace, and asked if they do not want a kitchen wench, and they have promised to try you. You will get your victuals free, at any rate.'

So the Princess became a kitchen wench, and had to wait upon the Cook and do all the dirty work. She fixed a pot into each of her pockets, and in them took home her share of the scraps and leavings, and upon these they lived.

It so happened that the marriage of the eldest Princess just then took place, and the poor Woman went upstairs and stood behind the door to peep at all the splendour.

When the rooms were lighted up, and she saw the guests streaming in, one more beautiful than the other, and the scene grew more and more brilliant, she thought, with a heavy heart, of her sad fate. She cursed the pride and haughtiness which had been the cause of her humiliation, and of her being brought to such depths.

Every now and then the Servants would throw her bits from

the savoury dishes they were carrying away from the feast, and these she put into her pots to take home with her.

All at once the King's son came in. He was dressed in silk and velvet, and he had a golden chain round his neck.

When he saw the beautiful Woman standing at the door, he seized her by the hand, and wanted to dance with her.

But she shrank and refused, because she saw that it was King Thrushbeard, who had been one of the suitors for her hand, and whom she had most scornfully driven away.

Her resistance was no use, and he dragged her into the hall. The string by which her pockets were suspended broke. Down fell the pots, and the soup and savoury morsels were spilt all over the floor.

When the guests saw it, they burst into shouts of mocking laughter.

She was so ashamed, that she would gladly have sunk into the earth. She rushed to the door, and tried to escape, but on the stairs a Man stopped her and brought her back.

When she looked at him, it was no other than King Thrushbeard again.

He spoke kindly to her, and said : 'Do not be afraid. I and the Beggar-Man, who lived in the poor little hovel with you, are one and the same. For love of you I disguised myself ; and I was also the Hussar who rode among your pots. All this I did to bend your proud spirit, and to punish you for the haughtiness with which you mocked me.'

She wept bitterly, and said : 'I was very wicked, and I am not worthy to be your wife.'

But he said : 'Be happy ! Those evil days are over. Now we will celebrate our true wedding.'

The waiting-women came and put rich clothing upon her, and her Father, with all his Court, came and wished her joy on her marriage with King Thrushbeard.

Then, in truth, her happiness began. I wish we had been there to see it, you and I.

Iron Hans

THERE was once a King whose castle was surrounded by a forest full of game. One day he sent a Huntsman out to shoot a deer, but he never came back.

'Perhaps an accident has happened to him,' said the King.

Next day he sent out two more Huntsmen to look for him, but they did not return either. On the third day he sent for all his Huntsmen, and said to them, 'Search the whole forest without ceasing, until you have found all three.'

But not a single man of all these, or one of the pack of hounds they took with them, ever came back. From this time forth no one would venture into the forest; so there it lay, wrapped in silence and solitude, with only an occasional eagle or hawk circling over it.

This continued for several years, and then one day a strange Huntsman sought an audience of the King, and offered to penetrate into the dangerous wood. The King, however, would not give him permission, and said, ' It 's not safe, and I am afraid if you go in that you will never come out again, any more than all the others.'

The Huntsman answered, ' Sire, I will take the risk upon myself. I do not know fear.'

So the Huntsman went into the wood with his Dog. Before long the Dog put up some game, and wanted to chase it; but hardly had he taken a few steps when he came to a deep pool, and could go no further. A naked arm appeared out of the water, seized him, and drew him down.

When the Huntsman saw this, he went back and fetched three men with pails to empty the pool. When they got to the bottom they found a Wild Man, whose body was as brown as rusty iron, and his hair hanging down over his face to his

317

knees. They bound him with cords, and carried him away to the castle. There was great excitement over the Wild Man, and the King had an iron cage made for him in the courtyard. He forbade any one to open the door of the cage on pain of death, and the Queen had to keep the key in her own charge.

After this, anybody could walk in the forest with safety.

The King had a little son eight years old, and one day he was playing in the courtyard. In his play his golden ball fell into the cage. The boy ran up, and said, 'Give me back my ball.'

'Not until you have opened the door,' said the Wild Man.

'No; I can't do that,' said the boy. 'My father has forbidden it,' and then he ran away.

Next day he came again, and asked for his ball. The Man said, 'Open my door'; but he would not.

On the third day the King went out hunting, and the boy came again, and said, 'Even if I would, I could not open the door. I have not got the key.'

Then the Wild Man said, 'It is lying under your mother's pillow. You can easily get it.'

The boy, who was very anxious to have his ball back, threw his scruples to the winds, and fetched the key. The door was very stiff, and he pinched his fingers in opening it. As soon as it was open the Wild Man came out, gave the boy his ball, and hurried away. The boy was now very frightened, and cried out, 'O Wild Man, don't go away, or I shall be beaten!'

The Wild Man turned back, picked up the boy, put him on his shoulder, and walked hurriedly off into the wood.

When the King came home he saw at once the cage was empty, and asked the Queen how it had come about. She knew nothing about it, and went to look for the key, which was of course gone. They called the boy, but there was no answer. The King sent people out into the fields to look for him, but all in vain; he was gone. The King easily guessed what had happened, and great grief fell on the royal household.

When the Wild Man got back into the depths of the dark

318

forest he took the boy down off his shoulder, and said, ' You will never see your father and mother again ; but I will keep you here with me, because you had pity on me and set me free. If you do as you are told, you will be well treated. I have treasures and gold enough and to spare, more than anybody in the world.'

He made a bed of moss for the boy, on which he went to sleep. Next morning the Man led him to a spring, and said, ' You see this golden well is bright and clear as crystal ? You must sit by it, and take care that nothing falls into it, or it will be contaminated. I shall come every evening to see if you have obeyed my orders.'

The boy sat down on the edge of the spring to watch it ; sometimes he would see a gold fish or a golden snake darting through it, and he guarded it well, so that nothing should fall into it. One day as he was sitting like this his finger pained him so much that involuntarily he dipped it into the water. He drew it out very quickly, but saw that it was gilded, and although he tried hard to clean it, it remained golden. In the evening Iron Hans came back, looked at the boy, and said, ' What has happened to the well to-day ? '

' Nothing, nothing ! ' he answered, keeping his finger behind his back, so that Iron Hans should not see it.

But he said, ' You have dipped your finger into the water. It does not matter this time, but take care that nothing of the kind occurs again.'

Early next morning the boy took his seat by the spring again to watch. His finger still hurt very much, and he put his hand up above his head ; but, unfortunately, in so doing he brushed a hair into the well. He quickly took it out, but it was already gilded. When Iron Hans came in the evening, he knew very well what had happened.

' You have let a hair fall into the well,' he said. ' I will overlook it once more, but if it happens for the third time, the well will be polluted, and you can no longer stay with me.'

On the third day the boy again sat by the well ; but he took

319

good care not to move a finger, however much it might hurt. The time seemed very long to him as he looked at his face reflected in the water. As he bent over further and further to look into his eyes, his long hair fell over his shoulder right into the water. He started up at once, but not before his whole head of hair had become golden, and glittered like the sun. You may imagine how frightened the poor boy was. He took his pocket-handkerchief and tied it over his head, so that Iron Hans should not see it. But he knew all about it before he came, and at once said, ' Take that handkerchief off your head,' and then all the golden hair tumbled out. All the poor boy's excuses were no good. ' You have not stood the test, and you can no longer stay here. You must go out into the world, and there you will learn the meaning of poverty. But as your heart is not bad, and as I wish you well, I will grant you one thing. When you are in great need, go to the forest and cry " Iron Hans," and I will come and help you. My power is great, greater than you think, and I have gold and silver in abundance.'

So the King's son left the forest, and wandered over trodden and untrodden paths till he reached a great city. He tried to get work, but he could not find any ; besides, he knew no trade by which to make a living. At last he went to the castle and asked if they would employ him. The courtiers did not know what use they could make of him, but they were taken with his appearance, and said he might stay. At last the Cook took him into his service, and said he might carry wood and water for him, and sweep up the ashes.

One day, as there was no one else at hand, the Cook ordered him to carry the food up to the royal table. As he did not want his golden hair to be seen, he kept his cap on. Nothing of the sort had ever happened in the presence of the King before, and he said, ' When you come into the royal presence, you must take your cap off.'

' Alas, Sire,' he said, ' I cannot take it off, I have a bad wound on my head.'

Then the King ordered the Cook to be called, and asked how

320

he could take such a boy into his service, and ordered him to
be sent away at once.   But the Cook was sorry for him, and
exchanged him with the Gardener's boy.

Now the boy had to dig and hoe, plant and water, in every
kind of weather.   One day in the summer, when he was working alone in the garden, it was
very hot, and he took off his
cap for the fresh air to cool
his head.   When the sun
shone on his hair it glittered
so that the beams penetrated
right into the Princess's bedroom, and she sprang up to
see what it was.   She discovered the youth, and called
to him, ' Bring me a nosegay,
young man.'

He hurriedly put on his
cap, picked a lot of wild
flowers, and tied them up.
On his way up to the Princess,
the Gardener met him, and
said, ' How can you take such
poor flowers to the Princess ?
Quickly cut another bouquet,
and mind they are the choic-
est and rarest flowers.'

' Oh no,' said the youth.
' The wild flowers have a
sweeter scent, and will please
her better.'

She immediately clutched at his cap to pull it
off; but he held it on with both hands.

As soon as he went into the room the Princess said, ' Take
off your cap ; it is not proper for you to wear it before me.'

He answered again, ' I may not take it off, because I have a
wound on my head.'

But she took hold of the cap, and pulled it off, and all his

321

golden hair tumbled over his shoulders in a shower. It was quite a sight. He tried to get away, but she took hold of his arm, and gave him a handful of ducats. He took them, but he cared nothing for the gold, and gave it to the Gardener for his children to play with.

Next day the Princess again called him to bring her a bunch of wild flowers, and when he brought it she immediately clutched at his cap to pull it off; but he held it on with both hands. Again she gave him a handful of ducats, but he would not keep them, and gave them to the Gardener's children. The

He called three times, 'Iron Hans, as loud as he could.

third day the same thing happened, but she could not take off his cap, and he would not keep the gold.

Not long after this the kingdom was invaded. The King assembled his warriors. He did not know whether they would be able to conquer his enemies or not, as they were very powerful, and had a mighty army. Then the Gardener's assistant said, 'I have been brought up to fight; give me a horse, and I will go too.'

The others laughed and said, 'When we are gone, find one for yourself. We will leave one behind in the stable for you.'

When they were gone, he went and got the horse out; it was lame in one leg, and hobbled along, humpety-hump, humpety-hump. Nevertheless, he mounted it and rode away to the dark forest. When he came to the edge of it, he called three times, 'Iron Hans,' as loud as he could, till the trees resounded with it.

The Wild Man appeared immediately, and said, 'What do you want?'

322

IRON HANS

' I want a strong horse to go to the war.'

' You shall have it, and more besides.'

The Wild Man went back into the wood, and before long a Groom came out, leading a fiery charger with snorting nostrils. Behind him followed a great body of warriors, all in armour, and their swords gleaming in the sun. The youth handed over his three-legged steed to the Groom, mounted the other, and rode away at the head of the troop.

When he approached the battle-field a great many of the King's men had already fallen, and before long the rest must have given in. Then the youth, at the head of his iron troop, charged, and bore down the enemy like a mighty wind, smiting everything which came in their way. They tried to fly, but the youth fell upon them, and did not stop while one remained alive.

Instead of joining the King, he led his troop straight back to the wood and called Iron Hans again.

' What do you want ? ' asked the Wild Man.

' Take back your charger and your troop, and give me back my three-legged steed.'

His request was granted, and he rode his three-legged steed home.

When the King returned to the castle his daughter met him and congratulated him on his victory.

' It was not I who won it,' he said ; ' but a strange Knight, who came to my assistance with his troop.' His daughter asked who the strange Knight was, but the King did not know, and said, ' He pursued the enemy, and I have not seen him since.'

She asked the Gardener about his assistant, but he laughed, and said, ' He has just come home on his three-legged horse, and the others made fun of him, and said, " Here comes our hobbler back again," and asked which hedge he had been sleeping under. He answered, " I did my best, and without me things would have gone badly." Then they laughed at him more than ever.'

The King said to his daughter, 'I will give a great feast lasting three days, and you shall throw a golden apple. Perhaps the unknown Knight will come among the others to try and catch it.'

When notice was given of the feast, the youth went to the wood and called Iron Hans.

'What do you want?' he asked.

'I want to secure the King's golden apple,' he said.

'It is as good as yours already,' answered Iron Hans. 'You shall have a tawny suit, and ride a proud chestnut.'

When the day arrived the youth took his place among the other Knights, but no one knew him. The Princess stepped forward and threw the apple among the Knights, and he was the only one who could catch it. As soon as he had it he rode away.

On the second day Iron Hans fitted him out as a White Knight, riding a gallant grey. Again he caught the apple; but he did not stay a minute, and, as before, hurried away.

The King now grew angry, and said, 'This must not be; he must come before me and give me his name.'

He gave an order that if the Knight made off again he was to be pursued and brought back.

On the third day the youth received from Iron Hans a black outfit, and a fiery black charger.

Again he caught the apple; but as he was riding off with it the King's people chased him, and one came so near that he wounded him in the leg. Still he escaped, but his horse galloped so fast that his helmet fell off, and they all saw that he had golden hair. So they rode back, and told the King what they had seen.

Next day the Princess asked the Gardener about his assistant.

'He is working in the garden. The queer fellow went to the feast, and he only came back last night. He has shown my children three golden apples which he won.'

The King ordered him to be brought before him. When he

appeared he still wore his cap. But the Princess went up to him and took it off; then all his golden hair fell over his shoulders, and it was so beautiful that they were all amazed by it.

'Are you the Knight who came to the feast every day in a different colour, and who caught the three golden apples?' asked the King.

'Yes,' he answered, 'and here are the apples,' bringing them out of his pocket, and giving them to the King. 'If you want further proof, here is the wound in my leg given me by your people when they pursued me. But I am also the Knight who helped you to conquer the enemy.'

'If you can do such deeds you are no Gardener's boy. Tell me who is your father?'

'My father is a powerful King, and I have plenty of gold— as much as ever I want.'

'I see very well,' said the King, 'that we owe you many thanks. Can I do anything to please you?'

'Yes,' he answered; 'indeed, you can. Give me your daughter to be my wife!'

The maiden laughed, and said, 'He does not beat about the bush; but I saw long ago that he was no Gardener's boy.'

Then she went up to him and kissed him.

His father and mother came to the wedding, and they were full of joy, for they had long given up all hope of ever seeing their dear son again. As they were all sitting at the wedding feast, the music suddenly stopped, the doors flew open, and a proud King walked in at the head of a great following. He went up to the Bridegroom, embraced him, and said, 'I am Iron Hans, who was bewitched and changed into a Wild Man; but you have broken the spell and set me free. All the treasure that I have is now your own.'

NOTE BY THE ARTIST

SOME years ago a selection of *Grimm's Fairy Tales* with one hundred illustrations of mine in black and white was published—in 1900, by Messrs. Freemantle and Co., and afterwards by Messrs. Archibald Constable & Co., Ltd.

At intervals since then I have been at work on the original drawings, partially or entirely re-drawing some of them in colour, adding new ones in colour and in black and white, and generally overhauling them as a set, supplementing and omitting, with a view to the present edition.

Of the forty coloured illustrations, many are elaborations of the earlier black and white drawings or are founded on them. The frontispiece, and those facing pp. 34, 70, 94, 104, 116, 118, and 190 are entirely new, and several of the text illustrations also have not been published before. The remaining illustrations in the text have been reconsidered and worked on again to a greater or less degree.

HAMPSTEAD, *September* 1909.   ARTHUR RACKHAM.